Cass's mind was about r̶ any more tonight. With a̶ ful the way the weekend was progressing so far, the electricity would be restored by morning. In the meantime . . . "Let's just get some sleep. About ten more guests signed up for individual readings before they went to bed, so I'm going to have to start earlier than planned." Hmmm . . . Maybe Stephanie was right. Maybe stories of the bungled séance would bring more business.

She snuggled down into the pillow, tucking the blankets beneath her chin. Beast's soft snores soothed her. Not that a dog was any defense against a ghost. But Beast was a really big dog, and he could be really scary when necessary. He was usually so easygoing, though. The only person he'd ever growled at had been Jay Callahan, when he'd threatened Cass. Until tonight. Why had Beast taken such an instant dislike to Conrad Wellington? Maybe because Bee disliked him. Weren't dogs sensitive to stuff like that?

Her eyes fell closed, exhaustion weighing heavily.

Bee's rhythmic breathing told her he'd already nodded off.

Blizzard force winds howled.

A scream jerked her from the brink of sleep. Real? Or imagined? The wind, maybe? It came again, accompanied by the pounding of footsteps in the hallway.

Ah . . . jeez. What now?

Titles by Lena Gregory

DEATH AT FIRST SIGHT
OCCULT AND BATTERY

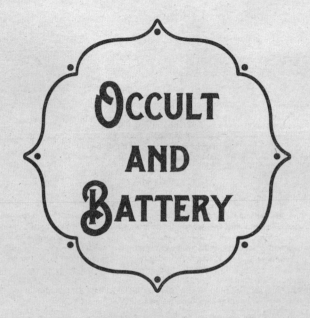

OCCULT AND BATTERY

LENA GREGORY

BERKLEY PRIME CRIME
New York

BERKLEY PRIME CRIME
Published by Berkley
An imprint of Penguin Random House LLC
375 Hudson Street, New York, New York 10014

ISBN: 9780425282762

First Edition: April 2017

Printed in the United States of America
1   3   5   7   9   10   8   6   4   2

Cover art by Griesbach & Martucci
Cover design by Adam Auerbach
Book design by Kelly Lipovich

To my brother, Chris, who fought harder
than anyone I know but lost his battle way too soon.
You will live forever in my heart!

ACKNOWLEDGMENTS

This book would not have been possible without the support and encouragement of my husband, Greg. We've built a wonderful life together, and I can't wait to see where our journey will lead next. I'd like to say a big thank-you to my children, Elaina, Nicky, and Logan, and to my son-in-law, Steve, for their understanding and help while I spent long nights at the computer. My husband and children are truly the loves of my life.

I also have to thank my best friend, Renee, for all of her support, long conversations, and reading many rough drafts. I still wouldn't know how to use Word without her help. I'd like to thank my sister, Debby, and my dad, Tony, who are probably my biggest fans and have read every word I've ever written. To my agent, Dawn Dowdle, thank you for believing in me and for being there in the middle of the night every time I have a question. Words cannot express my gratitude to Julie Mianecki for giving me this opportunity and for her wonderful advice and assistance in polishing this manuscript. And a huge thank-you to Bethany Blair for taking things over in the middle and making sure everything went perfectly!

1

"**S**top the car!"

Bee Maxwell slammed on the brakes, skidding to a stop on the sand-covered shoulder. Without loosening his white-knuckled grip on the steering wheel, he turned a glare on Cass. "Are you crazy? What's the matter?"

Cass released her hold on the dashboard and shot him a grin. "We're here."

A hand the size of a baseball mitt fluttered to Bee's chest, with all the drama of a true diva. "You nearly gave me a heart attack because we've arrived at our secret destination?" Gritting his teeth, he shifted gently into park. No way would he jam the shifter into gear, even though she could tell he badly wanted to. The black Trans Am was his baby, always to be treated tenderly. Cass, on the other hand, was a different story. Bee looked about ready to throttle her. "Wouldn't it have been easier to just tell me where we were going?"

Stephanie Lawrence poked her head between the seats to stare at Cass. "Not that I want to agree with Bee, but really, Cass, you could have just told him where to go. Then maybe this maniac wouldn't have nearly put us through the windshield."

She shrugged. "I didn't think he'd agree to take me if I told him where we were going."

Bee waved a hand in dismissal and glanced out the window, as if realizing for the first time where they were.

The old, supposedly haunted Madison Estate perched in the center of the highest ground on the island, amid dried-up beach grass, trees long since devoid of leaves, and garbage from whatever kids were brave—or stupid—enough to ignore their parents' warnings. Thick, grey clouds gathered overhead, lending credence to the haunted stories Cass had heard since childhood.

A dainty shiver ran through Bee's bulky frame. "Well, if your destination has anything to do with that house, you can just count me out."

"But it's perfect." She opened the door and shot him a quick grin over her shoulder.

"Hey. Where are you going?"

Ignoring Bee's protests, Cass climbed from the car. She closed the door behind her, effectively cutting off any further arguments. Bee happened to be deathly afraid of ghosts. Not that he believed in them.

As she stared up at the abandoned mansion, ideas chased each other around her head.

During the summer months, tourists flocked to the small island that sat nestled between Long Island's north and south forks. They rented cottages, swarmed the beaches, hung out until all hours in the beach bars, climbed to the top of the lighthouses, and swamped Mystical Musings—her small psychic shop on the boardwalk.

But with winter in full force, Bay Island was less than thriving. The murky waters of Gardiner's Bay were rough and choppy, the piercing wind a bitter enemy, making the ferry ride to the island less than comfortable. As much as Cass loved living on the tiny island, if she couldn't drive business into Mystical Musings during the harsh winter months, she wouldn't be able to stay. She'd have to go back to New York City and her once-thriving psychiatric practice.

An icy gust of wind tore through Cass, chasing the thoughts away. Something touched her shoulder, and she almost jumped out of her skin.

"Sorry, didn't mean to scare you." Stephanie laughed.

"Jeez, you could at least say something before you grab me."

Bee glared at them from inside the car.

"What are we doing here?" Stephanie zipped up her thick down coat, tucked her wild mane of frizzy brown hair inside it, and tried to pull the collar farther up around her ears.

"Come on. I'll show you." Cass shoved open the rusty wrought iron gate.

Screeeeeech!

Bee's muffled protests followed her through the gate and up the cracked cobblestone walkway.

She smiled.

Bee was one of her best friends, but he was also the biggest drama queen she'd ever met.

It was a house. Nothing more. Nothing less. At one time, people lived in it . . . and died in it. She swallowed hard.

A seagull shrieked as it dove toward the dark, churning waters of the bay behind the house.

A shiver raced through her, and she pulled her long coat tighter around her, failing to ward off a chill that had little to do with the near-freezing temperatures. Although Cass didn't consider herself psychic in any traditional sense— despite the fact she made her living reading people and "talking" to the dead—she had to admit the house gave her the creeps. *Perfect!*

The stone had long since weathered and cracked. Many of the shingles, which might have once been brown, were now a dull grey and hung precariously, if they weren't missing altogether. The front porch sagged, but the steps looked sturdy enough. She tested each one before putting her full weight on it. They creaked but held. She tiptoed across the porch, her heart hammering erratically, and cupped her hands around her eyes to peek into the large front window. Nothing. Dirt, grime, and salt made it impossible to see the dark interior. A chill crept up her spine.

This is ridiculous. No one has lived in this house for longer than I can remember. Using a crumpled tissue from her coat pocket, she rubbed a circle of dirt away and leaned closer.

"Cass Donovan!"

She jumped, whacked the back of her head against Stephanie's chin, and spun around, startled by Bee's booming voice from behind her. "Ouch." She rubbed the back of her head. "What's the matter with you?"

He stood just outside the gate, his gaze darting around frantically. "You get back in that car right this minute, missy, or I'm leaving you here. You and your sidekick." He gestured toward Stephanie, who was moving her jaw from side to side and rubbing her chin.

Cass pressed a hand to her chest, hoping to keep her heart from jumping out, and laughed. "You wouldn't dare."

At better than six feet tall—even without his platform shoes—Bee could have been an imposing figure. If not for the hand resting on his cocked hip. And the look of sheer terror marring his pale face. "Try me, sugar."

She started back toward the gate. A flicker of something, movement from the corner of her eye caught her attention, and she stopped short and turned. *What the . . . ?* A reflection? She squinted. But the sun was hidden behind the thick cloud cover. Her imagination?

"Oh, come on." Bee's whine followed her as she started around the side of the house.

The screech of the gate opening told her Bee had given up his threat to abandon them and decided to join them, or at least come closer to argue his point. He muttered to himself as he stalked toward Stephanie, likely figuring she was the more reasonable of the two. He was probably right.

Cass glanced up at the huge house. She'd never been inside, but from the number of wings and windows, she guessed it had a lot of rooms. Her gaze caught on the huge stone chimney running up between two quarter round windows, giving the impression of a face staring back at her. A flicker of movement grabbed her attention as a curtain rippled in the rounded cupola that sat slightly off-center on the roof.

Her heart stuttered, and she tore her gaze from the house and jogged back to the porch, where Bee and Stephanie stood arguing.

Ignoring them, she headed for the front door.

"What are you doing now?" The fear in Bee's voice made her pause, but only for a moment.

She'd been planning this for over a month and had already gotten permission and cooperation from the owners. Her idea might be nuts, but she was pretty sure it would be a big hit. *If* she could convince her two best friends to help her out. She forced a smile, waggled her eyebrows, and held the front door key up between them. A puff of condensation enveloped the shiny new key each time she exhaled.

"Are you crazy?" Bee's voice only hit that high note when he was completely shocked or extremely upset. In this case, it was probably a little of both.

"Look, Bee. I have to find a way to generate income during the winter."

He offered a quick look of sympathy. Before his designer dress shop, Dreamweaver Designs, had gotten so big, he used to have the same problem. Now that his designs were becoming more popular, and big names in the fashion industry had started attending his annual fashion shows, he had a steady stream of orders pretty much year-round.

Good, maybe he'd help her.

"You know how we do the group readings in the shop?" He eyed her suspiciously. "Yeah."

Although Bee didn't believe in psychic powers or talking to the dead, he stayed as far away from anything to do with it as possible, just in case. Cass had cajoled him into helping with the group readings since there were no dead people involved. She'd also convinced him it was all done very scientifically.

She shrugged, hoping to appear casual. "Well, I want to do a group reading."

He stuffed his hands into his coat pockets and rocked back and forth. The thought of him falling through the old boards of the rotting porch ran fleetingly through her mind. "In addition to the once-a-month readings you usually do?"

"Sort of?" She caught her bottom lip between her teeth and peered at him from beneath her lashes.

It only took a moment for him to figure it out. "No. Oh, no. Not happening, sugar."

"But—"

"Not on your life, sweetie. There is no way I'm going into that house while you . . ." He shook his head and waved his hand wildly. "Do whatever it is you do."

"It's just a reading, Bee. I'll do it the same way I do in the shop." Knowing she was perilously close to whining, she rushed on. "I need your help. You have a background in theater, plus you put on the best fashion shows." No need to remind him how much Cass had helped with those shows. *All right, now I'm getting catty.* She sucked in a deep breath of the frigid air, freezing her lungs. "How about if you just help with the setup? You don't have to stay for the reading."

Bee sighed.

Yes!

"I don't know." He glanced toward the front door, shaking his head. "We'll see. Okay?"

"Bu—"

He held up a hand to stop her. "Be happy with it, honey, it's the best you're going to get."

"I'm telling you, it'll work. A group reading at a haunted

house? Are you kidding me? People will line up for that."
Cass pushed the mansion's front door open and held it for
Stephanie, who followed her into the foyer.

Bee caught the door, holding it open and lodging himself
firmly between the door and the jamb without actually crossing the threshold.

"I rented the space fairly cheap, and I'll charge more for
the tickets than a regular reading. If I've figured it right, I
should be able to make a decent profit." She moved through
the foyer and peeked into the large living room, weaving
between several ladders, drop cloths, cans of paint, and paint
trays with remnants of several different colors splattered in
them. The inside of the house was in considerably better
condition than the outside.

Bee swallowed hard, his Adam's apple bobbing notice-
ably. "How did you manage to rent it cheap?"

She shrugged. "It's owned by Wellington, Wellington,
and Wellington." The same investment company her ex-
husband and ex–best friend both worked for. She tamped
down the flare of anger that always accompanied thoughts
of her exes.

She'd met Priscilla Wellington at a few holiday parties,
when staff were invited to bring their spouses. Though
they'd never shared more than a few words, Priscilla had
always seemed warm and approachable. "I called Priscilla
Wellington last month and she loved the idea. They've been
having work done on the house anyway, to turn it into a bed
and breakfast–style hotel, so they've decided to allow me
to do the reading next Friday, a few weeks before their of-
ficial grand opening is scheduled. They're hoping the guests
will stay the weekend."

Bee lifted a skeptical brow. "Why would they open a hotel on Bay Island in the dead of winter?" A cold gust of wind blasted through the open door, hammering home Bee's point.

Cass couldn't help the frown. She'd wondered the same thing but shrugged off any misgivings. She needed this to work. Whatever ulterior motives the Wellingtons might have were of no concern to her. "Who knows? Some people love stuff like this, Bee."

He scowled and remained in the doorway while she and Stephanie moved farther into the room. It had obviously not been cleaned yet. Cobwebs marred the corners, as she'd expected, and dust floated in the dim light filtering in from the front door. It could definitely use a few coats of paint. Priscilla had said the guest rooms were already finished, so apparently, this was next up on the agenda. She shuddered at the cracks running down several of the walls, hoping they were only cosmetic. Having the house tumble down around them was the last thing she needed.

Car doors slamming pulled her from her reverie, and she and Stephanie moved back toward the front door.

Bee stood blocking the doorway, his arms folded across his massive chest. "It's a crazy idea. For all you know, this house is falling apart. It's dangerous. Right, Stephanie?"

Stephanie bit her lip and stared at Bee, excitement lighting her eyes.

"Oh, don't even tell me. Not you, too." Bee slouched against the doorjamb, dropped his arms to his sides, and sulked.

"Why not make it a weekend? You could do a bunch of stuff. There are a gazillion rooms in this house. Do a psychic weekend. You said the Wellingtons were hoping guests would spend the weekend anyway, so they've probably worked that out already. You could offer individual readings, a large group reading, sell crystals . . ." Although Stephanie offered Bee a sympathetic smile, her enthusiasm grew the more she spoke. "And maybe on Saturday night, you could have a masquerade ball or something."

"I don't know." But ideas were already barreling through Cass's mind. It was brilliant. An entire weekend devoted to psychic events.

The voice of reason intruded in the form of Bee's whine. "Do you have any idea what something like that would cost? You'd have to have everyone stay over, have inventory to sell, feed everyone . . ." Bee ticked off the list on his fingers.

Stephanie waved off his concerns. "We can get Isabella Trapani to cater it. Her shop is dead in the winter, too. She'll probably give you a really good deal. As far as the guests, it's only going to make the Wellingtons money. Let the Wellingtons worry about it."

"Let the Wellingtons worry about what?"

Bee jumped, startled, and squealed as he closed the door on the man standing on the porch behind him and launched himself toward Cass.

She held her breath, waiting for all two hundred or so pounds of him to jump into her arms like a frightened child. Thankfully, he stopped just short of her.

"Will you calm down, Bee?" Stephanie stepped around him toward the man who'd pushed the door open and was now entering the house, eyeing Bee with suspicion. "Can I help you?"

"Are you Cass Donovan?"

"No." Shooting Bee a warning glare, Cass sidestepped him and held out her hand. "I'm Cass, and you are?" He had to be one of the Wellington brothers—with his neatly creased, pleated slacks, cashmere sweater, and short blond hair—but she had no idea which one.

"Conrad Wellington the third, Ms. Donovan." He gripped the tips of her fingers in a tentative hold, quickly releasing them to wipe his hand on his perfectly pressed pants. "And, in case my sister hasn't mentioned it, I'm completely opposed to this absurd idea."

Ooookay. "Uhh . . ."

"Marring our pre–grand opening weekend with a bunch of psychic drivel . . ." His face reddened as he glanced around the room. "Well, let's just say anyone with even the slightest amount of intelligence knows there's no such thing as ghosts, and having some sort of so-called psychic . . ." His gaze crawled up and down Cass, lingering on her chest. ". . . feed into the reputation this house has for being haunted can't possibly bring us the type of clientele we are hoping to attract."

She resisted the urge to pull her coat closed around her.

Bee stepped forward, chin lifted, broad shoulders squared, and tossed one end of his silk scarf over his shoulder.

Uh . . . oh.

Ignoring Cass's warning glare, he stood toe to toe with Conrad Wellington. "I actually agree with you about the whole no-such-thing-as-ghosts idea, but what exactly do you mean *so-called* psychic?"

Conrad's upper lip curled, and he looked down his nose as if Bee was something disgusting stuck to the bottom of his shoe.

Bee wasn't deterred. If anything, his haughtiness in-creased to match Conrad Wellington the third's. "And just what sort of clientele were you hoping to attract?" He tilted his head and lifted one bushy brow. "A bunch of snooty, stick-up-their—"

"Hi all." A woman breezed through the still-open front door. "I'm Priscilla Wellington." Although she had to be in her fifties, she appeared much younger at first glance. Her long blond hair was pulled back into a high ponytail, and she wore jeans, a grey pullover sweatshirt, and black boots. A stark contrast to her straight-laced brother. Ignoring the ten-sion, she strode through the room as if she owned the place.

Oh, right. She does own the place.

"Ms. Donovan." She approached Cass immediately and gripped the hand Cass managed to extend between both of hers. "It's a pleasure to see you again."

"It's . . . uh . . . nice to see you, too, Ms. Wellington."

She released Cass and waved a hand dismissively. "Please, call me Priscilla. Now . . ." She paused and glanced around, seeming to notice the tension for the first time. Purs-ing her lips, she turned her attention to her brother. "Do I even need to ask what this is all about?"

Twin spots of color blossomed on his pale cheeks. "Noth-ing, Prissy, just having a discussion with . . ." He gestured at Bee. "Seems he agrees with me about the psychic babble."

Bee harrumphed, folded his arms across his chest, and pouted.

"Now, dear." She patted Conrad's cheek as if speaking to a small, rebellious child. "I thought we'd already settled all of this." Her voice hardened. "We are launching the pre–grand opening celebration with a psychic reading on Friday night."

"Actually, you and *James* settled this." He spat the name with more contempt than Cass could ever muster. "I've disagreed from the beginning."

"Yes, dear, but Joan is so excited and so looking forward to the opening. Do you really want to disappoint your wife?"

Conrad scowled but offered no further argument.

Ignoring him, Priscilla returned her attention to the others. "Why don't I give you a tour of the mansion while you tell me about the reading? Turning the old Madison Estate into a bed-and-breakfast was a fabulous idea, if I do say so, but opening with a psychic reading was sheer genius, Cass. I'm just thrilled about it."

Cass stood with her mouth open, not sure what to say or do.

Thankfully, Stephanie found her voice . . . sort of. "Um . . ." Her gaze shot to Cass, who simply stared at Priscilla.

Even though she'd dismissed her brother so rudely, Cass liked the woman. She had a fresh, no-nonsense way about her that Cass appreciated. "Just before you got here, we were discussing the possibility of doing some additional events throughout the weekend," Cass said.

Bee sighed.

Conrad balked.

Stephanie smiled encouragingly.

Ugh . . .

Priscilla wove her arm through Cass's and started toward the stairs. "Come, dear, I can't wait to show you the guest rooms. They're all finished, and they look gorgeous." She crossed the room slowly, as if she had all the time in the world. A stark contrast from the whirlwind that had first blown through the door. "Tell me about your plans while we walk."

Stephanie fell into place at Cass's other side, while Bee and Conrad jostled for a position directly behind them.

"Well, I thought maybe we could make a weekend out of it."

The elaborate curved stairway gave way to the second-floor rotunda, which overlooked the living room and a ballroom behind it.

Cass's breath shot out. Stunning. She tried to imagine how it would look once it was fully restored. Would the Wellingtons eventually invest the money necessary to completely renovate the old place? Maybe, if the hotel was successful. "I'd like to move the group reading to Saturday." It would be easier to do a group reading after she'd gotten to know some of the guests. "Maybe have individual readings throughout the day Saturday, followed by the group reading that night."

Priscilla frowned. "What about Friday night?"

What had Stephanie said? A masquerade ball?

"A séance." With a quick wink at Cass, Stephanie continued, "She wants to do a séance on Friday."

Priscilla stopped walking and turned to face Cass.

Elbowing Bee aside, Conrad stepped between them and confronted his sister. "No way."

Bee leaned over and whispered urgently in Cass's ear, "Are you out of your mind?"

"What? It's a great idea." Stephanie pushed past Cass to get to Bee.

The sounds of their bickering faded as Cass tried to focus

on the confrontation between the Wellington siblings, their silent stare-off leaving Cass completely lost, until Priscilla stepped around Conrad to study her.

Cass held her breath.

Bee and Stephanie must have stopped arguing, because the hum of silence echoed loudly.

Cass waited.

Nothing.

The silence ate at her until she couldn't take it anymore. *What about Sunday? Hmm . . .* "Then maybe Sunday we could have a brunch with the opportunity for guests to buy crystals and essential oils." Lame? Too much info? She had no idea, but if Priscilla didn't say something soon, she was just going to give up. "You know the house is supposed to be haunted, right?" *All right, just shut up now.*

Priscilla cleared her throat. "It's brilliant."

"Huh?"

"It's brilliant. I love the entire concept."

Conrad huffed out a breath.

"This could be just the publicity we need to make this all work. Have you sold any tickets yet?"

"Uh . . . no, actually. I just came up with the idea, but I've sold tickets to the Friday night event, and if most of the guests were planning to stay the weekend anyway, it shouldn't be a problem."

"Do you think you can still pull it all together by next weekend, even with the additional events?"

Cass shrugged. Could she? Getting together some inventory to sell would only take a few hours. She'd already touched base with most of the people she planned to invite about Friday night's reading and knew they planned to attend, and Isabella was a miracle worker. This time of year, she'd definitely be able to put something together at the last minute. The only thing that would take some work would be the séance, and she could probably talk Bee into helping her set that up. "Sure. I can do it by next weekend." *I hope.* She crossed her fingers behind her back.

"Well, I'm quite intrigued. I'll tell you what, e-mail me a proposal listing the itinerary, the cost, and the number of tickets available, and I'll let you know how many I want."

"Excuse me?"

"I'll let you know how many tickets to put aside for me."

"Um . . . great. Thank you so much." Cass's heart raced. *What have I gotten myself into?*

2

Wind chimes tinkled as Cass pushed open the door to Mystical Musings.

Stephanie looked up from a paperback she was reading at the counter.

Great. Apparently she hadn't been swamped with customers. Cass sighed. She loved her small shop, with the gleaming driftwood countertops and the glass cases filled with trinkets, souvenirs, and crystals. She enjoyed the challenge of reading people, using her instincts, intuition, and years of psychiatric training to delve into their minds and offer advice and guidance.

Beast, the giant Leonberger puppy she'd sort of inherited from Marge Hawkins, and then again from Ellie Callahan, bounded in beside her, tracking mud across the polished hardwood floors. *Ugh* . . . She'd grown to love the clumsy pup, who was just starting to grow into his too-big paws, but he was a handful. "Thanks for keeping an eye on the shop while I went to pick him up. He only ate one cushion off a kitchen chair today."

Stephanie laughed. "I don't know when you're going to listen to me and crate this monster." She rubbed behind his ears.

Beast flopped over onto his back and bared his belly for Stephanie to pet.

Cass shrugged and grabbed a roll of paper towels and a bottle of cleaner from behind the counter, then bent to clean up the mess. She really should crate train him. Everything she'd read said so. "It just seems so mean to put him in a cage all day. As soon as it gets warm, though, he's going for obedience training."

The big, furry dog ignored her glare and simply rolled over toward Stephanie, content with the attention.

"I really have to run if you want me to stop at Bella's and drop off the deposit check for the catering."

To Beast's disappointment, Stephanie stood and brushed off her hands.

"I left the check in the register drawer."

"Got it," Stephanie said.

"Thank you."

With a quick hug for Cass and one last pat for Beast's head, Stephanie shoved the check into her pocket, pulled her coat tight, and ran out into the cold.

Cass dropped the wad of paper towels into the trash can, then surveyed the empty shop. Not a single customer had come in all day. This psychic weekend idea had to work. If it didn't . . .

Island life agreed with Cass. The front door of her shop

opened to the boardwalk, and the back door opened onto the beach. What could be more perfect? Sitting on the back porch looking out over the bay, feet propped on the railing with the scent of the sea invading her lungs soothed her in a way nothing else could. The thought of going back to the hustle and bustle of the city sent a shiver up her spine.

Beast stared at her and whimpered.

"Don't worry, boy. We'll make it work."

Cass lifted her gaze at the tinkle of the wind chimes she'd hung above the door of the shop. "Hey."

"Hey, yourself." Bee shivered. "It's freezing out there." Brushing a light dusting of snow from his hair, he stomped his boots off on the welcome mat.

With a yelp of recognition, Beast launched himself toward Bee.

"Stop right there, mister," Bee scolded as he juggled the armload of books he held to pet the dog's head. "What are you doing here? I thought you'd be over at the mansion." He hefted the stack of books to the other hand and slid his coat off.

"Nah. I'd just be in the way." She lifted the basket of lotions she'd been pricing, skirted the counter, and dropped the basket into its holder. "Priscilla Wellington is going all out." She shot Bee a grin.

"Seems a bit much, don't you think?" With a frown, Bee dumped the books onto the table in the corner and shook out his arms. "You want tea?"

"Sure."

"And why is she rushing so much? It hasn't been that long since you came up with this whole cockamamie idea." He dropped a tea bag into a foam cup and filled it with boiling water, then filled a second cup for Cass.

She'd wondered the same thing, but she wasn't going to argue. At this time of year, she was just grateful for the prospect of income.

Bee lifted a brow as he stirred milk into his tea. "Like I've said before, I don't know that winter is the time to open a hotel on Bay Island, but she sure seems gung-ho about all of this nonsense."

Laughter bubbled out of Cass. "Some people actually like all this psychic mumbo jumbo, Bee."

Bee harrumphed and dropped his bulky frame into one of the velvet-covered chairs surrounding the table.

Beast grabbed a toy from his basket and settled down beside him to chew.

"What have you got there?" Tilting her head to the side, Cass studied the spines of the books he'd dumped on the table. *The History of Bay Island, Bay Island: Past and Present, True Hauntings* . . .

"I told you I'd help with the preparations." He blew on his tea, sipped, then set it aside and shuffled through the books, settling on *Modern Day Hauntings*. "If you're going to put on a show, you may as well do it right."

Biting back a grin, Cass took her tea and sat beside him at the big round table. "You're the best, Bee."

"Yeah, well . . ." Twin spots of red tinged his cheeks. Of course, they could have been caused by the warmth in the shop after the below-freezing temperatures outside. "I figured if you know the history of the house, it would be more realistic if you *contact* an actual former resident."

"Does this mean you'll help with the reading and . . . uh . . . stuff?"

His pointed glare told her he probably wouldn't.

Time to pull out the big guns. She offered her best smile. "I've already worked out the menu with Isabella from Bella's on the Bay and ordered desserts from Tony's." She waggled her eyebrows, knowing he'd be tempted. If there were two things Bee couldn't resist, they were Isabella Trapani's Italian cooking and Tony's desserts. Especially . . . "Tony's bringing a nice big tray of cannoli balls Sunday morning." They were Bee's favorite dessert, and Tony only made them on Sundays. "If he brings me a huge tray, there might not be any left for the bakery. And even if there are a few, you'd have to get up awfully early to get some before he ran out."

Bee often worked on his dress designs through the night, and nothing short of an earthquake would roll him out of bed much before noon.

The chimes tinkled and he gave her a dirty look.

Beast's ears perked up as he lifted his head, but he went back to chewing when he didn't recognize the customer.

"Brrr . . . It's freezing out there." An older woman unwound her scarf. Something was familiar about her, but Cass couldn't quite place her.

"If you'd like, you can take off your coat and hang it on the coatrack in the corner." Cass stood and rounded the table to approach the woman. "Would you like a nice hot cup of tea?"

"Oh, sure, dear. That would be very nice. And could you pour one for my gentleman friend, too, please?"

Cass paused halfway to the counter, studying the woman, who was obviously alone.

Rich laughter poured through the shop as the woman removed her loose-knit hat and patted the tight, blue-grey curls clinging to her head. Why did she look so familiar?

"No, I'm not crazy or senile . . . yet, anyway. He dropped me off at the door and went to park the car. Didn't want me to slip on the ice and break a hip or anything." Her eyes sparkled with a smile.

Cass moved to the counter to pour the drinks. "He sounds like a real keeper."

"Yes, siree. And I have you to thank for him."

"Me?" Cass gestured to a small seating area and placed the cups on a scarred wooden coffee table between two chairs.

"That's right." The woman dug into the ruffled collar of her blouse and pulled out a small pouch tied around her neck with a leather cord. It rattled when she shook it.

That's it! Now she remembered. The woman had come in back before the holidays sometime, looking for a love potion. Cass had filled the small pouch with crystals and told her to wear it over her heart. Hmm . . . Maybe there was something to this hocus-pocus after all. She shot Bee an *I told you so* look, but he just rolled his eyes.

The chimes above the door tinkled, and a tall older man with pale blue eyes and a kind smile walked in. "Colder than a witch's—"

"Rudy!"

"Oops." His sheepish grin was adorable, emitting a warmth that made him instantly likable.

"This is the gentleman I was telling you about. Rudy Hastings. And, by the way, I'm Grace Collins. I figure since I'm planning to be a regular customer, you oughta know my name."

"It's nice to meet you both. I'm Cass Donovan, owner of Mystical Musings."

Grace shuffled to the seating area, Rudy's hand on her lower back to guide her.

With a quick glance at Bee, who was now perched on the edge of his seat, hunched over an open book on the table, completely engrossed in whatever he was reading, Cass grabbed her tea and joined the couple. "How can I help you today?" She sat across from them, sipped her tea, and set it aside. Leaning forward with her elbows resting on her knees, fingers laced together, Cass studied Grace.

Worry creased the woman's brow, unlike the last time she came in, when she'd been somewhat embarrassed, hoping to find love. Today's purchase would undoubtedly be of a more serious nature.

Rudy laced one hand with hers as he lifted a foam cup with the other. Grace's tea sat untouched on the table.

Cass bit back the urge to ask if everything was all right. She'd let Grace get to things in her own time.

"I was wondering if you have anything to help with fertility."

"Uhhh . . ." No way could she possibly think she could have a child at her age.

Grace laughed and waved her off. "Not for me, dear." She shook her head and lowered her gaze for a moment before continuing. "The thing is, my granddaughter has been a bit . . . sad . . . lately."

Cass frowned.

"She wants to have a baby so badly, and she and her husband have been trying for years. The doctors haven't found anything wrong, but still . . ." Grace shook her head, the granddaughter's pain etched clearly on the grandmother's face. "Nothing."

Cass's heart ached for her.

"I just thought, since things worked out so well with Rudy and me, well . . . Maybe you have something to help Sadie?" Hope filled Grace's turbulent grey eyes.

Cass smiled. "Sure. You two sit and relax and warm up. Give me a few minutes to get some things together."

Leaving them to drink their tea and thaw out, Cass went about collecting trays of crystals and placing them on the low coffee table in the center of the seating area. She pulled a small pouch and an extra-long length of leather cord from beneath the counter. After dropping those on the table, she grabbed some essential oils, a couple of candles, a basket, and a few sheets of pastel green tissue paper, changed her mind and switched it for pink, and added them to the growing pile.

Settling herself back in her seat, Cass reached for the large basket. "Okay . . ." She arranged the tissue paper in the bottom then pulled one of the trays toward her. "This is moonstone." She lifted a small crystal from the tray and twirled it in the light. Blue and brown swirls shifted in the translucent background as light shimmered across the surface, creating the appearance of ripples of motion. "The most powerful stone for fertility. In many countries, it's considered magical and sewn into the clothing of newly married women." She dropped the moonstone into the small pouch and set the tray aside.

Grace leaned forward, studying Cass intently. Rudy kept his gaze on Grace, his feelings for the woman clearly evident in his eyes as he watched her. Cass tucked the insight away.

Pushing the tray of moonstone aside, she lifted another crystal. "Rose quartz."

"Hey, I remember that one. It's in my bag too." Grace lifted a brow. "I hope that's not why it's in there."

Cass couldn't help the laughter that bubbled out. "Don't worry, you're safe. Rose quartz is used for a lot of things. It's considered the stone of love; family love, romance . . . It's a soothing stone that not only creates inner warmth but also reduces stress." She added it to the bag, along with a ruby, known to enhance fertility, and a jade, which supposedly aided in childbirth, and tied the pouch closed with the leather cord.

"I gave you a long length of cord so you can adjust it until the stones rest over your granddaughter's stomach." She placed the pouch in the tissue paper along with the mix of essential oils and a couple of candles. "Tell her to put a few drops of the oil into a warm bath, not too hot, light the candles, dim the lights, and soak in the tub until it cools before . . . uh . . ." Heat flared in Cass's cheeks, and she had no doubt they flamed red.

Grace laughed and patted her hand. "Don't worry, dear, I have six children, I know how they get made." She shifted toward the front of the chair, and Rudy jumped up and took her hand. She glanced over at Cass and winked.

Biting back a sigh at the thought of what it would be like to have such an attentive man, Cass took the basket to the counter and wrapped it in cellophane while Grace and Rudy got their coats. She rang up the purchase and added a business card to the side of the basket.

"How much, dear?" Grace propped her small handbag on the counter and counted out bills when Cass gave her the total.

"I know this is probably going to sound like a sales pitch,

but I promise it's not." She handed Grace her change. "When Sadie runs out of the oils, if she wants more, tell her she can either order them from me or do some research and be very careful where she gets them. Unfortunately, some of the same oils that can help fertility *might* also cause miscarriages if she uses them after she's pregnant."

Grace sucked in a breath. "Are they safe for her to use?"

"Oh, very. I don't use any of those in my mix, but some people do." Cass smiled and rounded the counter to hand Grace the basket. "They're not unsafe, but the way I figure it, why take any chances?"

"Thank you. I'll—"

Bee squealed—there was no other way to describe the sound that came from him—and launched himself from his chair, slapping a hand over his mouth and slamming his thighs into the table. "Ouch!" He massaged the fronts of his legs.

Beast jumped up and barked.

The heavy, velvet-covered chair teetered on its back legs for a second before Bee composed himself enough to grip the arm and lower it back down. "Uh, sorry," he whispered, flipping the cover of the book he'd been reading closed and shoving it across the table with one finger. "Don't mind me." He lifted his hands palms forward. "I'll just . . . uh . . ." He looked around the shop as if unsure what to do with himself.

Grace offered a smile and clutched her basket tighter, but Rudy just stared, mouth agape.

That was a pretty standard reaction to Bee.

Cass guided them toward the door, while Bee continued to wring his hands together.

She shut the door behind the couple and turned a glare on Bee. "What is the matter with you?"

He winced. "Sorry."

Curiosity won out over annoyance as she approached the table where Bee still stood staring at the book he'd been reading. "What freaked you out so bad, anyway?" She lifted the cover of the offending book, but Bee slammed a hand over hers, effectively closing it again.

"That house is haunted." A not-so-delicate shiver ran through him.

Cass laughed. She couldn't help it. "I thought you didn't believe in ghosts?" She folded her arms, cocked her head, and waited.

"I never said I didn't *believe* in ghosts. Exactly. I just don't believe in talking to ghosts."

"Mmm . . . hmm . . ."

"Weeeell." He sank back into his chair and pouted.

Cass grabbed her tea, popped it in the microwave for a minute, then joined Bee at the table. "So, what's the deal?"

"Did you know someone died in that house?"

"Sure. Everyone knows that." Cass tried to recall the stories from her childhood but couldn't bring any specific details into focus. "When I was a kid, there were rumors that people were murdered there, but I don't really remember who or how . . ." She shrugged and sipped her tea. "Maybe I never knew."

Bee was already shaking his head. "No. I don't mean a gazillion years ago."

Cass shot him a scowl.

"I'm talking about more recently. Back about ten years ago." Bee leaned forward, elbows resting on the table.

"I wasn't here ten years ago." Although she'd grown up on Bay Island, Cass had left to go to college and hadn't returned until a little more than a year ago, after a seventeen-year hiatus.

"Me neither, but apparently one of the Madisons had a heart attack in the house. That's why they sold it. Of course, it took forever to sell, because who wants to buy a haunted house? A house they proved was haunted." He slid back in the chair, crossed one leg over the other, and straightened his scarf.

Determined not to give in to his theatrics, Cass blew on the lukewarm tea and took a sip she no longer wanted. She set the cup aside and reached for the book. No way would Bee let her read it herself if he had good dirt to impart. Flipping through the first few pages, she waited patiently for Bee to cave first and tell her why he was so sure the house was haunted.

Bee studied his fingernails then buffed them on his shirt.

"Okay, fine. Spill it. How could they prove the house was haunted?" Cass asked.

"Well, it seems Horatio Madison and his wife, uh . . . Ellen?" Perking up considerably, Bee slid forward on the chair. He pulled the book toward him, flipped to the middle, and skimmed a few pages. "No, Abigail. They were walking through the house, taking pictures to send to some magazine or another, when the ghost appeared and scared them nearly to death." He lifted his gaze to meet hers, fear etched into the lines bracketing his mouth. "Or, I guess in Horatio's case, it actually *did* scare him to death."

Cass bit back a grin. Her interest was definitely piqued, and if she dared to laugh, Bee would get insulted and clam up for sure.

"And if that wasn't enough . . ." He paused, stretching out the drama. "Guess who the ghost was."

"Who?"

"Buford Wellington, who apparently died at the mansion about a hundred years ago."

This time she couldn't hold back the laughter.

Bee flopped against the back of the chair and folded his arms to sulk.

"I'm sorry, Bee, but how could they possibly know whose ghost it was?"

He shrugged, keeping the frown firmly in place. "How should I know? That's what the book says. One thing is pretty clear, though."

When he didn't continue, Cass sighed, propped her elbows on the table, and massaged her temples. "What's that?"

"The Madisons and the Wellingtons have some kind of history that dates back to before the siblings purchased the estate. And Priscilla is awfully anxious to have this psychic weekend." Bee eyed Cass, his brow lifted in challenge. "And awfully accommodating."

"I'm sure it's a coincidence, Bee. What else could it be?"

Next Friday morning came faster than Cass could have thought possible. She unlocked the front door of the old Madison Estate and entered the foyer, along with a blast of icy wind and flurries. Her stomach churned with tension.

Beast bounced happily at her side, darting and leaping to catch the swirling snow in his mouth, seemingly oblivious to his owner's distress.

After shouldering the heavy wooden door shut, Cass hit

the light switch, and the elaborate chandelier cast a brilliant light throughout the foyer and living room. She sucked in a breath. Stunning. Even the minimal amount of work they'd done had changed the atmosphere completely. The wooden wainscoting along the lower half of the walls had been polished until it gleamed. Fresh wallpaper featuring pink and peach flowers on a background of what appeared to be ivory lace covered the cracks in the walls, while still retaining the retro feel. The wood floors still remained scuffed and worn—there had obviously not been time to sand and restore them—but now they were clean and free of dust and dirt.

The door rattled, and Cass jumped and spun toward it, her nerves about shot. She danced out of the way as it swung open.

"Whoa . . . wicked weather out there." Bee stopped short, the dolly full of electronic equipment coming to an abrupt halt. "Wow. What happened here?"

"Can you believe it?"

He shook his head, pushed the dolly aside, and shut the door.

Beast pranced in circles until Bee patted his head. "What are you doing with this guy for the weekend? He staying?"

Cass shot him her most hopeful gaze.

"No way. I'm not having this behemoth in my house." He gazed affectionately at Beast. "He might eat it."

"Please, Bee. I don't have anyone else to watch him." She offered her sweetest smile. "Of course, you could stay here with him, if you prefer." She'd actually rather he stay and help, even if it meant keeping Beast with her.

He shook his head.

"Fine. You can stay at my house with him."

His expression softened.

"Pleeeease." She clasped her hands together and batted her eyelashes.

"Ugh . . . fine." He pointed a finger at Cass. "But you are gonna owe me *so* big time for all of this. And, I'm telling you now, I'm not responsible for anything he damages."

"Thanks, Bee. You're a lifesaver." She stood on tiptoe and plopped a loud kiss on his cheek.

"Yeah, well, don't you forget it." An adorable blush started at his neck and crept up his cheeks.

A gust of wind howled, vibrating the windows.

"Is the storm getting worse?"

Bee brushed the melting snow out of his hair and started forward through the newly renovated foyer and into the living room, his gaze darting around nervously. "Yeah. It's still only flurrying, but the wind is picking up, and it's brutally cold out there." He shivered. "It almost makes it comforting to be in here."

Cass grinned as hope flared.

His glare dimmed any flicker of optimism trying to surface. "Don't get excited. I said almost. And, no, I'm not staying."

"Okay, fine." She blew her bangs up off her forehead and hit the living room light switch.

Bee looked around. "Where is everyone?"

"Priscilla is only sending a skeleton crew for the weekend, and most of them will arrive on the first ferry."

"I can't believe what they've done in here. It looks really . . . good."

Cass turned to look at the living room. A lit fireplace on the far wall wrapped the entire room in cozy warmth.

"Hmm . . ." Bee walked a circuit around the room, fluffing pillows on the floral-print couches, stopping to study the ivory wallpaper, running a hand along the stone mantel. He turned to Cass, sympathy filling his eyes. "It's lost a lot of the spooky."

The frustration, which had been smoldering since she entered the mansion, ignited. "Can you believe this?" She gestured around the room. "What am I supposed to do now? Part of the draw of using the old estate was the creepy atmosphere. I may as well have the séance in broad daylight at the Bay Side Hotel at this point."

Bee's thick brows drew together, and he propped his hands on his hips. "All right. Relax."

"Relax? Are you kidding me?"

He held up a hand, palm facing her. "Listen, honey. I can't think with you freaking out. You go do what you have to do and let me take care of this." Eagerness danced in his eyes. "I'll take some of the bulbs out of the chandeliers, keep the flickering glow of the fireplace . . ." Bee loved a good challenge. "The gathering storm will help add to the creep factor. It'll be fine. Dim lighting, creepy music playing low in the background . . ." He gestured toward the pile of stereo equipment on the dolly. "Trust me when I tell you, this place will seem haunted again in no time, especially once it gets dark."

A tear began to trickle down her cheek, and she brushed it away. "Thank you." If there was one thing Bee did extremely well, it was put on a show.

Footsteps on the front porch made her stop short, and she held her breath and waited. *Hmm . . . Maybe the house is still a little creepy.*

Beast barked, and Bee grabbed his collar to keep him from tackling anyone.

A tall stranger stomped his boots off on the mat, pulled a black knit hat from his head, and raked his fingers through shaggy, dark brown hair.

"Mm mm . . ." Bee licked his lips and straightened the multicolored silk scarf Cass had given him for Christmas, while trying to contain Beast's wriggling form. "This weekend is certainly looking up."

"Oh, stop yourself."

Bee and Stephanie were constantly playing matchmaker, trying to fix Cass up with whomever they deemed hot and available.

"I'm seeing someone, remember?" Cass said.

He lifted a brow in challenge.

All right, so *seeing* might be too strong a term. She hadn't actually *seen* Luke in over a month, but they talked on the phone often. Sort of. She huffed out a breath.

"Exactly."

"Hi." The stranger closed the door behind him. "Cold enough out there?"

Bee nudged Cass with his elbow.

"Uh . . ."

Beast's wagging body made it difficult for her to concentrate. *Right . . . Can't be the handsome stranger interfering with my ability to focus.* Ignoring the internal reprimand, Cass stepped forward and gripped the hand the man extended toward her.

"I'm Jim."

"Cass. Cass Donovan. Are you here for the psychic

weekend? You're a little early. We have a few hours left before we begin." Were there really only a few hours left? She checked the clock over the mantle. About eight hours, really, but it still wasn't enough. Butterflies flitted through her stomach and into her throat.

He released her hand and reached for Bee's.

Thankfully, Bee shook hands with no drama.

"Yes, I'm here for the weekend. I wanted to make sure I got over here before they stop ferry service because of the storm."

"Are they already talking about shutting down?" The thought of canceling this whole cockamamie idea flitted through her mind, followed by a wave of relief. Then reality set in. There was no way out. The worst of the storm wouldn't arrive until close to midnight, hours after the guests were due to arrive.

"Nah. Not yet, at least, but they will soon enough." Jim dropped his black duffle bag on the floor in the foyer. "So, what can I do to help?"

Shooting Bee a—hopefully discreet—*shut up* stare, Cass struggled to figure out where to start. Isabella would be arriving with the food soon, so she had to check the kitchen. She had to find her room and stash her overnight bag.

Jim shrugged out of his coat. A brown sweater stretched across his muscular chest, and the muscles of his back rippled beneath the fabric when he turned to hang his coat on the rack beside the door. Okay, she was definitely not taking him up to her room. She'd have to take care of that later. "Did Priscilla send you?"

"Yup. She issues the commands, and I obey." His laugher echoed in the high ceilings. His calm, easy demeanor worked to soothe Cass's nerves. If he was an example of Priscilla Wellington's lackeys, she was one lucky woman.

"I guess you can take a walk with me to the kitchen. I have to check that everything is in order for the caterer, and the rest of the staff is due to arrive any minute."

Beast whimpered and barked, trying to pull free of Bee's hold.

"You can let him go." Jim's grin sparkled in the green of his eyes as he showered Beast with attention, petting behind his ears, then squatting down when Beast rolled over and bared his belly for a rub. "What a beautiful animal. He's got a great temperament."

Yeah, as long as you don't turn your back on him or leave him alone anywhere.

Bee caught Cass's gaze over Jim's head, bit his lower lip, and fanned himself.

Firming her mouth into a line, she narrowed her eyes in a warning glare.

The front door opened again. This time Priscilla blew in with the wind.

She opened her arms wide, and Jim stood and embraced her, kissing each of her cheeks.

Disappointment flared in Cass's gut, surprising her.

"Hello, dear." She offered Cass a quick embrace, which she awkwardly returned. "Don't you love what we've done with the place?"

"Umm . . ." *Not really.* "Sure. It looks beautiful." *That's true enough.*

"I see you've already met the third Wellington sibling." She gestured toward Jim.

Easygoing Jim was James Wellington? It didn't seem

possible that he was related to high-strung Conrad or in-constant-motion Priscilla.

Bee offered a sympathetic smile before easing the awkward moment of silence. "I have to run back to the shop for a few things, and I want to do it before this storm blows in and the roads get bad. Come on, Beast—want to take a ride?"

Beast yelped once and trotted toward Bee, tongue hanging out the side of his mouth.

Bee held out a hand to Cass, palm up.

"What?"

"You don't think I'm putting this monster in my car, do you?"

Huffing out a breath, Cass fished the keys from her pocket and dropped them in Bee's hand. *Pain in the—*

"Thanks, dear. Be right back. Go tend to whatever you have to do." He shooed them toward the kitchen.

Biting back a growl, she shut the door behind them and turned back to the Wellingtons.

3

Cass stood beside Priscilla at the open front door, greeting people. The more information she had about each of them, the easier it would be for her to "read" them, so she tried to study everyone who entered and pick out who seemed nervous, who seemed excited, who seemed skeptical—

Bee's curse came to her from the living room, followed by Stephanie's "Shush."

Cass winced as she glanced at Priscilla, who was shaking hands and smiling at a woman who had just entered. Good. Maybe she hadn't heard.

Half of the guests had already arrived, and Bee hadn't yet finished setting up the sound system. But, to his credit, the house definitely looked much spookier now. The lighting had been dimmed. He'd brought fabric from Dreamweaver Designs and dyed it to look age-stained—which was the reason he was currently running so late—and made slipcovers for the couches. Wispy cobwebs rippled in several corners, stirred by the wind from the open front door.

Priscilla had balked at first, but Jim had come to the rescue, convincing her that spooky would be better for their purposes. She'd agreed, but only for the séance. Tomorrow morning, before the readings, everything would have to be restored.

Conrad had simply looked at them with disgust, rolled his eyes, and walked away.

The woman moved on to shake Cass's hand. "I'm Joan Wellington. It's nice to meet you."

Ah, Conrad's wife. The mousy woman didn't seem as formidable as Cass had expected. She was thin to the point of being frail, her brown hair pulled into a tight bun, her features delicate.

"It's nice to meet you too. Thank you for coming." Cass released her hand and started to turn to greet the next customer.

Joan stopped her with a hand on her arm. "I've actually heard of you. A friend of mine went to your shop over the summer and had a reading. She asked me to pass on a message."

Cass waited, anxious to move on to the rest of the guests and get the front door closed before she froze to death.

"She and her husband came in when she first found out she was having a baby, and you told her she was having a girl. Her husband was skeptical, but Simone believed you completely."

Cass couldn't place the couple, since so many came in

asking the same question, but she held her breath waiting
to see if she'd been right.

Joan's grin answered the question before she said anything. "She gave birth to a beautiful baby girl two weeks ago."

Joy spread through Cass. "Tell her I said congratulations."

"I will. Thank you. I'm looking forward to having a reading from you."

She moved on. Conrad, who'd been hovering nearby,
placed a gentle hand on Joan's elbow and guided her toward
the back of the house, and Cass turned to greet the next
guest. The smile froze on her face.

In front of her stood Donald Larson, her ex-husband, and
Sylvia Marshall, her ex–best friend, arm-in-arm. Fear was
etched on Donald's face as he extracted his hand from Sylvia's grip and moved forward to greet Cass. His eyes held a
plea—for her to remain silent, maybe.

When he extended his hand, Cass took it automatically,
unable to even form a coherent thought.

He leaned over, her hand gripped in his, and whispered
in her ear, "I'm sorry. Priscilla forced all of us to come."
Then he released her hand and moved on, leaving her head
reeling.

Sylvia breezed past her with no greeting, her expression
smug, her long fur coat trailing behind her.

Cass greeted the rest of the guests automatically, a haze
of bad memories plaguing her. Sylvia had been her best
friend until the day Cass had gone home early. The day she'd
needed Donald's support after one of her patients had committed suicide soon after leaving her office. The day she'd

found Donald and Sylvia engaged in . . . inappropriate activities in Cass's living room.

"Are you okay?"

Cass jumped, the hand on her shoulder bringing her back to the present. The concern in Jim's eyes sent heat rushing to Cass's cheeks. "I'm sorry. I must have zoned out for a minute." The front door was already closed, and Priscilla was walking up the stairs with the last of the guests. "Is everyone here?"

Jim shrugged. "Most everyone, though a few haven't shown up. The ferry is shut down now, and the roads are getting bad, so I doubt anyone else will show." He grinned. "I do feel bad for those who didn't make it without a good excuse, though."

"Oh." Keeping her mind on what he was saying was a struggle, the image of Sylvia's self-satisfied smirk raking Cass's last nerve. "Why's that?"

He laughed out loud, a deep, rich sound that made her smile in spite of her ex's presence. "Priscilla can be a real sweetheart, but if she tells you to be somewhere, you're there. No excuses." He put a gentle hand on the small of her back, guiding her toward the ballroom at the back of the house. "Come on. It's time for the séance, and Priscilla doesn't tolerate tardiness." He released her when he spotted Priscilla and went to whisper something in her ear.

Cass's stomach heaved, its contents roiling and sending bile rushing up the back of her throat. She forced it back down. How was she supposed to do this with her exes sitting there staring at her? She glanced around the room for Stephanie. Bee would already be long gone—hopefully he'd remembered to get Beast from her room—but she needed some support if she was going to get through this. Entering the ballroom brought a small measure of comfort. A beautiful stone fireplace lent warmth as well as ambiance. The long table would easily seat everyone; she'd just have to make sure to have Stephanie seat her exes as far from her as possible. The wallpaper in the ballroom hadn't yet been replaced, and the yellowing paper was peeling at the corners. Sconces dotted the walls of the octagon-shaped room.

Cass drew in a deep breath, searching for calm, and fingered the small stones she'd put in her skirt pocket to help soothe her nerves. Did they really work? Who knew? But her customers sure seemed to think they did . . . plus, they couldn't hurt.

As she massaged the bridge of her nose between her thumb and forefinger, Cass studied the guests in attendance. It seemed at least half were already seated at the large table. Soft mood music played in the background, and she offered a silent thank-you to Bee.

Dessert and coffee would be served after the séance, but the thought of food set her stomach off again.

"Jeez, you look like you saw a ghost."

Startled by the voice in her ear, Cass jumped and turned.

"Hey. You all right?" Stephanie frowned and gripped both of Cass's arms.

"Yeah." Cass shook her head. "No. Ugh . . . I don't know."

"What's the matter?" Stephanie's urgent whisper echoed in the high-ceilinged room.

Blowing her bangs up off her forehead, Cass grabbed her hand and pulled her toward the corner. "Donald is here with Sylvia."

"What!" Stephanie's confused expression hardened into a scowl. "That snake."

Warmth surged through Cass. It would be all right. She'd get through this, with the help of one of her best friends, just as she'd gotten through the past year and a half. Donald's presence would probably be tolerable, especially since he'd had the decency to show some level of embarrassment. Sylvia's snide smirks could be a problem, though. She'd always been a bit condescending, especially where Cass was concerned, but it had worsened after she'd stolen Cass's husband.

Stephanie squeezed her hand, and Cass shoved the thoughts aside. This was her night. She'd built Mystical Musings from nothing, and she wasn't about to let Sylvia take anything else away from her.

"Don't worry, I'll dump coffee in her lap after the show." Stephanie's grin lightened Cass's mood.

Cass sucked in a breath, pulling her thick cable-knit sweater over her head. She untangled the chain of her good luck necklace from her wavy blond hair, tucked it back in place, and handed the sweater to Stephanie. She took the purple robe Stephanie held out to her and slid it over her black leggings, skirt, and camisole top. The coin belt jangled as she cinched it around her waist, the familiarity of the routine working to soothe her nerves.

Cass reviewed the information Bee had given her. But who should she contact? Buford Wellington, who'd died in the house a hundred years ago, or Horatio Madison who'd died more recently? Bee had suggested Horatio Madison, since he wasn't an ancestor of anyone in attendance, but Cass didn't have a copy of the complete guest list, so how would she know if any Madisons were among the guests?

Horatio had only died ten years ago. There was a chance,

however small, that someone in attendance could have known him. Buford, on the other hand . . . Well, there was no possibility anyone here had known him.

She rolled her hair into a bun and tucked it beneath the purple sash. With a deep breath, she smoothed her robe and started forward. Problem solved. She'd contact Buford.

Silence descended on the guests as Cass took her place at the head of the table. The crackling of flames and the soft music playing in the background were the only sounds in the room. An occasional gust of wind blowing off the bay rattled the windows.

Thankful Donald and Sylvia were seated at the far end of the table—but off to the side where she wouldn't have to look straight at them—Cass took a deep cleansing breath and stood. Everyone followed her lead. "I'd like to thank all of you for coming." She surveyed the faces staring back at her, some familiar from town or her regular monthly readings, but many strangers. She stared at Priscilla, who stood opposite Cass at the far end of the table, her brothers flanking her. "I'd also like to thank the Wellingtons for hosting this event. And wish them much success with the new Wellington Inn."

A smattering of applause as she lifted her glass of wine from the table in a toast, then the others followed suit.

"Please, be seated."

Cass sat, adjusting her purple satin robe to stall for an extra minute or two. She worked to clear her mind. With the unexpected props they'd needed, Bee had been busy all afternoon. By the time he'd finished, she was already greeting guests, so he'd never had a chance to go over everything with her. Hopefully, he'd told Stephanie what to do.

She heaved in a breath and began. "Please hold hands." Cass gripped Sara Ryan's hand on her right, thankful Stephanie had seated someone familiar beside her.

Rustling sounded, along with a few nervous giggles, as everyone moved to grab their neighbors' hands.

Stephanie leaned over the table and lit several candles then extinguished the lights. The music continued, but with the volume lowered. A few dim sconces on the walls remained lit. Their flames flickered, casting dancing shadows across the room.

Nice touch, Bee.

When Stephanie sat beside her at the table, Cass gripped her hand, closed her eyes, and remained quiet.

Someone shifted.

She tried to ignore it. Lowering her head, she searched for calm, tried to center herself, to find peace.

Someone coughed.

Pushing everything else away, Cass steadied her breathing. A séance was actually much easier than a reading. While doing a reading, she had to be fairly accurate, since the guests interacted. During a séance, she could say whatever struck her. Usually, something did.

Not this time.

Sweat sprang out on her forehead and crawled down the side of her hairline. *Oh, please. Not now.* A lump formed in her throat. *Don't let me choke. Not in front of Sylvia.*

Someone fidgeted.

Cass concentrated harder. Buford Wellington. He'd shown himself to Horatio Madison—supposedly—causing the man to have a heart attack. He must have wanted something. "I sense a presence." *Okay, corny, but better than nothing. Ugh . . .*

A soft gasp.

Hmm . . . maybe it would be okay. She resisted the urge to break the circle and wipe the sweat from her brow.

"An ancestor. A man. He died here, a long time ago." Cass tried to focus. "Hung. He died hanging in the cupola." The dome-shaped cupola, walled in by windows, had caught her attention when she'd first noticed the house. Was that where the idea came from? It didn't feel right. But, no matter, she was quite certain that was what had happened. She must have seen it in one of the books Bee'd brought to the shop.

A low rumble started in the distance. Thunder? During a snowstorm? Was that even possible? A snow plow maybe? Someone cleared their throat.

She regained her focus more easily this time, the words coming more readily. "He wants something." True enough, or he wouldn't have shown himself to Horatio. But what would he want after all these years? "A secret. Someone is hiding something important. He says someone has a secret that needs to be exposed."

The thunder rumbled again. Louder this time. Closer.

"This is ridiculous."

Cass opened her eyes. Conrad was standing, hands hanging at his sides, the circle broken.

Priscilla issued a warning glare. "Sit down, please, Conrad."

Wisps of smoke curled up the wall beside the fireplace behind the Wellingtons. Odd.

Conrad ignored his sister's warning. He propped his

hands on his hips. "This is the most asinine thing I've ever seen. What on earth would a hundred-year-old ghost know about someone having a secret?"

Priscilla stood and faced her defiant brother.

Jim jumped up and took her arm. "Let it go, Conrad. Just sit down."

The other guests looked on, more interested now in the conflict at the head of the table than anything Cass had to say.

The smoke coming from the fireplace increased, seeping throughout the room. If things hadn't gone wrong, she'd be in the middle of the séance by now. Had Bee set the timer on the fog machine he'd used in the fantasy section of his fashion show? Or was the fireplace backing up and going to kill them all?

The Wellington siblings' bickering was cut off by a huge boom, loud enough to shake the room, rattling the wineglasses on the table. Cass surged to her feet, knocking the chair over behind her. Many of the guests stood, too, fidgeting, twisting their fingers, gazes darting around wildly, obviously nervous. Unsure if this was part of the show. Unfortunately, Cass was just as much in the dark as they were.

She cast a quick glance at Stephanie, reluctant to tear her gaze from the Wellingtons gathered at the head of the table in front of the fireplace. Stephanie's expression was a mask of confusion. Apparently, she didn't know what was going on either.

The cloud of smoke billowed toward the high-domed ceiling, gaining form as it rose, taking on substance, forming a shape. The vague shape of a man emerged, his shoulders broad . . . Cass blinked rapidly, trying to dispel the image. It had to be her imagination. She rubbed her eyes.

A woman screamed. Another fainted. A man scoffed.

Cass stood with her mouth open, unsure what to do. Was this Bee's doing? He was a master at creativity, might even have the skill to pull it off, but she couldn't see how. A chill raced up her spine.

The next explosion of sound sent a tremor through the room. Cass gripped the table. A blast of ice-cold air gusted from the fireplace, eradicating the still-forming figure and extinguishing the roaring fire, as well as the candles on the table. The sconces flickered and died in a shower of sparks, leaving the room shrouded in blackness. The music abruptly stopped.

The momentary silence was deafening.

Chaos ensued.

"What the heck is going on here?" Conrad whined. "Whatever it is, I'm not amused."

People panicked, the harsh thumps of chairs falling over, people scrambling from the room. "Move."

"Get out of the way."

"What was that thing?"

"Was it really a ghost, Herbert? I want to go home. Now."

The heavy thud of footsteps overhead brought an immediate halt to the evacuation. The urgency of the voices dropped to frantic whispers.

"What is it?"

Someone was crying, the soft sobs echoing through the strained semi-silence.

Cass held her breath and listened through the harsh sounds of ragged breathing and soft whimpers. The noise seemed to be coming from directly above them. *Clomp, clomp, clomp* . . . accompanied by a strange scratching sound. Footsteps? Too fast. Whoever it was would have to be running.

"It's on the stairs." The shaky voice was barely decipherable. "It's coming down the stairs. What do we do?"

Stephanie grabbed Cass's hand, leaned over and whispered, "Is this part of the show?"

Cass shook her head then realized Stephanie couldn't see her in the dark, but she wasn't able to force the word *no* past her chattering teeth.

The pounding grew louder. The scratching came closer. Right outside the room. A deafening peal of . . . thunder? The ballroom door burst open.

Screaming, some of the men now joined the women.

Cass's heart jackhammered in her chest. She tried to suck in a breath. Couldn't.

"Sorry, Cass, but this is more than I signed on for."

Bee?

A dim light flickered to life as Stephanie lit a barbeque lighter and held it to one of the candles on the table. She went down the line, lighting every candle she could find, her hand shaking wildly each time she touched the flame to a wick.

Bee clomped across the room on his platform shoes, his intense gaze pinned on Cass. Beast clung to his side, tail tucked between his legs.

"What are you still doing here?" She pressed a hand to her chest, trying to control her erratic heartbeat.

As soon as they reached her, Beast whimpered and nudged her hand with his nose. Weaving the fingers of her free hand through the thick mane standing up around his neck, Cass took as much comfort as she offered.

Conrad stormed across the room, his demeanor aggressive as he approached Cass.

Beast growled low in his throat, baring his teeth, hackles raised.

Although Conrad stopped in his tracks, he didn't back down. Pointing a finger at Cass, he yelled, "That's going too far. I don't know what kind of cheap game you're playing, with your foolish parlor tricks, but I for one have had enough. I'm canceling the rest of the weekend."

"You can't do that." Panic clawed at her throat. No way was she refunding all of these people the price of their tickets.

"I can, and I just did." He spun on his heel and plowed into his brother.

Jim shoved him back with an open palm to his chest, his teeth clenched. His green eyes held a dangerous look she wouldn't have thought possible. "Let's all calm down."

Conrad tightened a fist at his side, but Priscilla stepped between them before he could take a swing. Cass couldn't help but wonder if he'd have had the nerve to do it.

"Enough." Priscilla spoke calmly, her voice pitched low, forcing everyone to quiet down if they wanted to hear her. And it definitely seemed no one wanted to miss what she had to say.

"Please excuse my brothers' behavior." She glanced around the room, making eye contact with each person. "It seems tension is running a bit high in light of the . . . events . . . that took place during the séance."

A few awkward chuckles followed.

A man approached Priscilla and spoke quietly to her.

She nodded and returned her attention to her guests. "It

seems the electricity is out throughout the mansion, so I have a suggestion." Her tone suggested it was more of a command. This was a side of Priscilla Cass hadn't seen, a forceful, dominant woman used to having her orders obeyed. "We'll retire to our rooms for the night. In the morning, we'll have breakfast, continue with the individual readings, and perhaps the group reading." She smiled, and more of the tension seeped from the room. "Then, if everyone is willing . . ." She stared directly at Cass. "We'll try the séance again tomorrow night."

Cass simply nodded dumbly, unsure what to say and unwilling to cross this new version of Priscilla Wellington.

4

"Scootch over." Bee lifted the blanket and slid into bed with Cass.

"What do you think you're doing?"

"It's your fault I'm stuck here, and I'm not sleeping on the cold floor."

Even though they had a lantern on the dresser between the two full beds—Priscilla had rounded up and distributed as many flashlights and lanterns as they could gather—the heat had gone with the electricity. Cass lay in the bed, shivering, fully dressed, with her coat spread across the top of several blankets. At least Bee would give her some warmth. "Fine. You can share, but it's not my fault you got stuck here. I can't control the weather."

Bee harrumphed. "By the time I finished setting everything up, the roads were already too bad to drive. There was no way I was going downstairs with that . . ." He waved a hand dramatically. "Stuff . . . going on. So I waited up here with Beast." A small chuckle escaped, and he pressed a hand to his chest. "I nearly had a heart attack when the lights went out."

The image of Bee running pell-mell through the dark hallways in his platform shoes popped into Cass's mind. She glanced at Stephanie in the bed next to hers, a pile of covers pulled up over her mouth and humor lighting her eyes. Cass couldn't bite back the laughter, and it bubbled out.

Bee scowled then joined her.

"Don't worry, Bee. I think half the guests had the same reaction." Stephanie sat up straighter and lowered the blankets. "Actually, once word gets around about this fiasco, maybe interest in Mystical Musings will pick up."

Cass shrugged. "Maybe." *Or maybe everyone will think I'm a fraud and stay away.* She sighed. "By the way, Bee. How did you make that figure form in the smoke?"

His bushy eyebrows drew together. "What do you mean? What smoke?"

"The smoke from the fireplace."

"I didn't do anything with the fireplace."

"You didn't use the fog machine from the fashion show?"

"Hmmm . . . I didn't think of it, but it would have been a good idea."

Stephanie shifted and pulled a blanket tighter around her. "So where did the smoke come from?"

A shiver ran through Cass.

Bee shrugged. "Probably from the fire."

But Bee hadn't been there, hadn't seen the man who'd

started to appear. Maybe Cass hadn't either. Maybe he'd been nothing more than a figment of her overactive imagination reacting to a room full of stress.

"And what about the image of the man that started to appear over the fireplace?" Stephanie asked.

Or, perhaps, mass hysteria? Is there even a remote possibility it could have been real? Cass did *not* want to examine that any closer. At least not tonight. "What about the rumbling noise? Was that your doing?"

He was already shaking his head. "I thought it was thunder."

"Can it thunder when it's snowing?"

"Sure." He didn't say anything for a minute as he seemed to ponder the answer more carefully. "At least, I think it can."

Cass's mind was about ready to shut down. She couldn't take any more tonight. With any luck, which seemed sort of doubtful the way the weekend was progressing so far, the electricity would be restored by morning. In the meantime . . . "Let's just get some sleep. About ten more guests signed up for individual readings before they went to bed, so I'm going to have to start earlier than planned." Hmmm . . . Maybe Stephanie was right. Maybe stories of the bungled séance would bring more business.

She snuggled down into the pillow, tucking the blankets beneath her chin. Beast's soft snores soothed her. Not that a dog was any defense against a ghost. But Beast was a really big dog, and he could be really scary when necessary. He was usually so easygoing, though. The only person he'd ever growled at had been Jay Callahan, when he'd threatened

Cass. Until tonight. Why had Beast taken such an instant dislike to Conrad Wellington? Maybe because Bee disliked him. Weren't dogs sensitive to stuff like that?

Her eyes fell closed, exhaustion weighing heavily.

Bee's rhythmic breathing told her he'd already nodded off.

Blizzard force winds howled.

A scream jerked her from the brink of sleep. Real? Or imagined? The wind, maybe? It came again, accompanied by the pounding of footsteps in the hallway.

Ah . . . jeez. What now?

She flung the covers back, grabbed her coat, and poked her foot around the floor in search of her Uggs. When her foot came to rest on something furry, she squealed and pulled it back.

"Will you be quiet?" Bee's sleep-filled voice helped bring her back to reality.

Slipping her arms into her coat, she stood, pushed Beast's head off her boots, and stepped into them. *Oh well, at least they're warm.*

Another scream tore through the night.

Bee shot from the bed as if he'd been cattle prodded. "What the . . ."

Voices accompanied the hurried footsteps, and Cass crept toward the door, with Bee clinging to her back.

"What do you think is going on?" Tremors shook his voice.

"I have no idea, but I can't imagine it's anything good."

"Should we wake Stephanie?"

"Stephanie's already up."

Cass jumped at the voice just behind her.

"Nice to know you guys were going to leave me here alone," Stephanie said.

Beast barked.

Ugh . . . Frustration shortened Cass's temper. "Fine. Let's just go find out what's happening, but don't let Beast out until we know what's going on."

Opening the door only as much as necessary, keeping Beast in the room, the trio slipped through into chaos. Oil lamps hung sporadically along the hall cast a soft, flickering glow over the melee, making the scene seem all the more surreal.

Priscilla stood sobbing at the bottom of a steep stairway in the middle of the hall. A stairway that hadn't been there when Cass had gone to bed. *What the* . . . A quick glance up explained why. An attic-style stairway had been pulled down from the ceiling, presumably after they'd started to fall asleep.

Jim held his sister against his chest, one arm embracing her, the other hand rubbing circles on her back. "You have to calm down and tell me what's wrong if you want me to help."

Priscilla sucked in a deep breath but didn't manage to form any sounds other than crying.

Many of the guests were now crammed into the narrow hallway, standing around in various states of undress, most wrapped in coats or blankets and holding an assortment of flickering lanterns, candles, or flashlights, looking as confused as Cass felt. She couldn't help but wonder why Jim didn't go up the stairs and see if anything was up there. It seemed like the most obvious course of action.

Would she have to do it?

She chanced a quick glance at the gathering crowd. Gazes darted frantically around, ultimately landing on the newfound stairway before not so discreetly shifting away. Feet shuffling and soft murmurs told her she wasn't the only one who'd had the thought. Of course, no one seemed too eager to go see what had the super-composed Priscilla Wellington sobbing like a baby.

Sucking in a shaky breath, Priscilla lifted her head from Jim's chest. She stared at her brother through eyes that were puffy and red, black makeup tracks running down her cheeks and circling her eyes. Her lower lip trembled, and she sniffed.

Someone held out a wadded-up tissue, and she reached for it and looked around, seemingly noticing the crowd for the first time. Her eyes went wide, fear etched into every line of her face. She'd aged ten years in the span of those few seconds, before she turned back to James. "Conrad . . ."

Cass had to strain to make out the harsh whisper.

She heaved in another breath. "He's . . ." *Sniff.* Her voice grew stronger, but not by much. She sighed. "He's . . . dead."

A collective gasp filled the hallway, then silence.

"I found him in the cupola."

Jim pushed Priscilla aside, grabbed a lantern from someone, and ascended the steps two at a time. Cass glanced around, then followed.

"Are you nuts?" Bee grabbed her arm and tried to hold her back.

Pulling her arm away, she leaned close so only he and Stephanie, who were practically glued together, could hear.

"I have to go. This could kill my reputation. I have to know what happened." She started up then breathed a sigh of relief when she felt their weight settle on the ladder-like stairs behind her.

"Wait."

Cass froze at the familiar voice and looked down into Donald's face.

"You might need this." He held a flashlight out to her, the beam of light bouncing around the hallway in his unsteady hand.

Coward. He never could take any kind of stress. Was she being unkind? Probably. Rolling her eyes, she grabbed the light and said, "Thanks."

Directing the light in front of her, she ascended quickly—before she could change her mind—and poked her head into the cupola.

It only took a moment to find Jim in the center of the small room, lantern lifted, staring at his brother's body hanging from a noose tied to a rafter.

Bee sucked in a breath from behind her and slapped his hand over his mouth.

Stephanie gasped.

Ignoring them, Cass moved toward Jim, gaze carefully averted to avoid looking at Conrad. "Are you okay?"

He shook his head but remained silent, staring at the body as it swung gently in the soft breeze probably coming through the old windows, the *creak, creak, creak* of the swinging rope hypnotic.

Unsure what to do, Cass hesitated. She didn't want to startle him, but she certainly wasn't going to stand there all night, or leave him there. "Jim? Are you all right?" She laid a gentle hand on his arm.

"You know what's weird?"

Cass frowned.

"He's had some sort of weird fascination with this cupola since the day we first looked at this house. With everything we had to do to get ready for this weekend, he still insisted on having the stairway installed before the séance so he could have access to it from inside the house." He finally pulled his gaze away from his brother to look at Cass. "Priscilla didn't know he'd chosen the room he wanted to stay in, and she accidently gave it to another couple who'd already checked in. Conrad freaked out. He wanted her to throw the guests out so he could have it, but she refused. They had a wicked argument over it. She finally caved when Joan approached her and told her how much it meant to him to have the only room directly beneath the cupola. She had no idea why, but Priscilla relented and relocated the other guests."

Cass didn't know what to say, so she simply remained silent.

Pain filled his eyes, and he lowered the lantern and sidestepped Cass without another word.

Bee and Stephanie shuffled out of the way so he could reach the stairway.

"You think he planned to kill himself all along?" Bee approached her without letting his gaze fall on Conrad.

"I don't know."

Screams and sobs reached them. "Where is my husband?"

They heard something unintelligible as someone tried to soothe the distraught widow.

"No. No. No! Conrad would never kill himself."

Cass reached up to massage her temples. What a disaster.

"Do you think anyone checked to make sure he's dead?"

Cass shined the light at Stephanie, who stood gripping Bee's hand, lower lip caught between her teeth.

"Huh?"

Stephanie shrugged. "Well . . . what if he's not dead? Do you think they checked or just freaked out when they saw him?"

"You think he could still be alive?" Bee pinned her with an incredulous look.

"How do I know? I'm just sayin' someone should check." She stared pointedly at Cass.

Crap. She was going to have to check. Blowing out a breath, she turned the light on the body. *Oh yeah. He's dead.* No doubt lingered as she started to shift the light away and get out of there.

The beam caught on something, and she played it back over the body, careful to avoid looking at his face. He wore no shirt, which seemed odd, given the temperature in the cupola was even colder than in the house, which was freezing. His slacks were still held up with his belt, and his socks and one shoe were on. She shifted the light across the floor in search of the missing shoe.

She found it in front of the window that faced directly out over the bay. She could barely make out a soft glow where the lighthouse beacon warned sailors they were approaching the rocky coastline. She bent to retrieve his shoe.

A hand gripped her arm. "Don't touch anything."

She looked up into Stephanie's worried frown.

"You can't touch anything. Even if he did kill himself, we're going to have to call the police. They're going to want to investigate."

Since Stephanie's husband, Tank, was a detective, Cass assumed Stephanie knew what she was talking about. She pulled her hand away but cast the light at the shoe and examined it more closely. Was the black dress shoe laying on its side the same one he'd been wearing all evening? She couldn't remember.

Tilting her head, she tried to shine the light beneath it. It seemed as if it had hooked on something, a protruding nail maybe? A raised board? She had to know.

"Are you crazy? I told you to leave everything alone." Stephanie huffed out a breath when Cass didn't pull away.

"Here." Bee shouldered his way between them. "Give me the light and see whatever you need to see so we can get out of here. Now." He held the light steady, sort of, as she toed the shoe aside. A piece of the floorboard lifted with it.

An empty space, about eight inches wide and a foot long, peered back at them.

"That's it. I'm outta here." Bee turned and headed toward the stairs.

"Wait. Give me the light for one more second." She grabbed it from him when he stopped and turned back and crossed back to the body. What was the reflection the light had caught the first time she'd looked at Conrad? Quickly running the light from his head to his feet, she didn't see anything. Then she moved it from side to side, and the same reflection glinted. Something clutched in his hand, a hint of gold just peeking out of his closed fist. She leaned closer but couldn't tell what it was, and there was no way she was touching him.

She started to back away.

"Hey. What's that?" Stephanie grabbed her hand and directed the light to shine on Conrad's arm. It fell on a large, dark bruise circling his bicep. No. More than one bruise.

Uh-oh . . . Cass quickly shot the light to the matching bruises on his other arm. A small patch of what looked like dried blood had smeared across his forearm, and she searched for an injury. Finding nothing on his arm, she let the light travel slowly up his body. When she reached his head, she stopped. A cut on his forehead had opened and dripped blood down the side of his face. Apparently, he'd wiped it with his arm . . . or it had dripped onto his arm and then somehow smeared. Either way . . .

Her heart stopped, and her gaze jumped to Stephanie, whose mouth was hanging open, fear filling her eyes.

"He didn't kill himself," Cass whispered, not wanting to alert any of the other guests.

Stephanie nodded.

A scowl marked Bee's features. "What are you talking about?"

"Shh . . . lower your voice."

"What?" He frowned, still keeping his gaze firmly averted from the body. "Why?"

"Because those bruises look an awfully lot like finger-marks, and he's got a nice knot on his head, which means someone might have helped him up there."

Bee's eyes went wide.

Swallowing the lump of fear clogging her throat, Cass squeezed her eyes closed, hoping the certainty would magically disappear. It didn't. "Someone who must still be here."

Her gaze jumped from Stephanie to Bee. Without another word, they turned and fled.

Cass stumbled down the last step, and Jim reached for her, catching her before she could face-plant on the hallway floor. Bee and Stephanie came to an abrupt halt behind her.

"Uhh . . ."

"Are you all right?" Jim stared at her, a frown marring his strong features.

Was she? No. Not really. "Uhh . . . yeah." How much should she tell him? She glanced at the group of guests staring openly at her. Was one of them a killer? He almost had to be, didn't he? He? Her gaze fell on Priscilla, who was quietly consoling Conrad's widow. Who said it had to be a man? The killer could just as easily have been a woman. But would a woman have had the strength necessary to haul Conrad's weight up into the cupola rafters?

Icy fingers of fear crept up her spine. She had to get out of there.

"Cass?" Jim still stood staring at her, his eyebrows drawn together, intensity deepening the green of his eyes. "Is something wrong?"

Her mouth dropped open, and he had the good grace to blush. "I mean, other than the obvious, of course."

All right. She was going to have to pull herself together. "Did anyone call the police?" Her voice held a tremor she wished she could have controlled.

"The police?"

"Yes. Stephanie's husband is a detective, and she said even in an apparent . . . uh . . . well. Someone should still call the police." Claustrophobia threatened to suffocate her. She'd left her cell phone on the nightstand in her room, the perfect excuse to escape the narrow confines of the dim, crowded hallway. She needed space to think. "I'll go call." With one last glance at Jim, she retreated, with Stephanie and Bee close on her heels.

"What are you going to do?" Bee asked.

"Shh . . ." She prayed fervently that Bee wouldn't say anything about their suspicions. At least, not until they reached the privacy of their room.

"Hey. Cass. Wait."

She stopped short and spun on her heel, then glared at Donald, who was standing next to Sylvia.

"If you're . . . umm . . ." His gaze darted around the hallway as if seeking help.

Sylvia ran a hand up his arm then clung to him as if he might run away. Or maybe she was just trying to keep warm. Everyone else in the hallway clutched robes, coats, or blankets around them for warmth. Sylvia's negligee and transparent robe left little—or nothing—to the imagination.

Donald cleared his throat. "I mean, if you're done?" He gestured toward the light she still held.

"Whatever." Cass tossed the flashlight, and Donald elbowed Sylvia in the chest when he fumbled to catch it.

"Hey, watch what you're doing, spaz." Massaging her injury, she spun on her heel and stalked off.

"Score." Bee's whisper sent a small thrill of satisfaction through Cass, and she bit back the grin that would seem highly inappropriate under such circumstances.

Cass stalked down the hallway and pushed their door open, and the three of them stumbled into the room.

Apparently oblivious to the commotion down the hall, Beast greeted her with his usual enthusiasm. Tail wagging wildly, tongue lolling out the side of his mouth, he jumped and planted his feet on her chest. Thankfully, she saw it coming and braced herself. "Down, boy." She nuzzled his head for just an instant, the scent of shampoo from yesterday's trip to the groomer still lingering, then pushed him down. Keeping a hand buried in his thick mane, she crossed the room and dropped to sit on the edge of her bed, then grabbed her phone. She dialed 911, hit send, and tapped her foot while she waited.

Nothing.

Frustration beat at her as she glanced at the screen. Two bars. She should be able to get a call out. She tried again. Silence, followed by the familiar *beep, beep, beep* of a dropped call. This time the announcement on the screen read CALL FAILED.

She slammed the phone down on the bed, shoved her hands into her hair and squeezed, desperate to relieve some of the tension.

"All right. Let's all just calm down."

Yikes. Bee as the voice of reason. This situation was way out of control. She pinned him with a glare and lifted a brow.

Undeterred, he held up his hands, palms forward, and sat on Stephanie's bed, facing her. "Look, we don't even know if he was murdered. You're assuming he was, but what do any of us really know?" He shrugged. "For all we know, he was up there with no shirt on and wrapped his arms across his chest for warmth." Bee demonstrated, wrapping his arms across his broad chest, gripping his upper arms. "Maybe he just squeezed a little too hard."

Stephanie laughed. "You've got to be kidding."

Lowering his arms, Bee pouted. "Well, it could have happened that way."

Cass stared at him, reclaimed her phone, and tried again.

"Okay, so it probably didn't, but I'm just saying there could be a perfectly logical explanation. Who knows? Maybe he got in an argument with someone earlier and they grabbed him by the arms. Just because there are bruises doesn't mean they were put there by a killer, or at the moment of his death."

Ugh . . . Giving up, Cass plugged the phone back into the charger before realizing it wouldn't charge with no electricity. She pressed the heels of her hands against her eyes. Something else was bothering her. A small niggle of something relentless, just out of reach, nagged at her. "So, who do you think could have killed him?"

Bee shrugged, seemingly forgetting he was supposed to be sulking. "Maybe his wife."

Cass tilted her head, willing to consider the possibility. "What makes you think that?"

"How would *you* like to be married to that man?"

She had to concede that point, but still, she couldn't see that frail woman killing her husband. Besides, she must have known what he was like when she married him.

Stephanie, who was still standing at the foot of the bed, began to pace the braided throw rug. "How about one of his siblings? They didn't seem to get along very well with him."

While that was certainly true, Cass knew plenty of siblings who bickered without murdering one another. Heck, Bee and Stephanie argued on a regular basis and didn't kill each other. At least, they hadn't yet.

"You know what?" Bee tucked his legs beneath Stephanie's blankets and rested his back against the headboard. "When I was working on the sound system earlier, I noticed Jim Wellington glaring at a couple who'd walked through the foyer. When he asked Priscilla what they were doing there, she just waved him off. It seemed as if he let it go, but he didn't seem happy about it when he stalked off."

"Do you know who they were?"

Bee shook his head. "Nah. No one said anything after that, and I was having . . . issues."

When Bee was concentrating on something, it took his full focus. That's why he preferred to work through the night: fewer distractions. Cass was surprised he'd even noticed that much.

Beast barked two seconds before a knock on the door interrupted them.

"Who is it?" Cass's gaze darted to the lock she'd forgotten to turn when they entered.

"It's Isabella."

"Come in."

Isabella Trapani cracked the door and stuck her head in. "If you guys want to come to the kitchen, I'm going to try to make some hot chocolate and something to eat."

"Is the electricity back on?" A small flare of hope ignited.

"No, but the stove is gas, and I have lanterns. A few of

the guests helped me move a lot of the refrigerated foods out to the sunroom when the electricity went out. I'm going to make a few trays of cookies. Want some?"

"Sure, thanks. We'll be down in a few minutes."

Cass waited until she'd left before saying anything. "What do you think the hole in the floor is? Do you think he had something hidden there?"

"I have no idea, but I can tell you one thing, I'm not going back up there to find out." Bee shivered and pulled the blankets up higher, tucking them beneath his chin.

Stephanie stopped pacing to stare at Bee. "Don't be getting too comfortable there, mister. You're not staying."

Bee pushed out his bottom lip. "Ah, come on. Why don't you sleep with Cass and let me have this bed." He jerked a thumb toward Cass. "She snores."

"Forget it, buddy. Not happening. That's my bed."

He huffed out a breath.

Cass worked to ignore their squabbling. What had James said in the cupola? "What was Jim saying about Conrad insisting on having that room?"

"When?" Bee frowned as if trying to remember.

"When we were in the cupola."

"He said Conrad and Priscilla fought because she accidentally put someone in the room he wanted," Stephanie said.

"That's what I thought. Why do you think it was so important he have that room? What could have been important enough to throw another guest out?"

Stephanie shrugged.

"Maybe it's a really nice room," Bee offered.

"It seems odd he'd need the room right at the bottom of the stairway. Just below the cupola."

"Maybe the view is really good from there? It is at the back of the house, overlooking the bay." Bee reached for Beast, who was still sitting between the beds, and gave his head a gentle rub. "Good night, boy."

"Hey. I said you're not sleeping there." Stephanie yanked the blanket back.

"Knock it off. Neither of you is going to sleep yet."

"What do you mean?" Bee only whined when he wasn't getting his way, which was fairly often. "I'm tired."

"Oh, please, Bee. You never go to sleep before it starts to get light out. You're the closest thing to a vampire I know."

He laughed. "That is true, but it's cold, and I don't like the cold. Besides, this house gives me the creeps. The sooner I go to sleep, the sooner I can get up and get out of here."

If the still-howling wind was any indication, Bee wasn't going anywhere any time soon. "Well, neither of you can go to bed yet. I need you to do me a favor," Cass said.

"What?" asked Stephanie.

She knew they were going to balk, but she was pretty sure she could convince them to do what she needed. She'd heard Isabella knocking on doors as she continued down the hallway, which meant many of the guests would probably be headed for the kitchen or dining room. "I need you to go have cookies and hot chocolate."

"Hmm . . . works for me." Bee swung his legs over the side of the bed. "Do you think she'll make the almond crescents?" He slid into his shoes.

Beast whimpered. "You can't come, boy, but I'll sneak

you back some cookies," Bee whispered conspiratorially. He grabbed his jacket. "Ready?"

"You guys go ahead. I'll meet you there in a little while."

"Why aren't you coming?" Stephanie asked.

"I will. I just need you to keep everyone down there for a while, so I can take a quick peek in Conrad's room." She winced and waited for the tirade. She didn't have to wait long.

"What is wrong with you?" Bee propped a hand on his hip.

Stephanie pinned her with a glare. "What makes you think Joan will go to the dining room?"

"You two are going to knock on her door and ask her to." Cass caught her lower lip between her teeth.

"And you don't think that'll look weird?"

"No." Cass jumped from the bed and lifted the lantern from the nightstand. "You both go to the door and tell her she shouldn't be alone. Tell her she shouldn't be in the room, because the police will want to search it, tell her anything, but try to get her out of there. Make sure one of you goes out behind her and leaves the door unlocked."

"I don't understand why you have to get in there so badly."

"You said so yourself, Bee. What if Joan killed him? We can't get ahold of the police. We don't know if anyone else did, but I don't hear sirens or a commotion, so I doubt it. Even if we do get in touch with them, we're at the farthest end of Bay Island and, in case you haven't noticed, there's a blizzard out there. Joan will have all the time in the world to get rid of any evidence before the police do get here."

"What evidence?" Stephanie frowned.

"How do I know if I don't look?"

Bee shook his head and rubbed a hand over his face. "I don't know. I don't like the idea of you searching the room by yourself."

"I have to. I need one of you to stay with Joan and the other to stand guard at the bottom of the main stairs and make sure no one comes up." She'd have to hope no one went through the kitchen and came up the back stairs.

Blowing out a frustrated breath, Bee stared at Stephanie.

"Please. I really have to see why he wanted that room so bad."

"Why?" Bee glared at her. "I don't see why you have to investigate."

She worked to control the tremor in her voice. "Don't you understand? My reputation is on the line. And, if I have to start refunding everyone their money and still pay all the expenses, I'll be broke. I'll have to leave Bay Island."

He sighed.

Yes!

"Fine." Bee tossed Stephanie her coat. "But you're getting ten minutes, that's it. Then I want you out of there, or I'll come get you."

"Thanks, Bee. You're the best."

"Yeah, yeah." He waved her off. "Give us a few minutes to get Joan out of there before you go out into the hall. And make sure no one's around before you go in."

"Sure."

"And one more thing, missy." He pointed his finger at her, his expression serious. "I'd better not find my name on that suspect list."

A pang of guilt surfaced. She feigned innocence. "What are you talking about?"

"Mmm hmm . . . Just sayin'." He spun around, opened the door, and sashayed down the hallway.

Stephanie shot her a sympathetic look before following him.

5

Cass resisted the urge to tiptoe down the hallway. All she needed was for someone to come out of their room and find her sneaking around. She gripped the flashlight Bee had given her tighter but didn't turn it on. There was no need with the sconces on the walls flickering a dim light. He was right, though she hated to admit it—the flashlight was better than the lantern since she could turn it on and off.

It seemed all of the other guests had either gone to the kitchen for snacks, or were perhaps holed up in their rooms, as she strolled purposefully toward Conrad's room. When she reached it, she held her breath and pressed her ear to the door. Silence. Hopefully, Bee and Stephanie had succeeded. She probably should have worked out some sort of signal for them to let her know, but she hadn't thought of it at the time. Maybe this whole amateur sleuth thing wasn't for her. She sighed.

With one last look around the empty hallway, she sucked in a breath and turned the knob. Easing the door open—wincing at the small squeak from the hinges—she slipped into the room, flicking the flashlight on as she shut the door gently behind her. She only took one step in before the beam of light landed on the image of a man. She choked back a scream—barely—squinting to bring the figure more clearly into focus.

Her breath shot out on a loud exhale when the shock of recognition punched her in the gut. Donald stood, frozen, beside the large dresser beneath the TV. The deer-in-headlights expression he wore would probably have been comical under other circumstances.

"What do you think you're doing?"

"Cass?"

Crap! With the light shining ahead of her, he wouldn't have been able to see who she was. If she could have just kept her big mouth shut.

"Cass. Is that you?" His harsh whisper grew more urgent. "What are you doing here?"

Uh . . . oh . . . that's gonna be tough to explain. "I asked you first." *Ugh . . . brilliant. I am so going to jail.*

He held up his hands in a gesture of surrender. A washcloth dangled from one closed fist. "Look, Cass. It's not what you think."

A tidal wave of memories—none of them good—slammed through her, crushing her chest. The pain of losing her patient after he committed suicide, the weight of the guilt, the longing for Donald's comforting embrace. But, when she'd pushed the front door open, there were Donald and Sylvia, naked, contorted on her living room couch.

Tears pricked the backs of her eyes. *Oh, no. Not now.* She couldn't fall apart again. The betrayal, the hurt . . . not only her husband, but her best friend. At least, that's what she'd thought.

"Cass. Please. You have to listen to me. I'm telling you, it's not what you think."

Past and present melded together. Shock, pain, emotions she had no hope of controlling. She took a step back and slammed into the door, the thud tearing her from the brink of panic. "Seems to me I've heard those words before, Donald." *Those exact same words.*

When he'd looked up and seen her standing in the foyer, mouth hanging open, he'd held up his hands in the exact same gesture and told her it wasn't what she thought. But it was exactly what she'd thought. There was nothing else it could have been.

His whispers grew frantic. "Are you ever going to get over that? It was one time, Cass."

"Oh, please." She struggled for calm. Worked to slow her racing heart. Fought to stay in the present. She wasn't that same weak woman anymore. She'd made a life for herself here. And Donald Larson was not going to take that away from her. "I asked what you're doing here. You have two seconds to answer before I go for help."

"You've got to believe me. It's different this time. It really isn't how it looks."

She studied his hands. What was he doing in a dead man's dark room with a washcloth in the middle of the night? Realization struck like ice water. "Well, it looks like you're wiping down the room."

He glanced at the offending rag, as if noticing it for the

first time, and winced. "All right, I guess it is what it looks like—sort of—but I can explain." Sweat had sprung out on his forehead and was now dripping down the side of his face. He used the rag to wipe it away. "I only used the washcloth so I wouldn't leave fingerprints. This was originally my room, but Ms. Wellington asked us to move so Conrad could have it. When we left, Sylvia must have forgotten her engagement ring, because she couldn't find it when we got to our new room. She begged me to come back and look for it, afraid the police would think she had something to do with Conrad's death."

The rapid tumble of words brought a dull ache to the base of her brain. It didn't make any sense. How would Sylvia know Conrad had been murdered? Unless . . . "You know what? I don't want to hear it." She fumbled behind her for the knob, not ready to turn her back on him, alone, in a dead man's room.

"No, wait. Please." He lunged toward her, and she clamped her teeth closed over the scream begging to escape. She had to stay calm.

"Stay away from me," she hissed. "Or I'll scream." She shoved the flashlight toward him. At least she had something to use as a weapon.

Maybe it was the tremor in her voice, or maybe it was the memory of how he'd charmed his way out of trouble with her time and time again during their marriage, but Donald's confidence seemed to increase the longer they stood there. Growing bolder, he took another step toward her, until they stood toe to toe. "Don't be silly. This is all just a misunderstanding." He spread his arms to the sides. "I'm sure we can work things out." Another bead of sweat dripped along the side of his face, belying the smug grin he now wore. "Come on, Cassie." He reached toward her, stroking a finger down the side of her jaw.

That was going too far. Rage tore through her. Bracing herself on her right foot, she swung her left knee with all of her strength, landing a crushing blow squarely between his legs. Donald crumpled to the floor with an "*oomph*."

She leaned over him, not even bothering to lower her voice. "Don't you ever touch me again. And do *not* call me Cassie." He was the only one besides her parents to ever use that nickname, and she wouldn't have it tarnished by passing over his lips now. "As far as what you're doing in here, you can just explain that to the police, because I don't care."

"Fine," he wheezed. "You . . ." He huffed out a breath and rolled over with a moan. "Can explain . . . too."

Great. She hadn't thought of that. How could she explain what she was doing in Conrad's room? "I'll just tell them I heard a noise and found you in here wiping the dresser." Would that work? Probably not. She'd worry about it later. Right now, she just had to get out of there.

Shoving his leg aside with her foot, she turned and cracked the door open. She certainly couldn't search the room now. She peered down the hallway, first one way then the other, flicked off her flashlight, and fled.

Cass strode through the doorway and into the dining room as if her heart weren't beating five hundred miles an hour and threatening to launch itself out of her chest. She hunted for Bee and Stephanie immediately, on a mission to get one or both of them alone and tell them she'd found Donald wiping down Conrad's room.

Could he have been telling the truth? Had Sylvia really sent him to search for the ring she'd left behind when they changed rooms? Was the washcloth really a lame attempt not to leave fingerprints? Her head spun with questions. Uppermost on her list was: had Conrad Wellington really been murdered? Followed closely by: if so, who killed him?

An engagement ring. Huh. She wouldn't bother to examine how she felt about Donald and Sylvia getting engaged. The hurt and betrayal ran too deep.

She didn't have to search too long to find Bee, as all six-foot-something of him was frantically waving both arms over his head and gesturing her toward him. He glanced pointedly at Priscilla, Jim, and Joan Wellington seated together at a small round table in the farthest corner of the room. Apparently, he'd kept watch from his current vantage point.

Her body sizzled with adrenaline as she tried to avoid talking to anyone on her way across the room.

"Cass?"

Crap. Maybe if she just kept walking . . .

"Cass." Sylvia's tone was sharper that time. If Cass wanted to avoid a scene, she'd probably best stop and answer her.

Ignoring her, Cass kept on walking.

Bee had returned to his seat, leaning forward, elbows on the table, hands clasped together in eager anticipation, as he continued conversing with a couple Cass didn't recognize. She headed toward them.

A firm grip on her elbow brought her up short. "Did you not hear me calling you?"

Cass huffed out a breath, shaking Sylvia's hand off as she turned to face her. Better to just have this out once and for all. She caught the other woman's gaze and held it firmly. "I heard you." She had no doubt the challenge was evident in her stance and her attitude, but she didn't care.

Sylvia held her gaze but didn't take the bait. She swallowed hard before continuing. "Where is Donald?"

A small flicker of suspicion ignited in Cass's gut and began to burn its way up the back of her throat. "What are you talking about?" If Sylvia sent Donald in search of the ring, wouldn't she know where he was? Cass looked over at Bee, hoping to get his attention and have him rescue her, but he was too engrossed in whatever discussion he was having.

"Don't play dumb with me, Cass. You're missing. Donald's missing. I wasn't born yesterday, you know." She folded her arms, pushing up her cleavage considerably, and scowled.

A surge of satisfaction shot through Cass at her former friend's jealousy, but it was short-lived. If she admitted to seeing Donald, she'd have to admit she'd been in Conrad's room. If she didn't admit to seeing him, Sylvia would think she was lying anyway. A no-win situation really. Except for the small rush of pleasure at Sylvia's obvious insecurity. Cass tilted her head to the side and lifted a brow. "Gee, Sylvia. I have no idea where Donald is. Do you have any friends here?"

A frown creased her brow, wrinkling the twelve pounds of foundation she had to be wearing. "Yeah. Why?"

"Well . . ." She couldn't resist the small smirk tugging at the corners of her mouth. Leaning closer, she whispered in Sylvia's ear. "Maybe you should check their rooms."

Sylvia fumed, her face turning a bizarre shade of reddish purple, before she spun and stalked off.

Cass expected to feel some sort of satisfaction at Sylvia's discomfort, but all she really felt was tired. Maybe she was finally leaving Donald in the past where he belonged. Interesting. She'd have to look at that more closely. Later. Now, she had to find Bee and Stephanie.

With renewed determination, Cass crossed the rest of the dining room, weaving her way through clusters of tables and chairs where small groups of guests sat with mugs of something steaming between their hands. Hopefully, it was Bella's hot chocolate. Her mouth watered.

Bee jumped up as she approached the table. "Here, honey, have a seat." He pulled the chair beside his out, and Cass dropped into it. "Is everything okay?"

She nodded, hyper-aware of the audience they now had.

"Have you met Mitch and Carly Dobbs?" Excitement flowed from him as he rambled on, not giving Cass an opening to get him alone. "Carly actually has a personal interest in this old place. She even met Horatio Madison's wife, and she's been giving me a wonderful history lesson."

Unable to work up the same level of excitement Bee obviously felt, Cass settled for being grateful she'd decided to contact Buford instead of Horatio. "It's a pleasure to meet you both." Reaching across the table, she shook hands with each of the Dobbs' in turn.

"It's a pleasure to meet you too." Carly smiled, but her eyes remained cold and calculating, reminding Cass of a snake.

"Cass, you just have to hear all about the sordid past this place has." Bee's gaze held a newfound appreciation for the old house, and something else as well, but she couldn't quite put her finger on what. Suspicion? Distrust? His stomach growled.

Hmm . . . maybe he's just hungry.

"Isabella should have the cookies ready by now. I'll get us a plate and bring you some hot chocolate while Carly catches you up." He patted her folded hands then gestured toward Carly. "Don't keep going without me, though. I can't wait to hear the rest."

Before Cass could protest, he was gone, leaving her alone with the two strangers staring openly at her. She shifted, dropping her gaze under the pretense of getting more comfortable. When she looked up, they were still both staring at her. *Oookaaay.* "So, tell me, what has Bee so fascinated?"

With a quick glance at each other, they launched into the story. "Well . . ." Carly sat back and settled more comfortably.

Apparently this wasn't going to be a short tale. Cass held back the sigh and contented herself with studying the middle-aged couple. Carly was a big woman, both in stature and personality. She was loud, forward, and built like an Amazon. She was also quite attractive, despite the dark, reptilian eyes. Her husband matched her in size, but he was much less animated than Carly. His receding hairline and beer belly made him appear quite a bit older than his more muscular wife. Who knew? Maybe he was.

Struggling against the urgent need to run after Bee and tell him about Donald, Cass tried to focus on Carly's words.

". . . direct descendent of the woman Buford was having the affair with."

Affair? Huh? "You'll have to forgive me, my mind wandered. Would you mind repeating that?"

With a frown and an unhappy huff, Carly backed up. "I said, Buford Wellington was having an affair with a young servant at the time of his death. A nineteen-year-old girl named Celeste Garnier."

Ahh . . . now it made perfect sense. Bee wasn't enamored with the *history* of the mansion, he'd simply dug up some old dirt. Bee thrived on gossip. He lived for it. Even hundred-year-old gossip would completely enthrall him.

Carly leaned forward, forearms resting on the table, and stared at Cass. Apparently content to find her paying attention, she rushed on. "When good ole Buford was found swinging from the rafters, there was a letter in his pocket. Turned out he left a note bequeathing everything he owned, including this estate, which was called Wellington Manor at the time, to his teenage mistress."

Cass squirmed, wishing Carly would lower her booming voice. How would the Wellingtons feel if they caught wind of the insensitive way she referred to Buford's death? A death that too closely mirrored that of Conrad. The siblings and Conrad's widow remained engrossed in whatever conversation the three of them were having. None of them looked happy. Then again, under the circumstances . . .

"Hey, maybe someone oughta check Conrad's pockets." Carly's hearty laughter echoed through the somber atmosphere as she slapped the table then waved a hand in dismissal. "Anyway, after Buford's death, his wife, Annalise, ran Celeste off and sold the estate to the Madisons."

Despite Carly's inappropriate good humor, Cass couldn't

help her piqued interest. "If there was a note, how did she get away with that?"

Carly shrugged. "Celeste was just a kid, and she was the one to find her lover's body. Annalise was a prominent woman in society. When she threatened to tell everyone Celeste had murdered him . . . well . . . there was no doubt who'd be believed."

"Was he murdered?" Nothing could have pulled her attention from Carly's story at that moment.

"No one knows. They called it a suicide, especially with the letter in his pocket, but rumor has it his wife had him killed after she found out about his mistress."

"So, whatever happened to Celeste?"

"Oh, good. I made it back in time." Bee placed a steaming mug of hot chocolate in front of Cass and a platter of cookies in the center of the table.

"Thanks, Bee." She blew on her drink and returned her attention to Carly, then shook her head and laughed at herself. She was no better than Bee, hooked on ancient gossip like it was happening in real time.

Grabbing a cookie, Carly continued, "Celeste wound up being pregnant with Buford's child, a son. She fled, disgraced and afraid, and moved in with a well-to-do older couple. She cared for them in exchange for a small servant's cottage on their property. When her son was grown, she passed the letter on to him and told him of his birthright. He, in turn, passed it on to his children. As far as I know, none of them ever tried to get the estate."

"What about Buford's wife?"

"After Celeste left, Annalise sold the estate to the Madisons and moved away. I don't know what happened to her."

Carly bit off half her cookie then gestured with the other half while she went on around her mouthful. "But I do know what happened to the letter."

Mitch, who'd been quietly turning his mug in circles on the table until then, perked up considerably, his attention suddenly fully focused on his wife.

"I am a direct descendent of Celeste Garnier, and a copy of the letter has finally been passed on to me. I've already initiated a lawsuit demanding the house be turned over immediately."

Was this woman out of her mind? Did she really think a court was going to turn a mansion over to her based on a century-old letter? One glance at Mitch's eager grin was all the answer Cass needed.

Bee perched on the edge of his seat, nibbling daintily on his almond crescent, hanging on Carly's every word. "Lucky for you the Wellingtons own the house again, huh?"

She sneered. "Luck has nothing to do with it. When Horatio Madison keeled over after seeing Buford's ghost . . ." She elbowed her husband in the ribs. "Ahh . . . to have been a fly on the wall for that episode, huh, Mitch?" Laughter bellowed out, and this time her husband joined in. Tears streamed down her cheeks, and she pulled her sleeve down over her hand and wiped them away. "Anyhow, his wife closed up the house and let it sit. When I got the letter, I went to see her. I told her everything, about Celeste and her right to the inheritance, about the curse she put on the house before she left—"

Bee held up a hand. "Wait. Back up. What curse?"

"What'd you think, she just walked away with nothing and left Annalise to live happily ever after in *her* house?

Nah, she cursed Buford and the house. Supposedly, Buford's ghost is trapped here forever. And everyone who lives here is doomed to bad luck. That's why the house has stayed empty for so long. One catastrophe after another befell everyone who tried to live here. And when poor Horatio tried to do the magazine spread featuring the house, hoping to get rid of the bad rap the house had, it didn't turn out so well for him. Who knows? Maybe they wanted to move in and live here. Anyway, his wife refused to turn over the house to me, but she did contact the Wellingtons and sold it back to them pretty cheap. Said it could be their problem." Snatching another cookie from the plate, she heaved in a deep breath and flopped against the back of the chair.

"They should just turn it over and not make us drag this out in court," Mitch whined, greed shining in his eyes.

"Don't worry, dear, we'll get what's coming to us, one way or another . . ."

What a couple of crackpots. Cass leaned forward, rested her elbows on the table, weaved her fingers into her hair and squeezed, blocking out any more of the conversation.

Bee leaned close to her ear, pitching his voice low. "Well, well, well. Look what the cat dragged in."

She looked up just in time to lock gazes with Donald. Her heart stopped. Panic clawed at her throat.

He approached Sylvia, who stood at the far corner of the room in an animated conversation with someone Cass didn't recognize. Keeping his gaze firmly on Cass, he leaned close and said something to Sylvia.

Sylvia's attention shot instantly to Cass, just before the two of them turned and left.

"I cannot even believe the amount of gaudy jewelry that

woman has weighing her down, not to mention that dress. Can you say tacky! Puh-leease!" Bee rubbed Cass's arm, offering her what comfort he could.

She patted his hand and dropped her head onto his shoulder then whispered, "I found him in a compromising position. Again."

Bee gasped.

"This time in Conrad's room."

6

After making their excuses, then extricating themselves from the Dobbs', Cass and Bee hurried toward the kitchen in search of Stephanie.

"Did you really find him in Conrad's room? Who was he with?" Bee hammered her with questions she wasn't yet ready to answer.

"Yes. And he was alone." She strode purposefully toward the back of the house.

"Alone? Really? Hmm . . . doesn't sound very compromising to me." He hurried beside her, struggling to keep pace.

Cass stopped and faced him. "Look. I don't want to have to go through the whole thing twice, so let's just leave it at I found him wiping down Conrad's room." She frowned, remembering Donald's plea and wanting to give him the benefit of the doubt. *Nope. Not happening.* He'd made a fool of her once. No way was he going to do it a second time. Still . . . "At least I'm pretty sure that's what I found. Now, let's find Stephanie so we can figure out what we're going to do."

A pang of regret hit Cass the instant hurt crossed Bee's face. The same hurt she saw any time she was short with him. She should know better, but her nerves were frayed beyond rational thought. *Sigh* . . . "Come on. It's good dirt, well worth waiting for."

"Oh, yeah, speaking of good dirt." He grinned, her momentary lack of judgment apparently forgiven. "What do you think of the Dobbs'?"

Resuming her trek toward the kitchen, Cass shrugged. "They can't really think they're going to win that lawsuit."

Bee waved her off. "Of course not. I meant, do you think they could have killed Conrad?"

"Hmm . . . I wouldn't think so. Then again, I wouldn't think anyone would file a lawsuit based on a letter written a hundred years ago, either."

Bee laughed. "Well, let me tell you, James Wellington nearly had a conniption when the two of them walked in."

Cass paused. "That's the couple you were talking about earlier? The ones Jim got angry over—"

"And Priscilla blew him off. Yup, that's them."

"Hmmm . . ." Cass resumed walking, their footsteps echoing in the empty corridor. "Do you know if anyone's reached the police?"

"I have no idea if anyone's even tried. I was keeping an eye on the remaining Wellingtons so you could . . . you know . . . do your thing."

This time, Cass grinned. No matter what she got herself

into, Bee was always there to take her back. "You know you're awesome, right?"

"Kissing up will get you everywhere, my dear."

She pushed open the door to the kitchen. Stephanie was drying dishes while Isabella washed.

Bee shot her a glance, lifting a brow in question, and Cass just shrugged, certain it would be safe to talk in front of Isabella. It wasn't like she was a stranger, and she obviously wouldn't have killed Conrad. She didn't even know him.

"How did you get the water working with the electricity out?"

When Stephanie turned and saw them, her breath shot out in a rush. "There you are."

Cass massaged the bridge of her nose between her thumb and forefinger. Her friend must have been worried sick it was taking so long while she'd been hanging out with the Dobbs'.

Isabella obviously didn't notice the tension with her back to them. "I just turned it on, and it worked. I figured they probably had a well, but I guess they must have run city water at this end of Bay Island too. I can't get hot water, though, so I'm washing everything in cold just to get it cleaned off and out of the way. When the electricity comes back on, I'll run it all through the dishwasher."

Stephanie tossed the towel onto the counter and rubbed a circle on Isabella's back then shot Cass a look filled with sympathy. "You okay, Bella?"

Nodding, Isabella shut the water off and turned to Cass, her eyes red-rimmed and puffy. "I know it's probably foolish, but . . ." She lowered her gaze to her hands, which were fidgeting with the zipper on her jacket. "I just can't believe he's gone."

Stephanie led her to a stool at the breakfast bar. "Here, sit. I'll get you a cup of hot chocolate."

"Thanks."

Cass and Bee slid onto the stools on either side of her. "I didn't realize you knew Conrad Wellington." Cass glanced over Isabella's head at Bee, who shook his head. Apparently he hadn't known either.

Taking a deep breath, Isabella swiped at her cheeks with the heels of her hands. "Yeah, well . . ."

Stephanie placed the steaming mug she'd poured from a large carafe in front of her.

"I haven't seen him in a long time. It's just . . . well . . . I know it's stupid, but I always held onto the hope we'd get back together."

"Uh . . ." Bee scratched his head. "I don't mean to be insensitive, but . . . isn't he married?"

Isabella blew out a breath. "I guess you could call it that."

When she didn't elaborate, Bee frowned but didn't press the issue.

Nothing Cass had ever seen of Isabella indicated she'd date a married man, but still . . .

"You weren't still seeing him, were you?" The words blurted out before Cass could censor them, and a pang of guilt stabbed through her with the glare Isabella sent her. "I mean . . . umm . . ."

"No, it's all right." She waved a hand. "I'm sorry. I'm just a wreck right now. I can't help thinking he wouldn't have killed himself if he'd never gotten involved with that witch he married."

Bee opened his mouth, but Cass shot him a *shut-up* look, and he snapped it closed.

Isabella twirled a spoon in her hot chocolate, staring into the mug and watching the contents swirl round and round. "He loved me." She spoke so softly Cass had to lean forward to make out the words. "We had talked about getting married." She shook her head and wiped her tears. "Anyway, none of that matters now."

Bee was hanging on every word, leaning so far forward that Cass worried he'd fall off the stool. "Of course it matters, honey. If you're this upset, he must have meant a great deal to you."

A small laugh bubbled out, but it held more scorn than humor. "At one time he did. Not really anymore. I've been over him for a while now, but that little bit of hope he'd come back one day stayed buried deep in my heart, you know?"

Bee nodded, his eyes filled with sympathy. "Do you mind if I ask how he ended up with Joan?"

"That gold digger!" Isabella set her mouth in a firm line, teeth clenched together, then sucked in a deep breath and let it out slowly.

Cass could almost hear her counting to ten.

"She set her sights on Conrad and didn't stop until she had him. I'm not sure what the deal was, but I'm pretty sure she had something on him." She blew on her hot chocolate, then took a sip and lowered the mug. "Whatever. It doesn't matter now. It just makes it harder that he killed himself, you know what I mean? If he'd just come to me, well . . . whatever the problem was, I'd have helped him work it out. Not because I wanted to be with him, or wanted anything from him, just because that's what friends do. You know?"

Bee and Stephanie both stared at Cass.

She caught her lower lip between her teeth. Indecision beat at her. Obviously, Isabella didn't have anything to do with Conrad's death and, truthfully, Cass couldn't even be sure he'd been murdered. But could she trust her to stay quiet about their suspicions until the police could be contacted? "Do you know if anyone has been able to alert the police?"

Bee finally sat back on his stool, apparently deciding the story had ended.

Isabella shrugged. "I'm not even sure if anyone has tried." Her pain tugged at Cass.

"You know, just because he was found hang . . . uh . . . like he was . . . It doesn't mean he killed himself. Until the police get here to investigate, we can't be sure no one gave him a hand."

Hope lit Isabella's eyes, followed almost instantly by fear. "You think someone—"

"Shhh . . ." Cass looked around the deserted kitchen then leaned closer.

Isabella lowered her voice to a frantic whisper. "You think someone killed him?"

"I'm not saying I think it. I'm just saying we can't assume he killed himself."

"So what do we do?"

Cass blew out a breath, blowing her hair up off her forehead. "I have no idea."

Cass strode down the hallway toward her room, with Bee and Stephanie keeping pace on either side of her, casting what they thought were discreet glances back and forth over her head, but remaining silent. "Knock that off."

"Knock what off?" Bee feigned innocence.

Stephanie just laughed.

Cass rolled her eyes, pulled the phone from her pocket, and dialed 911. Again. Nothing. Frustration beat at her. The thought of Conrad swinging back and forth above her head sent a shiver up her spine, and she quickly dismissed the image. She shoved the phone back in her pocket.

Pulling her room key from her pocket, Cass aimed the flashlight beam at the keyhole then jiggled the key in the lock and turned it.

The frantic scraping of Beast's nails met her through the door as he undoubtedly scrambled to his feet to greet her. She braced herself for the onslaught and shoved the door open. A blizzard of white flakes flew everywhere. Had she left the window open? No blast of cold air rushed from the open door.

She sucked in a breath and a mouthful of . . . feathers? *Ugh . . .*

"What on earth did that boy get into this time?" Bee peered over her shoulder as she trained the light on Beast.

He stood in the center of the room, tail tucked between his legs, a torn comforter hanging from his clenched teeth, head tilted in his best imitation of innocence.

Bee laughed as he pushed past her, and Cass handed him the flashlight. He patted the big dog's head and stage whispered, "Let me give you a tip, sweetie. Next time, drop the evidence."

"Great. How am I supposed to clean this up?" She wove her fingers into her hair, squeezing the strands to relieve the tension. It didn't work.

Stephanie dropped a hand on her shoulder and squeezed.

"I saw a vacuum in the closet off the kitchen when I was getting dishes. I'll run and get it."

"That's all fine and good, but how are you going to run it without electricity?" Bee lifted one of the bedskirts and shone the light under the bed, then repeated the process on the other bed.

Stephanie huffed.

"Besides, you may have a bigger problem than you think." He directed the light at the corner and ran it along the base of the wall.

Great. Just what Cass needed, another problem. Maybe if she didn't ask it would go away. Or, maybe Bee would keep it to himself. *Yeah right.*

Bee aimed the light at Cass and stood, waiting.

With a sigh, Cass relented. "What now?"

He handed the flashlight to Stephanie and held up what was left of the comforter. Unfortunately, a large section was missing from one corner.

"Where's the rest of it?"

Bee turned a glare on Beast, who let out a sound that sounded suspiciously like a belch.

Ahh . . . jeez. If she squeezed her hair any harder, she was going to tear out two large chunks. Tears leaked from the corners of her eyes. Blowing out a breath, she released her hair and rubbed her hands over her face. "Do you think he'll be all right?"

"He'll probably be fine." Stephanie took a turn re-examining the same small spaces Bee had already searched. "I had a golden retriever once who swallowed most of a sweatshirt, and she was fine." She shrugged. "Of course, she needed a little help . . . uh . . . getting it out."

"There's something to look forward to." Cass sat on the edge of the bed and pushed her hands through Beast's mane. "I'm sorry, boy. I don't think I'm cut out to be a pet owner."

Beast nuzzled her leg and dropped his head into her lap.

Bee rolled up the remnants of the comforter and stuffed it in a small trash can in the corner. "Aww . . . You'll be fine. You just have to be a little stricter . . . and maybe get him some obedience training and a crate."

"Really?" A small shred of hope flared. "You really think it'll help?"

"I don't see why not. The two of you certainly love each other enough."

Such a casual, offhand comment, but it struck a spark of realization. The big, sometimes dopey dog had really grown on her. She couldn't imagine not having him. But she was going to have to get a handle on the whole discipline thing before he got hurt. "As soon as we can get out of here, I'll take you to the vet and have him check you out." She stroked a hand down his back again and again, his warmth giving her comfort as he snuggled closer.

"Okay, I've been patient long enough." Bee flopped onto the other bed and swung his legs up, crossing his ankles and propping his hands behind his head against the headboard. "Spill, girlfriend. What was Donald doing in Conrad's room?"

"What?" Stephanie shot the beam of light at Cass.

The reminder snapped Cass back to reality. Covering her eyes against the bright stream of light, Cass brushed a bunch of feathers onto the floor and slid over—with Beast firmly attached—making room for Stephanie to sit. "Actually, I have no idea. It didn't make any sense. He said he went back to look for Sylvia's . . ." She struggled to force the words out. ". . . engagement ring."

"Oh, honey. I'm sorry."

"Me too." Stephanie patted her arm. "He's not worth worrying over, though. Let her have him."

"Yeah, she deserves him," Bee added.

Cass shrugged, even knowing they probably couldn't see the gesture in the dim light from the lantern. "It is what it is. Anyway, he had a washcloth in his hand and was standing in front of the dresser. In the dark." She struggled to think back through the shock of finding him there, wanting to make sure she relayed the events exactly as they'd happened. If she wanted Bee and Stephanie's opinions, she had to be careful not to put her own spin on things.

"That makes no sense." Stephanie frowned. "If it was originally his room, his fingerprints should be there. No?"

Bee held up a finger to stop her. "Not necessarily."

"What do you mean?" Cass slid back and pulled one of the blankets around her.

"Well, if he was touching the dresser or bed or something like that, his fingerprints would be expected. But what if he had to move something that belonged to Conrad or his wife? He certainly wouldn't be able to explain his fingerprints turning up on any of their possessions."

"Hmm . . . I hadn't thought of that." Part of Cass really wanted to be able to excuse his presence, but another side of her—the side that still bore the scars of his betrayal—didn't believe a word he said. "But what difference did it make if the ring was there or not? If it was, they could have just asked Joan Wellington for it."

"Yeah, but what if the police come and seal off the room? Then they wouldn't be able to get in to look for the ring."

Stephanie had a point, and yet, doubt still assailed Cass.

A soft buzzing sound intruded on her thoughts an instant before the lights flickered once and came on.

"Thank goodness, now maybe they can warm this place up a bit." Bee shivered and pulled his coat tighter around him.

"What you really need to figure out is if Donald had any reason to kill Conrad." Stephanie reached down to pet Beast when he nudged her leg.

"Did you not meet the man?" Bee scoffed. "Talk about obnoxious. Opening his mouth was reason enough." He stood and pulled the remaining covers back, then turned off the overhead lights, slid into bed, and tucked the blankets tightly under his chin.

Stephanie aimed the flashlight at his eyes. "Hey. What do you think you're doing? I told you that's my bed."

"Watch where you're shining that light."

"Get up."

"No way, sugar. You share with Cass. I'm already comfortable."

Stephanie growled but let it go, went around to the other side of the bed, and climbed in next to Cass.

The barest hint of grey light peeked between the curtains. It would be morning soon. One glance at her cell phone told Cass she wouldn't be able to contact the police tonight. No bars. That meant she couldn't contact Luke either. If anyone would know how to handle this whole mess, Luke would. As a detective on the mainland, and her sort-of boyfriend—well, *boyfriend* might be too strong a word—his advice would be invaluable. Too bad she had no hope of reaching him. She plugged the charger into the phone and left it on the nightstand.

The small beam of light disappeared when Stephanie clicked off the flashlight.

Cass tossed and turned as best she could, trying to find a comfortable position while crammed into the full-size bed with Stephanie. Useless, since the discomfort keeping her awake had nothing to do with the bed, the pillow, the cold, or Bee's incessant snoring.

7

The peal of sirens screamed through the morning, ripping Cass from a fitful half sleep. "Ugh." She rolled over, grabbed the pillow from the other side of the bed, and pulled it over her head.

"Hey." Stephanie yanked the pillow back from her. "No wonder Bee didn't want to sleep with you."

"Sorry." Sirens pierced the silence again. Cass popped her head up. "You think someone reached the police?"

Stephanie threw her pillow at Bee, hitting him square in the face. "Get up. I think the police are coming. And tonight, you can sleep with Cass."

He slit one eye open. "What time is it?"

"I have no idea."

"And what do you mean, tonight?" He threw the covers back and sat up. "If the police can get in, that means we can get out." He slid his shoes on, stood, and raked his fingers through his bleached blond hair. "And let me tell you, I am so outta here."

Beast scrambled to his feet, dancing in a circle between the beds.

"He has to go out." Smoothing her hair, Cass stood, then grabbed the leash from the dresser.

"Here." Bee held his hand out palm up. "I'll take him. Not like I'm in any big rush to talk to the police."

Bee's past had left him somewhat wary of law enforcement, so Cass handed over the leash. "Thanks."

Beast danced around in circles while Bee tried to clip the leash onto his collar. "Will you stay still already?"

"Sit."

Beast ignored Cass's command/request/whatever.

Bee paused for a minute to stare at her, brow lifted in a *you've-got-to-be-kidding-me* look.

She rolled her eyes and turned to open the door.

Beast shot through the gap before she had it fully open, dragging Bee behind him. Even with his two-handed grip on the leash, Bee couldn't slow the fleeing animal.

Ugh . . .

Stephanie burst out laughing.

"Not funny," Bee called over his shoulder as he tried to stop Beast before they reached the back stairway. They rounded the corner at the end of the hall, and Beast launched himself down the stairs.

Bee's shoulder hit the wall, and he ricocheted off. A tremendous racket—filled with bangs and curses—followed.

Ah jeez. Resisting the urge to go back to bed and pull the covers over her head, Cass ran down the remainder of the hallway. She skidded to a stop, with Stephanie breathing down her neck, when she reached the top of the stairs.

Bee lay in a heap at the bottom, leash tangled around him, Beast licking his face.

"Are you all right?" Cass yelled down.

"That *is* a rhetorical question, right?" Bee pushed up to sit, lifted one foot, and started untangling the leash.

Cass and Stephanie pounded down the stairs. When they reached him, they each grabbed one arm and helped haul him to his feet.

Once he was standing, Bee smoothed his jacket, adjusted his scarf, and tousled his hair.

"Are you hurt?" Grabbing the leash, Cass helped him disentangle himself.

Beast dropped his tongue out of the side of his mouth, panting frantically.

"I don't think so."

Stephanie handed Bee one of his shoes.

He took it and bent to put it back on.

With a quick look over Bee's back at Cass, Stephanie caught her lip between her teeth to keep from laughing. She couldn't stop the laughter from reaching her eyes, though.

Cass bit the inside of her cheek.

"Don't think I don't know what the two of you are doing," Bee said. If looks could kill . . .

Laughter blurted out, and Cass slapped a hand over her mouth. "I'm . . ." She sucked in a breath and tried to control herself. "Sorry."

"No you're not." He pointed at her. "You. Better. Get. This. Dog. Trained!"

She nodded, her head shaking like a bobblehead, tears streaming down her cheeks.

Stephanie hiccupped as she tried to contain her own outburst.

A smile tugged at the corners of Bee's mouth. "I think it was the shoe bouncing down that made all that noise."

"Really?" Laughter erupted. This time Cass made no attempt to restrain it. "Was it the shoe cursing up a storm too?"

"Ha-ha." Finally Bee joined their laughter. "Just schedule some kind of obedience classes for this animal. Before he hurts somebody."

Beast tipped his head innocently to the side, his eyes wide.

"Yeah right." Taking the leash from her once more, Bee eyed the dog warily. "That innocent routine doesn't work with me, buddy."

"Are you sure you still want to walk him? I can do it." Cass said.

He waved her off and headed for the back of the house. "Even a tumble down the stairs is better than a conversation with the police."

The peal of the door chimes, followed by pounding and shouting from the front door, forced her attention from Bee. Reluctantly, she turned away and headed for the front of the house, with Stephanie at her side.

Jim Wellington reached to pull the door open just as Cass and Stephanie rounded the corner and entered the foyer.

Detective Taylor Lawrence—Tank to his friends—strode through the door before Jim could even step back. "We got a call about a death." He held up his badge and moved past

Jim, scanning the foyer as he moved. When his gaze landed on Stephanie, his shoulders dropped. "Are you all right?"

She nodded as she crossed the foyer. The instant she reached him, he pulled her into his arms, and she leaned into him, resting her head on his massive chest.

Enfolding her in his arms, he kissed the top of her head. "You have no idea what my insides have been like since I got that call. Then I couldn't get to you. I had to get Emmett to plow in front of me all the way up here." He pinned Cass with a glare. "She's not allowed to hang out with you anymore."

"Hey. What'd I do?"

"You're a magnet for trouble."

Cass pushed out her bottom lip in her best pout and peered at him from beneath her lashes.

He opened one arm and gestured for her to come to him then pulled her into his embrace with Stephanie. "Are you okay?"

Cass shrugged, comforted by his presence. "I think so. Just shaken."

Stepping back and releasing both women, Tank turned to Jim. "What happened?"

Cass cringed. Tank tended to be a little overprotective of his wife, and his temper showed in the shortness of his tone.

Jim's chest inflated before he answered.

When Tank was angry, he often elicited that defensive reaction in men who didn't know him. Named for the vehicle he most resembled, Tank bore little resemblance to the teddy bear he actually was.

"My sister found my brother . . ." Jim pointed up through the ceiling. "In the cupola."

"Has anyone touched anything?"

Jim shrugged and glanced at Cass. "I didn't, but I wasn't the last one up there."

Cass's heart raced as Tank turned slowly toward her. "Do you want to tell me what you were doing up there?"

"Well . . ." She scratched her head and looked to Stephanie, pleading with her eyes for help. When none was forthcoming, she gave her a dirty look and turned her attention back to Tank. "I . . . uh . . ." Why had it made so much more sense to go up there in the heat of the moment? Should she mention she'd moved the shoe and tell him about the secret compartment? "The thing is . . ."

"Spill it."

She blew out a breath, flipping her bangs up off her forehead. He was a detective; he'd figure it out. "I thought I should go up and see what happened. I was concerned it would affect my reputation and hurt my business." She kept her gaze firmly on Tank, afraid to search Jim's expression and see how he felt about her somewhat selfish motives.

"All right." Tank rubbed his hand over the back of his neck and turned at the sound of tires crunching on the driveway. He moved to open the door, and more police officers filed in. An ambulance pulled in behind them, and Cass closed her coat tighter against the chill from the open door.

With Tank issuing orders, and members of the crime scene unit scrambling up the stairs and toward the back of the house, the scene became somewhat chaotic.

The attendants pulled a stretcher from the back of the ambulance and headed toward the house but left it on the front porch when they entered and pushed the door shut behind them. That thing would be freezing when they put Conrad on it.

Oh. Right. Cass cringed. When Jim led Tank up the stairs, she started to follow.

Tank stopped and turned to face her, his expression softening. "You don't have to come up, Cass. I'll be down to ask questions in a little bit. Why don't you and Stephanie go sit and have a cup of tea or something?"

She nodded, in no hurry to go back up to the cupola, but made no move to leave. Instead, she watched them ascend the stairs, then stood staring at the empty stairway.

"Come on, Cass." Stephanie laid a gentle hand on her arm and steered her away from the stairs and toward the dining room. "Tank's right. There's nothing you can do up there."

"I guess." The memory of Conrad's body would haunt her no matter what, but the thought that he might have been murdered by someone they'd been trapped in a house with all night chilled her to the bone.

Stephanie pushed the dining room door open then stepped aside for Cass to enter first, rubbing her arm in a gesture of support as she passed.

Cass braced herself and tried to shrug off the feeling of unease creeping in. As she entered the almost-empty room, Joan Wellington stood, knocking her chair to the floor behind her.

The police officer who'd been sitting across from her stood as well. He lifted his hands, palms toward her in a gesture of surrender, obviously trying to calm the irritated woman. Shaking her head, she backed away from him, tripping on the overturned chair. The officer made a grab for her, but she shook him off, regained her footing, and started across the room.

Tears streamed in a steady line down her cheeks. If her puffy, bloodshot eyes were any indication, they weren't the first tears she'd shed through the night.

Cass reached toward her. "Are you all right, Joan?"

Lifting her head, she spotted Cass. Her eyes widened, and her mouth fell open. Fear? But what would she have to be afraid of from Cass?

"Joan?"

With a soft sob, she pulled her gaze from Cass's, turned and fled.

"What do you think that was about?" A frown creased Stephanie's brow.

"I have no idea."

"She looked terrified."

Cass shrugged the strange incident off. The woman had just lost her husband, maybe it was grief marring her features. "Yeah . . . weird."

The police officer had moved a few tables over and now sat in deep conversation with Priscilla. Jim stood behind her, his hands on her shoulders, his stance defensive.

"He sure is protective of his sister. Don't you think?" Cass stopped at a table across the room from them where she had a good view of the action.

Pulling out her chair, Stephanie kept her gaze glued to the Wellingtons. "Even before Conrad . . . well . . . you know . . . Almost as if it were the two of them against Conrad."

"It did seem as if Conrad gave Priscilla a hard time, but she struck me as strong enough to deal with him."

"She pretty much blew him off when he objected to the séance. Apparently he didn't have as much power as the other two." Resting her elbows on the table, Stephanie propped her chin on her clasped hands. "At least not when they teamed up."

"Hmm . . ." Cass rested her cheek on her hand. Jim gently massaged his sister's shoulders. He'd rolled up his sleeves to his elbows, leaving the corded muscles of his forearms visible.

"Hey." Stephanie snapped her fingers in front of Cass's face. "Aren't you listening?"

"Uh . . . sorry. I must have zoned out for a minute."

"Uh-huh." Stephanie made no attempt to hide her smirk as she nodded knowingly.

Ugh . . . great. Now she'd tell Bee, and Cass would never hear the end of it. "Don't *uh-huh* me. How can you even tell what I'm thinking about?"

"Might have something to do with that bit of drool running down your chin."

"What? You're crazy." Cass waited for her to glance back toward the Wellingtons then discreetly checked her chin for drool. Stephanie's soft laughter told her she'd been played.

"Smart aleck." Cass couldn't help but laugh. Between Stephanie and Bee trying to play matchmaker, it was a wonder she wasn't married off ten times already. Speaking of married . . .

She sat up straighter and nudged Stephanie as Donald and Sylvia entered the dining room. With a glance at Priscilla and Jim talking to the cop, they skirted the table and sat one table away.

Cass worked hard to ignore them. "Can you do me a favor, Steph?"

"Sure. What do you need?"

"Could you not mention me going into Conrad's room to Tank?"

Stephanie sighed and stared at Cass. "Come on, Cass. You know I don't like lying to Tank. Besides, it might be important. You have no idea what Donald was doing there. How do you know he didn't kill Conrad? Besides, what if Donald tells the police he was there?"

No matter how she felt about Donald, it was hard to see him in the role of a killer. Still . . . "Technically, it's not really lying. You're just neglecting to mention something that probably doesn't matter anyway. Plus, we don't even know for sure Conrad was killed. If he committed suicide, Donald's presence doesn't matter. And I highly doubt Donald will confess to being there. He was a nervous wreck about me catching him."

"You know, I don't get you. I'd think you'd want to rat good ole Donald out after what he did to you."

"It's not really Donald I'm worried about." Shooting Stephanie a sheepish grin, Cass shrugged. "I don't want Tank to get mad at me."

"Oh, please. He's not going to . . ." Stephanie paused for a moment. "No. You're right. He's gonna be pissed." They laughed together, keeping their voices low out of respect for the Wellingtons.

"Hey. What's he doing here? I thought he'd stay as far away from any chance of interrogation as possible."

Cass looked in the direction Stephanie indicated. Bee was striding toward her, a tray in his hands. He slowed for a few seconds as he passed the Wellingtons' table.

"I don't know. I figured he'd stay away, too."

When he reached them, Bee lowered the tray to the table. "Hey, beautiful." He handed Cass and Stephanie each a cup of tea. "You too, Stephanie."

"Ha-ha." Stephanie smacked his arm. "What are you doing here?"

He perched on the edge of a chair, feet flat on the floor, looking ready to bolt at a moment's notice. "I brought Beast back upstairs."

Cass groaned.

"Don't worry. I'm pretty sure diving and tunneling through all that snow tuckered him out. I think he'll sleep, for a little while, at least." He stirred milk into his tea, then handed it to Stephanie. "And don't worry about taking him to the vet. I found the missing piece of comforter."

"You did?" A sigh of relief escaped. One less thing to worry about. "Where was it?"

"You don't want to know." Bee cleared his throat and glared at her. "But trust me when I tell you, you do *not* want it back."

"Oh . . . uh . . . nah. I'm just glad you found it."

"Yeah, me too. Anyway, I went down to the kitchen to see if Isabella had anything hot to drink—by the way, she said to tell you to keep Beast out of the garbage."

"When did he get into the garbage?"

Bee did his best not to appear guilty. It didn't work. "It could have been on my way back in with him." He fluttered his lashes then tilted his head in an imitation of Beast's innocent look.

Cass laughed.

"Anyway, when I saw Bozo and his sidekick there . . ." He nodded toward Donald and Sylvia. ". . . coming in, I wanted to make sure you were okay."

"Aw, thanks, Bee." Cass leaned her head onto his broad shoulder. "You're a real sweetheart."

"Yeah, well . . ."

"How'd you know we were here?" Placing the milk back on the tray, Stephanie absently stirred her tea.

"I always make it a point to know where my girls are."

Warmth surged through Cass. She didn't always appreciate Bee enough. Not only was he a good friend, he was the most sensitive, caring man she knew.

Bee was quick to change the subject. "Jim sure looks unhappy."

Jim Wellington's mouth had firmed into a thin line, and the creases in his face had deepened. The muscles in his shoulders bunched as he gripped the back of Priscilla's chair tighter.

"I'll say. Did you hear anything on your way past?" Cass asked.

"Nah. Couldn't hear a word. Seemed to me the Wellingtons and the cop were glaring at one another without saying anything. Priscilla looked like she'd been crying, but she seems to be over it now."

The anger etched on her face chased away any signs of the prior grief. Jim helped her to her feet and, with one final glare at the poor cop, he led her from the room.

"Hmm . . ." Bee stared openly, making no attempt to

disguise his interest. "Somebody just made a couple of enemies."

"He's getting on everyone's bad side. We ran into Joan on our way in, and she looked like she was running from a monster." Cass watched the small whirlpool as she swirled her spoon around and around. A shadow passed over her, and she sucked in a breath.

"Well, well, well . . ."

Cass jumped, startled by Donald's voice so close to her, and the spoon clattered to the table. How long had she zoned out that she missed him approaching? Though Bee and Stephanie eyed him suspiciously, they didn't seem surprised he was standing there with Sylvia hanging on his arm.

Donald ignored them, focusing his full attention on Cass. "Apparently our dearly departed Conrad may not have climbed up into those rafters himself. Who do you think could have helped him up there?"

Cass bristled. "How would I know?"

"Oh, I don't know, but I bet the police would be interested to know you were lurking around his room after the fact." Donald stood tall, hands in his pockets, no indication of his former fear remaining.

Scanning the room to be sure no one was listening, Cass gritted her teeth.

Bee slid back in the chair, hooking his arm over the back and crossing his legs. Pressing a hand daintily to his chest, he batted his long eyelashes. "I bet they'd be more interested to know she wasn't alone in there. Could be hard to explain to *some people* what the two of you were doing together . . . in the dark . . . alone." He tilted his head and aimed a lifted brow at Sylvia.

Anger reddened Donald's face as he turned on Bee, then just stopped and gaped. Bee in full diva mode was quite a sight to behold.

Without taking her glare from Bee, Sylvia straightened and released her hold on Donald. "Donald already explained why he was in there, and I think it was really sweet he went back to look for my engagement ring."

Wait a minute. Hadn't Donald said Sylvia sent him back to look for the ring?

"This may come as a surprise to someone as *loyal* as you . . ." Bee leaned forward and gestured for Sylvia to do the same. "But to some people, a ring doesn't mean anything." Then he gestured toward Donald's groin. "By the way, how are the boys feeling?"

Donald winced and covered himself.

With a huff, Sylvia turned and stalked away.

Cass made no attempt to hide a smirk.

"You ought to think about having another séance, Cass." Donald's sneer shot right to her gut. "Maybe you can ring up good ole Conrad and ask him who offed him."

Bee stared after them as they stormed from the room. "What a jerk. How were you ever married to that guy?"

Cass was saved from having to answer, or even think about it, when Tank strode into the room and straight toward them. He didn't look happy.

"Well, that's my cue." Bee stood.

"Uh-uh. You're not going anywhere." Tank pointed to the chair Bee had been sitting in. "Why don't you stick around and we'll have a little chat."

"Oh, that's okay. I have things to do, places to go, people to see. You know how it is." He only got as far as the next table.

"Sit, Bee."

He grumbled but did as he was told.

Tank frowned. "What are you doing here anyway? Stephanie said you weren't staying."

"I wasn't, but there were some issues when we got here." He shrugged it off as if it were no big deal, though everyone sitting there knew it was. "I hung around to help out and got caught in the storm."

Tank nodded then turned the remaining chair around and straddled it, folding his hands on the table. "What happened?"

The question wasn't aimed at anyone in particular, but since Bee and Stephanie sat staring at Cass, she sighed and started from the beginning. She talked Tank through going into the cupola, told him about the open space she'd stumbled across in the floor—then stared at Bee and Stephanie in turn, hoping they wouldn't mention she'd accidentally opened it while moving Conrad's shoe. Satisfied her secret was safe, Cass continued to walk him through what she remembered of the crime scene. When she finished up with her thoughts about the knot on his head and the bruises on his upper arms, Tank lifted a brow but remained silent.

Exhausted, Cass reached for her tea. "And that's it. Then we came down and had hot chocolate while we tried to call the police." A bead of sweat trickled down her back. Had Donald told anyone she'd been in Conrad's room? If he had, Tank would surely know by now. She lowered her gaze and sipped the now lukewarm tea, praying he'd accept her explanation and let it go at that.

Tank cleared his throat and ran a hand over his buzzed

hair. He pinned her with a gaze, his steel-grey eyes locking onto hers, searching for something. "You're sure?"

"Positive. Why?" She feigned innocence—at least she hoped it came across as innocence. She was a terrible liar, so it could possibly come across as hiding something.

"You didn't notice anything else at all while you were up there?"

Cass shook her head, her heart racing. Could he see it pounding against her ribs? She pulled her coat tighter around her, even though the room had warmed considerably.

Finally releasing her from his captive gaze, Tank stood. "Okay. Get your things."

Cass's heart lurched. "What are you talking about? I can't leave."

"What do you mean you can't leave? Of course you're leaving. All three of you." He pointed a finger and gestured at Cass, Bee, and Stephanie.

"Tank, please. This weekend is really important to me. I have to stay."

With a quick glance around the almost-empty room, Tank sank back onto his chair. "Cass . . ." He ran his thumb and forefinger over his goatee. "Do you understand what's going on here?"

She swallowed hard. Should she ask, or simply continue to go about her life without knowing? If she chose the latter, she could convince herself Conrad committed suicide. Probably. While sad, that would mean they hadn't spent the better part of the night holed up with a killer. She pitched her voice as low as she could. It wasn't hard, since she could barely suck in enough air to force out any sound. "Conrad didn't kill himself, did he?"

Tank shook his head.

"Are you sure?"

"Positive."

Fear clutched her heart. "How can you be positive?"

"The rafters are eight feet high. Conrad was less than six feet tall." He waited.

She stared blankly then spared a quick look at Stephanie and Bee. Neither of them seemed to have any sort of epiphany, so she turned her attention back to Tank. "And?"

"There was a stepladder in the back corner of the room."

Cass walked through the crime scene in her mind. She remembered the shoe lying on the floor across the room. Weird. But she couldn't recall seeing any sort of ladder, or stool, or chair. Nothing overturned beneath Conrad as he swung at least two feet off the floor. *Ah . . . jeez . . .*

"Obviously, Conrad didn't put it away himself, no matter how much of a neat freak he was."

"Neat freak?"

Tank shrugged. "At least that's what everyone says."

An image of the mess spread across Conrad's dresser flashed into her mind. Overturned bottles, discarded napkins and jewelry. Whoever left that was far from a neat freak. Had Donald made the mess while he was searching the room?

Tank stood, interrupting her thoughts. "There's no way I'm leaving my wife or my friends in danger. Not happening."

Bee sat up straighter, his fluttering eyelashes a good indication he was holding back tears. He and Tank had clashed numerous times, only recently reaching some sort of tentative truce, but this was the first time Tank had referred to him as a friend. It obviously meant a lot. Bee considered Stephanie one of his best friends, family really, and it always hurt that her husband couldn't accept him.

Tank's expression softened for just an instant. "I'm sorry, Cass. I really am."

"I'm going to have to refund everyone their money and still pay for the food and everything." Her throat strained with the effort to hold back her tears. "In the long run, this could end up *costing* me money. You don't understand, Tank." She had to struggle to force the words past the lump blocking her throat. "It could ruin me. I might lose the shop."

The confession didn't come easy. She'd poured her heart and soul into Mystical Musings, as well as all of her savings, but Bay Island just didn't thrive in the winter. She wiped away tears.

"It'll be all right, honey." Bee was at her side in an instant. He wrapped an arm around her and squeezed, pulling her into his embrace. "Since Dreamweaver has picked up and I've gotten some big-name buyers to come to my shows, I've been able to put a little money away. It's not much, just a small nest egg, but . . ." Twin spots of crimson spread across his cheeks. "You're one of my best friends, Cass. I'll help you any way I can."

A vise squeezed her chest. "Thank you."

He hugged her closer, and she wrapped her arms around his waist. "Of course, dear."

Stephanie rubbed a circle on her back. "Tank and I will help too."

"Come on, guys." Tank gently untangled her from Bee. "We'll work it all out, Cass. You're not going to lose the shop. Now, let's get you out of here. I'm closing down the bed-and-breakfast as soon as we can safely transport everyone to the Bay Side Hotel."

"Can we go up and get our things? I have to get Beast, too."

Tank's face paled. "You brought the dog?"

"Well, Bee was supposed to watch him, but when he got stuck here, so did Beast."

Tank propped his hands on his hips and blew out a breath. "We can't unbury all of the cars, so he'll have to ride back with us in my truck." He lifted a finger in warning. "Do not let him eat any part of it."

8

Cass unlocked the door to Mystical Musings the next morning and shoved it open with her hip, while digging through her oversize bag in search of the muffled ringtone coming from it. Using her elbow, she held the door for Beast to enter. "Ha. Got it." She yanked the phone from her bag and hit the button. Nothing. "Dang. After all that, I missed it anyway." Letting the door fall shut behind her, she crossed the store and dropped her bag onto the counter, then smiled when she read Luke's name above the missed call message. Heat crept up her neck and into her cheeks. She'd call him back as soon as she got settled.

She hadn't seen Luke in close to a month. With the holidays, his work schedule, and his other commitments, he hadn't been able to make time for the trip over to Bay Island. She could probably make time to get over to the mainland, but she didn't have anyone to leave Beast with.

Beast. The big dog stood near the front door licking puddles of snow from the floor. Cass sighed. Could be worse. At least he wasn't doing any damage, and she'd have to mop the floors before she opened anyway, before the residue from the salt in the parking lot and the porch damaged the wood. Actually, she should probably throw some more salt on the steps too. Maybe she'd do that first. The bright sun beating down had melted the snow and ice, turning everything to slushy puddles, only to have it all re-freeze again as soon as the sun dropped below the horizon.

With a sigh at the thought of going back out into the cold, she pulled the ice melt out from beneath the counter and trudged back onto the porch. A small niggle of depression crept in. Why even bother? Would anyone come into the shop today? The diner and Tony's bakery had opened this morning. And she had no doubt the deli had managed to open yesterday, since the owner's son lived in an apartment above the store and didn't have to wait for side roads to be cleared. Word of her failure would have spread to almost everyone by now. Especially with everyone pretty much snowbound for all of Sunday. They'd all be desperate for their daily dose of gossip by this morning. Cass might have been, too, after being cooped up for almost two days, if she wasn't the topic of the week. Again. *Ugh . . .*

She grabbed the shovel from beside the door and pushed the slushy mess off the porch and steps, then did the walkway, too. *Wouldn't want the mad dash of customers to slip.* The crunch of tires on the icy mess intruded on her pity-fest, and she glanced up. Emmett Marx was pulling in, driving his tow truck.

Emmett was a sweetheart. He owned the garage at the

other end of the island, and most islanders took their cars to him because he was practically a miracle worker. He was also known as the local handyman. Emmett hopped out of the truck and strolled toward her with his hands tucked into his sweatshirt pockets.

"Hey, Emmett. What are you doing out without a coat? It's freezing out here."

"Nah. Not that bad. 'Sides, my coat's in the truck. Too bulky while I'm driving."

Cass narrowed her eyes. As sweet as he was, Emmett wasn't known for his social skills. That was more than he usually said in an entire conversation. Hmm . . . maybe being stuck in the snow made him talkative.

"Thanks for digging my car out yesterday." If he hadn't plowed out the bed-and-breakfast, she'd still be stuck home with no car.

He waved her off and tucked his wild mane of long hair farther under his black knit cap. "If you give me your keys, I'll move your car out and tidy up the parking lot a bit." He held out an ungloved hand.

"Come on in for a minute. I have to get the keys." She propped the shovel beside the door. "Thank you. I was just thinking about shoveling it. I was worried this would all freeze over again by tomorrow."

Emmett grunted. Apparently his chatty streak was over.

Beast scrambled to get his feet beneath him on the polished wood floors, giving Emmett a second to brace himself before the onslaught.

"Beast!" Cass's command fell on deaf ears as the dog landed his front paws on Emmett's chest.

Emmett backpedaled, but caught himself before he

toppled over the coatrack behind him. "Hey, fella." He ran his fingers through Beast's mane before pushing him down.

"I'm sorry, Emmett." Cass pulled the keys from her bag and ran toward him. She picked up a bone from the floor and tossed it to Beast. "Are you all right?"

"Fine. I'm used to big dogs." Brushing the dirt from his sweatshirt, Emmett grinned. "Love that big fella, right, Beast?"

Beast barked once in answer then returned to chewing.

"Can I get you something to drink? Coffee, tea, hot chocolate?"

Emmett shrugged.

"Come on in. Sit and warm up for a few minutes." She led him to the table at the back of the shop. "I was just going to make some coffee."

"Sure." Emmett pulled out a chair and sat. He cleared his throat, something obviously on his mind.

"You okay?"

Fidgeting with the keys, Emmett shrugged. "Fine."

Cass busied herself preparing the coffee. Emmett was one of the shyest people she knew; though, he'd come out of his shell a little since he'd been seeing Sara Ryan. Cass couldn't be happier. The outgoing woman was good for him, and her daughter, Jess, and his son, Joey, were great friends.

"Actually, I wanted to talk to you about the other night."

She waited, stirring milk into the two cups. Hopefully, he didn't want his refund right away. Bracing herself for the possibility, she lifted the cups and turned to him. "I'm sorry. I know it didn't work out so well." Heat flared in her cheeks.

"No big deal. At least I got to spend the night with Sara."

He jerked his head up, a look of sheer horror twisting his features.

Cass laughed.

"I didn't mean . . . uh . . . well . . . you know what I mean." His entire face flamed red.

"Don't worry. I understand. I know you guys don't get to spend a lot of time together." Everyone knew Emmett was a perfect gentleman. Cass placed one cup in front of him then walked around the table and settled herself opposite him, giving him a second or two to compose himself.

"Anyway." He wiped his brow with the back of his hand. "We were in the dining room talking after most everyone went to bed. We talked for a long time. When we were done, I walked Sara back to her room and said good night at the door."

When he didn't go further, Cass waited. This wasn't like Emmett. He was usually blunt to the point of rudeness. He was never nasty. On the contrary, he was almost childlike in his innocence.

"When I was walking back to my room, I heard crying." He pulled his cap off and smoothed the staticky mess of hair down. "You know I mind my own business, Cass. I don't get involved in stuff. Everyone does their thing, know what I'm sayin'?"

"Sure, Emmett." She reached across the table and patted his hand, hoping to soothe some of his agitation. "I know that. Everyone does."

"Yeah, well." He lifted his coffee then set it back down without taking a sip.

"Did something happen?"

"When I was walking past the Wellingtons' door, I heard

a woman crying. Then two people yelling. A man and a woman." Lowering his gaze to his hands, clasped on the table in front of him, Emmett shook his head. "By then I was right outside the door. I would have kept walking. None of my business, you know? People fight all the time."

He stared into her eyes, and she just nodded, afraid to interrupt, for fear he might change his mind about talking. "But then I heard a slap. Loud. I don't put up with women getting hit by men. Got no tolerance for that."

"Of course not. You're too much of a gentleman to condone that."

His face burned so red it was almost purple. "Well, I put my ear to the door to make sure she was okay, you know?"

Cass nodded and held her breath. Her interest level shot through the roof.

He leaned forward and lowered his voice as if not to be overheard in the empty store. "It wasn't her that got hit."

"How do you know?"

"He said to her, 'no need to get violent, Joan.'"

Cass's heart stuttered. Joan Wellington, that mousy little woman, hit her husband? Emmett had to be mistaken.

"Then she said, 'I told you not to take it.'"

"Told him not to take what?"

Emmett's eyes narrowed, and he looked at her as if she had ten heads. "No idea. That's when I left. As long as I knew no woman was getting beat on, the rest was none of my business."

Cass wanted to scream. *Are you crazy? How could you leave just at the good part?* But she controlled herself. Barely. "So you didn't hear anything else?"

"Nope." Emmett lifted his cup and took a long drink, apparently relieved now that his story was told.

"What about before the slap? Did you hear anything to indicate what they were fighting over then?"

He was already shaking his head before she finished asking the question. "Nah."

"Did you tell the police?"

"Nope."

Uh . . . oh . . . Emmett was back to his old self again. She sighed. "Why not?"

"They didn't ask."

Cass frowned. "Why'd you tell me?"

He shrugged. "Didn't know if I would, but you seemed interested, so . . ."

Right. Of course. She rubbed her hands over her face. "Would you talk to Tank if I sent him over?"

"I guess." He pulled his cap back on and tucked his hair underneath.

"Thanks, Emmett. I appreciate you trying to help."

He shrugged. "Better get to plowing. I still got a lot to do." He pushed back from the table and stood. "Thanks for the coffee. Almost as good as Bella's." He winked. Cass couldn't help but laugh, and decided to consider the statement a huge compliment.

Once Emmett had gone, Cass called Tank and passed on the message. He promised he'd track down Emmett this afternoon and see if he could get any more information, but they both doubted it.

A few hours later, she crossed rose quartz off her list as she added it to the order form. She'd been unexpectedly busy this morning. With everyone from the séance stuck on the island until ferry service resumed, a lot of them wouldn't be heading home until tomorrow. There'd been a fairly steady stream of traffic in the shop all morning. She'd already done three readings and sold several baskets. Things were looking up. Now if it could just be that busy all the time, she might be okay.

And to top things off, not one person had asked for a refund. Yet. Of course, she'd have to refund at least part, if not all, of the money, but it was comforting to know she had a little time to figure it out.

The wind chimes tinkled a second before Beast charged the door.

"Stop right there, mister." Bee tossed a french fry over the dog's head while Stephanie cowered behind him.

The big dog skidded to a stop, then backpedaled and squirmed to change direction. Somehow he caught the fry midair.

Bee laughed. "You never miss, do you, boy?" He stamped his feet off on the mat, then turned and took the cup holder from Stephanie. "Okay, it's safe now."

Wiping her feet, Stephanie held up three McDonald's bags. "Hungry?"

Cass's stomach growled in answer. "I haven't had a chance to eat anything today. I'm starved." She took the bags from Stephanie so she could take her coat off, and put them on the table.

Bee slid drinks onto the table, hung his coat on the rack, and sat. "Me neither. Of course, this is *my* normal breakfast time."

"Well, some of us have been up for hours." Cass ran the

mop over the floor by the door, her need for organization winning out over her need for food.

"Come eat before it gets cold."

Beast sat beside the table staring at Bee, his tail wagging wildly.

"No more. You only get when you don't beg."

Making a noise similar to a whine, Beast slid his back end out and laid on the floor, head cradled on his front paws.

"Oh, fine." Bee tossed him another fry. "But that's it."

Seeming to understand, Beast took a toy and settled down to chew.

"Hey. How come he listens to you?" Cass asked.

"Because I mean it when I say no." He started doling out food. "Got you a Big Mac. Is that okay?"

"A Big Mac is always okay, Bee." Cass sat and opened her food. "You'll never guess who came in this morning."

"Emmett." Stephanie tossed Bee a couple of ketchup packets.

"Thanks, hon."

"Tank called?" Cass asked Stephanie.

Stephanie laughed. "Yup."

"So, what do you make of it?" Bee asked around a mouthful of food, then patted his mouth daintily with a napkin.

Cass shrugged and swallowed a fry. "I don't know. They were obviously fighting about something."

"Who says it was Conrad?"

Cass stilled, her drink halfway to her mouth. "What do you mean?"

Placing his burger in the cardboard box, Bee sat back. "Well, just because it was the Wellingtons' room doesn't mean Conrad was in there with her."

She hadn't thought of that.

"Maybe Conrad was already in the cupola."

Hmm . . . "Emmett seemed to think it was him."

"Yeah, but did he just assume it was because it was the middle of the night and Conrad's room? Or did he recognize the voice?" He grabbed a fry. "For that matter, who's to say it was Joan Wellington?"

"Emmett heard him say 'Joan.'"

"Still, could have been a different Joan."

The chances of that were slim, but Cass made a mental note to check the guest list and see if there were any other women named Joan on it. She tried to think through her visit with Emmett. Had he ever actually said he thought it was Conrad Joan had been arguing with? Or had Cass just assumed?

When Beast stood and started pacing, Cass hurried to finish her meal. She'd just taken the last bite when he started to whine. "Okay, boy. I'm coming." Leaving the mess on the table for now, Cass grabbed her coat.

"I'll take a walk with you, if you want." Bee patted his hard stomach. How he managed to stay in such good shape and eat the way he did never ceased to amaze Cass. "Need to walk off that Big Mac."

"Sure. You want to come, Steph?"

"Yeah, just let me lock the door and turn the 'Back in five minutes' sign over."

Cass started to clip the leash to Beast's collar while Stephanie and Bee put on their coats, then changed her mind. The beach was empty, and Beast loved the chance to run free now and then. When she pulled open the back door, a foot of snow stared back at her. Beast didn't even hesitate, just barreled through it at full speed.

They followed him as he dove through snow banks and headed toward the beach.

"The bay is still pretty rough," Cass said. "Have they restored ferry service yet?"

"Not that I know of," Bee replied.

Beast ran back toward them and stopped. They all stopped with him, huddling together in a small circle to keep warm. It was unusual, even in winter, for the bay to be so empty. Fishing boats, or people coming and going from work on the mainland, were common at all times of year. But today, the churning, choppy waves made it too danger-ous for most.

"Is he almost done yet?" Bee wrapped his arms around himself, his teeth chattering.

Cass glanced at the dog, who was still hunched over. She tilted her head for a better look. "Maybe you shouldn't have fed him those french fries."

"You've got to be kidding. That dog eats everything he sees. I doubt the french fries did anything to gum up the works."

"There he goes." Stephanie leaned over. "Hey. What is that?" She started to laugh. "Don't even tell me . . ."

Cass and Bee bent for a closer look at something sticking out of the mess Beast had finally managed. "Oh . . . oh no." A large diamond stuck out of the steaming pile.

"No way." Bee lurched back, laughing so hard he almost fell over in the snow. Tears clung to his cheeks. "Do you think she wants it back?"

Cass just stood, staring at the ring.

"That's quite a rock," Stephanie said through fits of laughter.

"I don't understand how he got it." Cass shook her head. There was no way she was digging that ring out.

"Who knows? How does he get anything?" Bee rubbed his cheeks.

"She probably dropped it in the hall and he sucked it up. That dog is like a vacuum cleaner." Stephanie started walking back toward the shop.

Bee followed, leaving Cass to decide what to do. She pulled a small garbage bag from her pocket and scooped up the mess—ring and all—then dropped it in a trash can on her way back to the shop. Let Donald buy another one. If the jewelry and furs Sylvia had been sporting were any indication, Donald was much better off now than he'd been when they were married. Or at least more generous. Figured.

Maybe she'd give Sylvia a call and tell her where she could find the ring. At least then she'd get the satisfaction of watching Donald dig it out.

9

Cass pushed through the back door of Mystical Musings, scattering snow across the floor as she entered. Maybe she should have shoveled the back porch too. It hadn't seemed necessary with all the snow drifts along the beach. She doubted too many people would trudge through that. But it would make walking Beast easier.

"Hey, Cass." Stephanie held the phone out to her. She covered the receiver and mouthed something Cass couldn't make out. If the anger furrowing her brow was any indication, it wasn't going to be a happy phone call.

Taking the phone, Cass shrugged out of her coat. "Hello?"

"Cass?"

"Yes." She worked to place the voice but couldn't think of any grown man who whined like that.

"Mitch Dobbs here."

Ahh . . . "Hi, Mr. Dobbs. How are you?"

"Well, you know, I'm not real happy."

Uh-oh. "Is there something I can do for you?"

"I paid a lot of money for this weekend, and I didn't get anything out of it. I want a refund for the whole weekend. I paid for readings for me and my wife, a group reading, a séance, not to mention the cost of the room, which I might add, wasn't worth the price I paid. Robbery, I tell you."

Cass dropped into a chair, propped her elbow on the table, and lowered her head, massaging her temples with her free hand. "I'm willing to work something out with you regarding the readings, Mr. Dobbs, but I can't refund the cost of the hotel." This guy had to be kidding if he thought the fees for his accommodations were her responsibility.

"I already talked to Jim Wellington about the cost of the room. I told him I'm adding it to the list he already owes me."

Don't ask. Don't ask. "Already owes you?" *Crud.* One of these days she was going to learn to keep her big mouth shut. Maybe. Probably not.

Mitch snorted. "Are you kidding me? Do you have any idea how much we've already laid out in legal fees trying to get what's rightfully ours? I deserve some compensation. Don't you think?"

Cass pulled the phone away from her ear and stared at it. This guy was stark raving mad. She glanced at Bee and Stephanie. Stephanie must have filled Bee in, because his expression filled with sympathy and he rolled his index finger in circles beside his head.

Shaking her head, she put the phone back to her ear. "Look, Mr. Dobbs—"

"Before you go getting your panties all in a twist about giving back the money, we all had an idea."

This time she bit her tongue until the coppery taste of blood forced her to stop. No way was she asking who *we all* were.

"We're holed up here at the Bay Side Hotel until at least tomorrow, so we figured you could come on up here and do the group reading sometime tomorrow. Then if anyone wants an individual reading, like me and Carly paid for, you could do those, too."

Actually, she had to admit the idea wasn't half bad. If she could do the readings, she could get away with keeping the money. What difference did it make where she did them? At least she'd be off the hook for some—hopefully most—of the refunds. Plus, she really wanted to make the event successful. The thought of sending all those people home disappointed burned a hole in her gut.

"You there?"

"Uh . . . yes. Sorry. I was just trying to think if that would work." At most, Henry Stevens might charge her to rent a ballroom. She'd still come out ahead. "Sure, Mr. Dobbs. I can do that." Of course, if she could get the customers to come into Mystical Musings, she might have a hope of selling some of the extra inventory she'd ordered for the weekend. "I'll tell you what. I'll see if I can work something out with Mr. Stevens to rent some space for a group reading tomorrow night at the hotel, but if anyone wants to have an individual reading, they can come by the shop during the day tomorrow. I open at ten, and I'll clear my schedule for the day to do the readings." *Because I'm so swamped with clients all day long. Ugh . . .*

Static hissed in her ear over the silent line. Had he hung up? She pressed the phone harder to her ear. Muffled voices carried through the line. Apparently he was discussing the plan with whoever *we* were. He could have at least told her to hold on.

"Sure. That'll work. And you should get Mr. Stevens to give you a ballroom for free, with what the Wellingtons are paying to put us all up in this place."

"Wait. The Wellingtons are footing the bill for the Bay Side Hotel? For everyone?"

"Yup."

She should probably just let it go. She knew that in her head. Unfortunately, nosiness got the better of her. It usually did. "So, if they're paying for your new hotel room, how do you figure they owe you money for the other room?" Was it just her? She looked at Stephanie and Bee and lifted a brow.

They both nodded emphatically in agreement.

"Duh . . . are we staying at the bed-and-breakfast?" He didn't wait for an answer. The dial tone sounded in her ear.

She hit the off button and put the phone on the table, then turned to Stephanie and Bee. "The guy's a lunatic . . ."

"Yeah, but his idea was brilliant." Bee grinned.

Stephanie stood and grabbed a colored pencil and a sheet of paper from the shelf behind the table. "See, I told you it would work out." She sat back down and smoothed the paper. "Okay, now, what are you going to need?"

Cass's heart warmed. "You're the best."

"Hey, don't forget me." Bee winked. "This is something I can do."

"You're both the best." Her smile was short-lived. "But first I have to call Doc Martin."

Bee swiveled to look at Beast, lying quietly on his dog bed in the corner. "Is he all right?"

"I don't know, but he usually doesn't lie on the bed."

"No . . ." Bee agreed. "He usually eats it."

With a vet appointment made for four o'clock and Bee and Stephanie running errands for tomorrow's impromptu readings, Cass started to re-stock her shelves and bins. If she hurried, she could probably get the store cleaned up before she had to leave with Beast. Then she would only have to come in a little earlier tomorrow to make a couple of big pots of coffee and set out the snacks and stuff. With Stephanie helping, it wouldn't take long. Bee probably wouldn't make an appearance before noon.

The tinkling of wind chimes announced a customer. Cass straightened and arched her back, pressing a palm to the ache. She slid a tray into the glass case. "Hi. Can I hel—"

"I hope so." Joan Wellington pulled off her hat and twisted it in her hands. She glanced over her shoulder then walked farther into the shop. "I was wondering. Well. I'd like to know if you can do a reading?"

"For you?"

"Yes. Please. Everyone says you can talk to the dead. And . . ." She lowered her gaze, and a tear dripped onto her wrist. She made no move to wipe it away. "I thought you might be able to talk to Conrad, to ask him who . . . you know."

Ah jeez. She did know. How could she explain to this woman that she didn't exactly *talk* to the dead? Easy. She couldn't. At least, not without ruining her reputation. She blew out a breath, fluttering her hair up off her forehead. "Sure. Of course. Please, come in and sit. Take your coat off and get comfortable. Would you like something to drink? Tea, coffee, hot chocolate?"

"Do you have any water?" Joan pressed a hand to her throat.

"Sure." Cass took Joan's coat and guided her to a chair. She placed a box of tissues in front of her then left her alone, giving her a little privacy to compose herself. After hanging the coat on the coatrack by the door, Cass took a small bottle of water from the fridge and handed it to Joan. She placed a comforting hand on her shoulder. "Are you okay?"

Joan reached up and patted her hand. "I'm fine. Thank you." She sipped the water.

"Are you sure you're up to this?"

Joan took another sip of water and nodded. "Yes. I'm very sure. I need to know."

"Okay, then." Cass lit the candles at the side of the table. A color reading would probably be best, the most peaceful. Perhaps it would help soothe Joan's nerves, ease some of her tension. Customers often told her they felt calm and at peace after having a color reading.

Cass pulled the basket of colored pencils and a small stack of paper out and brought them to the table, then sat across from Joan. Taking her time, she selected several pencils without bothering to look at them. It didn't matter. She had no doubt the random selection of colors would give her the results she needed. Instead, she studied Joan.

This was a large part of her business. Her uncanny ability to read people, to gain insight from their actions. It was obvious Joan was a nervous wreck. Anyone could see that. But Cass had to look deeper. Why was she so nervous?

Cass lined her selection of pencils beside the paper then rolled them back and forth.

With another quick glance over her shoulder, Joan finished off the water. Shifting the chair just the slightest bit, she glanced toward the door from the corner of her eye. The movements were so subtle—disguised as everyday fidgeting—most people might have missed them. But Cass was trained to see them and had spent years looking for those small tells in her patients. If you watched people enough, you learned they were very rarely completely still. Many were in a constant state of motion, without even realizing it. A scratch here, a cough there, hair swiped behind an ear, foot tapping to some imagined rhythm. It was Cass's job to differentiate between those small fidgets and actual telling behavior. And she was very good at it.

"Who are you afraid of?" The question blurted out before she could censor it. Would she have asked it if she'd realized sooner? In all honesty, probably not. While waiting for Joan to answer, Cass lifted a grey pencil, tilted it to the page, and slowly moved it back and forth. She wasn't surprised to have chosen grey first, the color reinforcing her observations of distrust. Or had she knowingly chosen the color, having already observed Joan's tear? Hmm . . .

"Afraid?" Joan forced an obviously uncomfortable chuckle. "I'm not afraid of anyone. Who would I be afraid of?" She punctuated the denial with a glance over Cass's shoulder.

Cass resisted the urge to turn and look behind her. Beast wouldn't still be sleeping fitfully on the floor if someone had entered the shop. Besides, the chimes would have tinkled, announcing the intrusion immediately. Intrusion? She frowned. Odd word choice. A client coming in wouldn't necessarily be an intrusion. Was it Joan's paranoia she was picking up on?

She returned the pencil to its place in the line and studied the blob she'd drawn.

Joan's hand shook as she spun the water bottle in circles. "When are you going to talk to Conrad?"

"It doesn't really work that way. I can't just call him up and have a conversation. He will send me . . . impressions, for lack of a better word, and I'll have to interpret them with your help. I won't necessarily understand what he's telling me but, hopefully, I can help you make sense of it."

Joan's shoulders relaxed a little, but she continued to pick at the label on the water bottle.

Cass chose a purple pencil and started to scribble. Another unsurprising color choice—the color of wealth and luxury.

"What is that you're doing?" She gestured to the page Cass was coloring on.

"It's a color reading. It helps me—"

Joan gripped her wrist, stopping the pencil mid-stroke. "Look, I don't have much time. I'm not as much interested in a reading for myself as in contacting Conrad." She pitched her voice low, even though the shop was empty. "I absolutely must ask him something. It's of the utmost urgency."

Cass sighed and set the pencil down among the rest. The urge to lift the red pencil was strong, but she ignored it. Red was a color of passion, power, and anger. The choice would have surprised Cass only a moment before. "All right, we can try something else." She stood and went to the counter behind the table. With one last glance over her shoulder at Joan, she lifted the crystal ball and returned to the table with it. Now to find out what in the world was going on here.

"I might be able to contact Conrad more easily through the crystal ball." Cass closed her eyes, the ball resting on the table in front of her. She conjured an image of Conrad, his hand resting on the small of Joan's back as he guided her toward the back of the house to prepare for the séance. "What do you want to know?" When she was met with silence, she opened her eyes.

Joan sat staring at her, thumbnail caught between her teeth.

"You have to ask him something if you want an answer."

"Is he here?"

Was he? Who knew? Maybe. "I won't know until you ask your question. Then we'll see if he answers."

"Fine." Joan slid up and perched on the edge of the chair. She leaned forward and looked into the crystal ball as if she expected to see her dead husband in there. "Where is it?"

Cass jumped, startled by the intensity of the command.

"I said, where is it, you rat?"

Shocked, Cass jerked back. A vision popped into her mind. A small compartment or hole. The same opening she'd seen in the cupola? She couldn't tell. No matter how hard she tried, she couldn't bring any of the surrounding space into focus. Was it her memory surfacing or some sort of cryptic message from beyond? She had no idea, but now she had to decide how much to tell the infuriated widow. "I see a cubby of some sort." True enough. Since she didn't know if it was the same one, she couldn't say with any degree of certainty where it was located.

"A cubby?"

"Well, sort of an opening or a hole." Cass shook her head. The image stayed firm.

"Can you be any more specific?"

Could she? She shook her head. "No. I'm sorry. That's all I can see. He seems pretty insistent on showing me that same vision continuously." True enough, since she couldn't seem to rid herself of the image.

"Hmm . . ." Joan stood. "Not surprising. I guess he's as useless dead as he was alive." She tossed, a twenty-dollar bill onto the table. "Thanks for trying."

Cass stared after her, mouth agape, as Joan crossed the room, grabbed her coat, and left.

10

Cass opened the back door of the small car, and Beast dove out. "Come on, boy. Time to see the doc and make sure you're all right. Again." Crossing the icy parking lot with Beast tugging on the leash proved to be treacherous. With the snow that had melted all day now freezing over, it was definitely time to get home before the roads got any worse.

She stamped her feet off as she entered the waiting room. Trying to keep Beast from jumping on anyone, she approached the counter. "Hi, Sue."

The receptionist looked up from the computer. "Oh, hey, Cass." She slid her glasses up onto her head and eyed Beast. "What'd he eat this time?"

Sue was a regular customer at Mystical Musings. She often attended group readings and had been at the Madison Estate for the disastrous weekend. They'd become quite friendly since she'd inherited Beast. "A ring."

The other woman winced. "I hope it wasn't a good one."

Hmm . . . "Nah. Nothing important." *True enough.* "Sorry about the weekend."

"Are you kidding me? People are going to be talking about that for years."

"You think?"

"For sure. When I stopped at the deli this morning for a roll and coffee, it's all anyone was talking about."

"Ah . . . jeez . . ." Cass massaged her temples between her thumb and forefinger, while gripping Beast's leash tightly in the other hand.

"Nah, no worries. It's fine. Actually, interest in Mystical Musings is through the roof. I heard at least three women and one man mention they were going to stop by the shop this week."

Sue's smile was contagious, and Cass couldn't help joining her. "Yeah, well, let's just hope the fascination keeps up."

Sue sobered. "Not sure the Wellingtons are going to fare as well, though. No one can stop talking about the way they bicker like spoiled children. Not appealing."

Bay Island was a small community of hardworking people. Being lazy or spoiled didn't earn you any points. The fact that one of the Wellingtons committed suicide might have earned them sympathy, the fact that someone was murdered there might have banded the community together to help, but the fact that they argued like a group of unruly children would do nothing to further their cause.

"They did bicker a lot, huh?"

Grabbing Beast's chart from the holder, Sue skirted the desk and gestured for Cass to follow. Beast pranced beside her while they walked down the small hallway. "No kidding. The four of them were at it constantly."

Wait. "Four?"

"The siblings and Joan. I guess she fits right in."

Cass frowned as Sue pushed open the door to an exam room and patted Beast on the head. Holding the door open with her back against it, Sue gestured for Cass to enter the room, then dropped Beast's chart in a wire holder beside the door.

"Who did Joan fight with?"

Sue scoffed. "Please. Who didn't she fight with? Before the séance started she was the main topic of conversation. She was bickering with Priscilla on the way to the ballroom. Then she went at it with James."

Cass was having a hard time connecting this woman— the same woman who'd come in demanding to speak to her dead husband—with the meek woman who'd introduced herself on her way into the estate. How had Cass missed all of that arguing? She was usually so accurate in her observations of people. The success of her readings depended on her spot-on assessment of people's personalities and moods. *Oh, right.* She'd been too preoccupied with Donald and Sylvia when she should have been making notes on each of the guests.

Sue folded her arms and leaned back more comfortably against the door. "And let me tell you, it's not like she was taking up for Conrad either. That woman didn't have one nice word to say about her husband. And nasty as he was to other people, he doted on her like you wouldn't believe. Poor guy—may he rest in peace." Sue made the sign of the cross. "No wonder he killed himself."

Hmm . . . If Sue had been in the deli, and with the number of people who were in and out of the vet's office all day, her gossip was probably pretty reliable. The general consensus must be that Conrad killed himself. Cass bit her tongue. No sense fueling any talk about murder.

"Anyway, I gotta run. Work to do and all that." She smiled and petted Beast's head. "Let me know when you reschedule the weekend." The door started to fall shut, but she grabbed it and pushed it back open enough to stick her head in and lowered her voice. "By the way, how on earth did you make that man appear in the smoke? That's the real topic of conversation, and people are pretty much divided on whether you did it on purpose or if it was a real ghost." Sue waggled her eyebrows. "Come on, you can tell. Your secret is safe with me."

Sue was a real sweetheart, and Cass liked her a lot, but truth be told, no secret was safe with her. "Sorry." Cass grinned through her fear. "My lips are sealed."

The grin slipped away as soon as the door fell shut, and she closed her eyes, massaging the bridge of her nose between her thumb and forefinger. Apparently everyone had seen the figure in the smoke. But what caused it? Bee swore he didn't, even when she'd asked him again and again, and she believed him. Could one of the Wellingtons have been behind the strange phenomenon? If not, there was only one alternative she could think of. She swallowed the lump of fear threatening to choke her.

The doorknob rattled, startling her from her reverie. She jumped and pressed a hand to her chest.

Doc Martin laughed as he entered. "Sorry, dear. Didn't mean to scare you."

Cass forced a chuckle. "Not your fault."

Beast jumped up and propped his front paws on the exam table while Doc Martin scratched behind his ears. "How are you doing, fella?" He dropped the chart onto the table, opened it, and scanned the front page. "A ring this time, huh?"

"Is he going to be all right?" Cass unclipped the leash and rolled it up, more for something to do with her hands than anything else.

"Why don't we have a look? Generally, these guys are pretty sturdy, but we'll see." He pulled on gloves and bent to feel Beast's stomach. "Any blood in the stool?"

"Not that I saw." She fidgeted with the clasp, opening it, letting it flip closed, opening it . . .

When he finished, he stripped off the gloves and rubbed a hand across the back of his neck. "I'll tell you what. I think he's going to be fine."

Cass sighed in relief.

He held up a hand. "But . . ."

Of course.

"I'd like to keep him overnight—"

"But, I thought—"

"Just for observation. It's already late, the roads are going to be bad tonight, and I don't want to risk you having a problem and not being able to get him back here." He crossed the room and tossed the gloves in the garbage. "This way, I'll be able to check on him throughout the night, do an X-ray and make sure everything looks okay, and you can pick him up sometime tomorrow morning." Pulling a treat from a cookie jar on the counter, Doc turned his attention to Beast, who propped his front paws on the counter and nudged the cookie jar with his nose. "No."

Beast dropped to the floor and looked quizzically at the doctor.

Doc held the treat in his hand and said, "Sit," while moving the treat toward Beast and above his head.

Beast promptly dropped his butt to the floor, tail wagging wildly, and Doc handed him the treat.

"Hey. How'd you get him to do that?"

"That brings me to the next order of business." He offered her a sympathetic look and scratched the back of his head. "You have to get this animal some kind of obedience training. He's too big to run around doing whatever he wants."

"Bu—"

He held up a hand to stop any argument. "No buts, Cass." His tone softened. "He's going to get hurt, or hurt someone else, if you don't get him under control. He's a great dog, with a fantastic temperament, but what's going to happen if a child comes into the shop and Beast gets excited and jumps on him? He's going to weigh well over a hundred pounds full-grown. You must be able to control him. It won't be his fault if he hurts someone."

It would be hers. He didn't have to say the words for Cass to get the message. Cass lowered her gaze to Beast, happily crunching his treat. "I'm sorry, boy." She ruffled his mane. "I was planning to take him to Herb in the spring." Herb Cox was the only dog trainer she knew of on the island, and he ran classes from the corral behind his house, which meant no classes when it was below freezing with a foot of snow on the ground. "I guess I could look for somewhere on the mainland."

"You can wait for Herb but, in the meantime, there are things you can be doing. He should be able to obey basic commands. If he learns sit, and he launches himself at a child or runs toward a busy road . . ."

A vise gripped Cass's chest at the image.

"All you have to do is yell sit, and he'll stop." Doc opened the top cabinet and pulled out a sheet of white paper. "Here's a list of websites that have good information on training. Work on one command at a time. Set aside fifteen minutes every day and work on teaching him to sit." He finally smiled, filling his ice-blue eyes with warmth. "This guy's smart. You'll be surprised how fast he learns."

"Thank you, Doc. I'll make sure to work with him."

He patted her arm. "I'll give you a minute to say good night, then Sue will come and take him back. Don't worry. I'll check on him all night. He's going to be fine."

She knew the doctor was right. And a breezeway connected the veterinary office to his home, so he'd be close by all night. But it didn't make it easier to leave Beast. She hugged him. "I'm sorry, boy. We'll work harder to make sure you're safe. I love you, ya big teddy bear."

After checking out at the front desk, she headed out. Cass pulled her hood up, opened her car door, tossed her bag and Beast's leash onto the passenger seat, and climbed in, then wrestled the door shut against the wind. Once she started the car and blasted the heater, she just sat, staring out the window. Wind rocked the car, the sensation bringing a small surge of nausea. At least, she thought that's what turned her stomach. Could also be stress . . . or guilt.

Now what? The thought of going home without Beast brought a wave of sadness. She pulled her sleeves down over her hands and pressed her hands to the vents, letting the warmth blow up her arms. At least the visit hadn't taken long, and the heat was already blowing warm. She lifted the coffee cup from the cup holder and took a sip. Yuck. She'd been gone long enough for it to become ice-cold. She returned the nearly full cup to the holder and dropped her head forward onto the steering wheel.

Okay. She was going to have to make a decision. The snow had stopped, but the wind still whipped the existing accumulation wildly, reducing visibility to nearly nothing. She'd closed Mystical Musings early to take Beast to the vet, but if what Sue said was true, she might still get a few customers. A gust of wind rattled the car. Probably not.

A truck passed the parking lot, spreading sand onto the road.

Cass wiped a few tears from her face, shifted into reverse, and backed out of the parking spot. With darkness beginning to fall, she'd just go home. She braked and hesitated before shifting into drive. Of course, Emmett's Garage wasn't that far out of the way. She could swing by and ask if it was Conrad whom Joan had been arguing with.

The ringtone from her purse allowed her another moment of procrastination as she put the car back in park and dug the phone from her bag. One glance at the screen chased away some of the chill. Luke. A small smile formed as she swiped the screen and answered. "Hey there."

"Hey, beautiful."

Heat surged. Why did the same phrase Bee often used turn her insides to mush when Luke said it? Oh. Right. That sexier-than-anything southern drawl of his.

"How's the weekend going? Are you wowing them with your superior psychic abilities?"

"Uh . . ." The image from above the fireplace flickered through her mind. "I guess you could say I was."

"Was? Not anymore?"

"Nope. The weekend got cut short because of the . . . um . . ." Surely it was okay to tell Luke about the murder. He was a detective on the mainland, so he couldn't have possibly been involved.

"Cass?"

The concern in his voice eased the gap between them, stirring feelings she wasn't ready to think about. Heat was one thing, tenderness something else entirely.

"It got cut short when Conrad Wellington was found hanging in the cupola."

"Hanging?"

"Dead."

"He hung himself?"

"Not exactly."

"What do you mean, not exactly? How do you not exactly hang yourself?" A slight touch of frustration crept in to overshadow the concern.

"It seems someone helped him get up there."

"He was murdered? Cass!"

She ripped the phone away from her ear. She could still hear his voice as clearly as if he were in the car next to her. She allowed one moment to wish he were, to envision laying her head on his hard chest, to feel the strength of his arms surrounding her as he pulled her into his warm embrace. She shook her head, dispelling the image. *Okay. Enough of that. Now, what was he saying?*

"Do they have whoever killed him?"

She cringed. "No."

Luke took a deep breath and let it out slowly. She imagined him counting to ten in his head. "Okay. I'm sorry, hon. I didn't mean to get upset. I'll give Tank a call and get the details of the case." Luke and Tank had become fast friends over the past few months. "Now. Are you all right?"

"I guess."

"What do you mean, you guess? Were you hurt?"

Cass shook her head, then remembered he couldn't see her. "No. I'm fine, just a little . . ." What was she? "Sad." She gave him a brief rundown of the weekend—he flipped a little when he found out she'd been trapped in the mansion overnight with a killer—then told him about the incident with Beast. After she assured him Beast was going to be okay, he had a good, deep belly laugh over that one.

"I'm sorry I haven't been able to get there to see you. Things have been crazy here."

"I understand." Except, she didn't. Not really. Or she did, but she just wanted to see him, so it didn't matter.

"Forgive me?"

She avoided answering that one. "The ferry's not running right now anyway."

"I'll tell you what. I'll see if I can get away next weekend. We'll do something special."

"Sounds good."

Usually, when she hung up the phone with Luke, she was left feeling pleasantly relaxed—even a little tingly—by his southern-boy charm. The thick drawl reaching some part of her that hadn't been touched in a long time. But if she never got to see him, what was the point? She tossed the phone on the seat, pity her new companion.

She once again shifted into drive and slowly navigated the empty parking lot. It had been a long time since she'd driven on icy roads. Too long. She'd lost her touch. Living in New York City all those years had spoiled her. Why bother driving on ice and snow when you could hop on the train or bus and let someone else worry about the slippery conditions?

She made it to the edge of the lot and sat at the exit, indecision taunting her. She could make a left and go straight home to a warm, cozy house. An empty house, now that Beast wasn't there. She hit the turn signal, pulled out, and made a right. It'd be just as easy to go the long way and swing past Emmett's Garage, then loop around and head home. It wasn't that far out of the way. Besides, she'd pass the old Madison Estate, and she was curious if anyone was still staying there or if they'd all moved to the Bay Side Hotel.

As soon as she got home, she'd make a cup of hot tea, pull out her laptop and research the dog training sites Doc had given her. There had to be some way to train this dog without having to put him in a cage. The idea just didn't sit well in her gut.

Flurries drifted onto her windshield, dragging her concentration to the road ahead. New snow seemed to be falling, in addition to what was already blowing. All of the slush that had melted under the bright sunlight was now re-freezing. Cass eased off the gas, the darkness making the icy road more difficult to navigate. As the road inclined toward the mansion, her tires slipped. Fear clutched her chest. Squeezed. Maybe this wasn't such a good idea. The tires gripped a clear section of blacktop, and Cass slowed a little more. She probably should have gone straight home.

The populated residential section of the island, where Doc Martin's office was located, gave way to a more secluded, wooded area. Darkness encroached. The snow increased, the drifting flakes changing to a more steady snowfall. The snowflakes flew at her, limiting visibility. If she didn't speed up, there was no way she'd make it up the hill. Holding her breath, she eased her foot down on the gas, accelerating slowly, but steadily. So far, so good.

As she rounded the curve at the top of the hill and the street leveled out, she blew out a breath. With a shaky hand, she pushed her hair back out of her face. "Well, that was scary." Nervous laughter escaped. She'd have to make it a point to practice driving in bad weather. Last year's unusually mild winter had spoiled her. Though they didn't get as much snow as upstate New York, Bay Island still got its fair share of winter weather, and she couldn't freak out every time she had to drive in it.

She lifted sweaty strands of hair off the back of her neck, then turned down the heat. Squinting through the snow as she came upon the Madison Estate—she still couldn't think of it as a bed-and-breakfast—she slowed to a crawl and tried to make out any cars parked in the driveway. None that she could see, but a light shone in the cupola. Was someone up there? Sweat trickled down the side of her face, but this time it had nothing to do with driving on the slick roads. Every other window stood dark and empty, yet she couldn't shake the feeling she was being watched. *Definitely time to go home.*

Forcing her attention back to the road, Cass continued on toward Emmett's. Darkness had fully descended, and she glanced at the clock on the dashboard. Five thirty. She might still catch him locking up if she hurried. She picked up a little speed heading down the hill, the intensity of the snow coming at her dizzying, giving the illusion of rocketing through space. Her stomach lurched.

The back end of the little Volkswagen Jetta slid again.

Her heart hammered. She gripped the wheel tighter, fighting her mind's commands to relax. She was going too fast, her back end fishtailing with half the length of the hill still ahead. Grappling with the steering wheel, Cass struggled to straighten the car.

Panic clawed at her throat, and a surge of adrenaline shot through her. She slammed on the brake pedal, remembering too late she shouldn't have. *Ah jeez . . .*

All four tires released their tentative purchase, and the Jetta careened out of control. The passenger side door hit something. A tree? Then ricocheted toward the snow bank on the opposite side of the road. Trees whirled by as the car spun, caught on something, and started to roll. The sensation of being airborne assailed her, an instant before her head smacked the window.

Dizziness left her unable to tell if the car was still in motion. Her stomach roiled. Bile surged up the back of her throat. An eddy of darkness invaded her peripheral vision, and everything went black.

11

"Hey."

Cass fought to ignore the voice intruding on her peace. She floated in darkness, reality nothing but a blur.

"Hey. Are you okay in there?"

Pain sliced through her head, dragging her forcefully from her tranquil slumber. *Ugh . . .*

Bang, bang, bang. "Hey. I'm gonna help get you out. Can you open the window?"

Could she? She had no idea. She didn't even know which way was up. She seemed to be suspended in midair. Ridiculous. She tried to push back the disorientation. Had to focus. Feeling around with one hand, she struggled to make sense of where she was. Pressure on her chest and shoulder. The seat belt?

The driver side door screeched open reluctantly.

"Are you all right?"

Cass pried open her eyes and glanced up into the face of . . . an angel? It had to be. He was perfect. The strong features, intense eyes . . . eyes . . . something familiar about those eyes.

"Hey. Wake up." A hand gripped her shoulder.

Clarity started to intrude on her dream of angels. And with it came pain. She reached up to touch the side of her forehead, and her hand came away wet. Blood? Too dark to tell. Her eyes couldn't focus. Eyes? Hadn't she just been thinking about eyes?

"Grab onto my arm."

Her body obeyed without her mind's approval, wrapping her arms around his arm as she struggled to see what he was doing. A glint of light. She squinted. Just a reflection, a streetlight reflecting off the blade of a knife.

Knife?

The knife plunged toward her.

She sucked in a breath. Her last? Figured her hot angel rescuer would turn out to be a psycho serial killer. She squeezed her eyes closed tight.

Without warning, the pressure against her side and chest released. If not for her hold on the stranger, she'd have tumbled over when he cut the seat belt.

He grabbed her shoulder and started to pull. "Come on. You have to try to help."

Ice pellets hit her face, clearing some of the fog from her brain. Her eyes flew open.

"Cass?"

She pressed her feet against something solid and pushed herself up, half climbing as he dragged her from the car.

"Cass Donovan?"

She opened her mouth but couldn't force any sound over her dry tongue, so she settled for nodding. *Ouch!* She winced. *Note to self: no nodding.*

"It's Jim. Jim Wellington." He helped her to sit on the driver's side of the car, which was now the top. The car had rolled on its side and come to a stop when it plowed into a tree. "Are you all right?" He pulled off a glove and pressed it to her head. "This is all I have right now. Hold it on that cut until I can take a look at it. Come on, now. Swing your legs around, and let me help you down."

She did as instructed, leaning toward his open arms as he helped her down from the car.

"Just stay still for a minute and make sure you're okay." He put an arm around her shoulders, waiting, concern etched in the creases at the corners of his eyes.

The cold seeped into her bones, and she started to shiver. She pulled her coat closed tighter. *What the . . . ?* Both hands came away wet. Jeez. How badly was she bleeding? She lifted a hand toward the streetlight. Not blood. She sniffed her fingers. Coffee! Relief and nausea rushed through her.

"Come on, hon. Let's get you to the car."

She frowned and turned to stare at the car on its side. He couldn't possibly think they were going anywhere in that.

Jim started to walk, slowly guiding her around the back of her Jetta. A dark SUV sat idling. She tried to shake off some of the confusion as he guided her into the passenger seat and helped her with her seat belt.

A jolt of terror pierced her heart. "Beast?"

"Beast? Was he in the car?" Jim spun toward the Jetta.

"No. Wait." A memory surfaced.

He stopped and looked back at her.

She'd been so upset when Beast had to stay with the vet overnight. Now, she couldn't be more thankful. "No." She shook her head. *Ah jeez. Okay. No shaking either.* Trying to keep the headache at bay and keep from bleeding to death, she pressed the glove harder against her head. "Beast isn't with me."

"Is anyone else in the car?"

"No." This time she was careful to keep her head still.

"Are you sure?"

She tried to think. She'd gone to the vet alone. Hadn't she? Stephanie had gone to dinner with Tank, and Bee had to start work on a dress design for a shop in the city. "I'm sure."

"All right, then. Let's get you back to the house."

"House?"

"The bed-and-breakfast. I want to see how badly you're injured, then we can decide if you need to go to the hospital."

Hospital? No way. She narrowed her eyes, forcing her gaze to focus on the dashboard. With a little effort, she was able to force both dashboards to merge together and become one. *There. No need for a hospital.*

Jim closed the door quietly then rounded the front of the SUV and climbed into the driver's seat. He brushed the snow out of his soaking wet hair and shifted into reverse. Placing his arm across the seat behind her, he started to turn and back up. Then stopped. His gaze caught on hers. He held her stare, the intensity darkening the green of his eyes.

Cass tore her gaze away to look out the windshield.

A second later, Jim backed onto the road and started slowly back up the hill. "What were you doing out in this weather?"

"I had to take Beast to the vet. He ate . . . something."

"You're sure he's not in the car, right?"

"I'm sure. The vet kept him overnight for observation."

"Lucky thing."

"Yeah."

With that, she ran out of energy for small talk. Sliding down in the seat, she rested her head against the back. Her eyes drifted closed.

"No sleeping." Jim rubbed his hand down her arm and gripped her hand.

Cass opened her eyes and stared at him.

"When we were little, Mother never let us sleep after a bump to the head." He frowned. "Not sure why, but there you have it. I guess some things just stick." He released her hand and returned his attention to the road, his comfortable laughter easing her frayed nerves a bit. If he was having trouble driving, he wouldn't be so relaxed. Right? Although, Jim seemed like the type of guy who took everything in stride, the kind who could walk into the most hostile situation and diffuse the tension in seconds with his carefree, laid-back attitude.

"What were you doing out in this mess?"

He shrugged. "I'm supposed to leave sometime tomorrow, but I had a few things to do up at the mansion. I figured I'd run over and take care of them tonight." He turned that easygoing grin on her, melting a little more of her stress. "Guess I should have checked the weather first, huh?"

She laughed with him. "No kidding."

He hit the turn signal—even though there was no one around for miles—pushed a button on his visor, waited for the gates to open, and turned into the driveway. His tires slid a little as he made the turn, but he easily regained control without even a hitch in his breathing.

She sighed and glanced at the lit cupola. Darkness drifted over her, and she pressed the glove tighter to her head and held her breath, afraid she might pass out. Then it lifted. *Oh . . . oh no . . .* She'd experienced the sensation of a shadow crossing her vision before, and it never ended well. She searched frantically for anything that could have caused the sensation—branches blowing in the wind, a bird flying overhead, a cloud slipping in front of the moon—anything other than the fact that someone nearby was going to die soon. Nothing. *Oh crap.*

"Let me have a look at your head." Inside the house, Jim leaned over Cass, the subtle scent of his aftershave—a hint of citrus—intoxicating.

She straightened in the chair, leaning an elbow on the table for support, and tentatively lifted the glove aside, afraid blood would start gushing the instant she removed the pressure. "Is it bad?"

"Nah. Not really. Head wounds bleed a lot, and that's already slowed to a trickle." He took the glove from her hand. "I'll be right back. Just sit here, don't try to get up, okay?"

She nodded slowly, afraid of setting off another wave of pain. So far so good. Though her head was tender, the more intense pain had faded to a dull headache. The rest of her body was a different story. Pretty much everything ached. Tomorrow would probably not be pleasant.

Cass glanced around the dining room. All of the tables and chairs that had been brought in for the weekend guests were still in place. Some of the chairs had been pulled to other tables to accommodate larger groups, while some sat with their backs facing the tables. Coffee mugs and plates still remained on some of the cloth-covered tables. The scene was surreal, giving the impression everyone had disappeared at the same time, leaving everything as it was.

Her mind raced. Were the police any closer to finding the killer? Last she'd heard, there were no real suspects, but she hadn't talked to Stephanie since this afternoon.

"Here you go. Hold this to your head." Jim returned and handed her a clean cloth filled with ice, then lifted her hair off her forehead. His fingers grazed her head, sending a jolt of electricity shooting through her. Jeez. She really had to get a life. Maybe she was finally ready to let go of Donald and her past and move on to a healthy relationship. An image of Luke flashed before her, his cocky grin sending a flare of heat rushing through her. Yeah. Maybe. Too bad she'd probably never trust another man.

She pressed the cold compress to her head and shivered.

"Are you cold?" Jim stood and turned to look at the pile of wood stacked beside the fireplace. "I could light a fire if you want."

"No. That's okay. Thank you." She shivered again as icy fingers of fear crept up her spine. "And thank you for stopping to help. If you hadn't . . ." No sense torturing herself with what could have happened if no one had come by and noticed her car.

"It's a good thing I was on my way back up here when I was." He crouched in front of her, reached out, and tucked the hair that had fallen back onto her face behind her ear. He was too close. This time his touch brought no jolt, other than a small spark of fear. But why? He hadn't done anything wrong. Why should she be frightened of Jim?

Hel-loooo. Maybe because someone killed Conrad in the middle of the night, someone who was staying at the mansion, and that someone is free right now. And what did she really know about Jim? She shifted to lean her back against the chair, allowing herself a little more space.

Jim apparently took the hint. He stood and propped his hands on his hips. "If you're okay for a few minutes, I'd like to run up to my room and get a few things I forgot."

"Sure. Would you mind if I used your phone? I left mine in the car."

Jim spread his arms. "Sorry. The police confiscated it, and as far as I know, the landline is still out from the storm. I can check when I run upstairs."

"Thank you." She would definitely feel a little better if someone knew where she was. She pulled the ice away from her head and looked at the small red stain on the white cloth. Barely anything. Gripping the table, she stood. Actually, other than the throbbing headache and the aches and pains everywhere else, she felt okay. No dizziness, no nausea, no piercing pain in her head. Good. She took her time crossing the room, brushing one hand along table edges and chair backs to steady herself, but she really didn't need it.

She dropped the ice pack in a garbage pail on her way out the door. While she was here, she had to have a look at the fireplace. There had to have been some sort of special effect used. When she entered the ballroom, a cold blast of air hit her square in the chest. Weird. Nothing was open that she could see. Had it come from the fireplace that now stood empty?

As she walked past the long table, she kept her gaze firmly glued to the area just above the mantel, where some-one's ghost—Buford's maybe—had appeared. Or the spot where the whole group's mass hysteria had conjured the figment of their collective imaginations. Cass held onto hope that the latter was true.

"What are you doing?"

Cass screamed and whirled to face the door, then grabbed the back of a chair for support. She froze. Was she dizzy? Nope. Nothing. She was fine. "Jeez. You scared me half to death."

Jim's laughter chased the lingering fear. "Sorry. I didn't mean to scare you. You probably shouldn't be walking around though."

Hmmm . . . If he didn't want her walking around, how was she going to convince him to let her go upstairs to check out Conrad's room? Which she was definitely going to do. No way could she let this opportunity go to waste. How would he feel about her digging through his dead brother's things? He didn't seem too upset, but you never knew.

Jim frowned, his brows drawing together. "Are you all right?"

How long had she been standing there lost in thought?

Long enough for him to grow concerned, obviously. "I . . .
um . . ." How could she get rid of him long enough to search?
"Do the phones work?"

"Nope. Still dead."

"How long are you planning to stay?"

Jim shifted a backpack she hadn't noticed to the opposite
shoulder. "Not sure. I was hoping to get things cleaned up
a bit. The police brought two buses to escort everyone to the
Bay Side Hotel, and everyone up and left. I want to go
through and make sure there's no food lying around or
anything."

"I hate to ask you this, but is there any way you could
run back to my car and see if you can find my phone?" She
caught her lower lip between her teeth and tried for her best
vulnerable expression. She couldn't dispel the image of Bee
rolling his eyes. "Bee was expecting me to meet him, and I
don't want him to get worried and come looking for me in
such bad weather." Okay. Total lie, and Cass was a terrible
liar. Would he know?

He held her gaze a moment longer than necessary. "Sure.
No problem. But promise me you'll sit still somewhere and
wait for me to come back? I don't want you falling or anything while I'm gone."

Cass pulled out a chair and sat, then slid her crossed
fingers behind her back. "I promise. I'm a bit tired anyway."
She propped her elbow on the table and lowered her head
into her hand, his footsteps retreating. Wind whipped
through the fireplace, howling fiercely in the empty room.
She waited, unable to hear any sound from Jim. How long
should she wait? Even if he found the phone right away, he

should be gone at least fifteen or twenty minutes. If she remembered correctly, everything had tumbled out of her purse when she crashed.

The sound of the front door slamming propelled her into action. She jumped up and headed for the stairs.

12

The image of the hole Cass had kept seeing during Joan's reading was haunting her. She had to search Conrad's room for any hidden compartments and get a quick glimpse into the secret space in the floor of the cupola. Thankfully, the attic-style stairway was still in place. At least she wouldn't have to waste time pulling it down. Lanterns glowed along the hallway walls but with all of the doors closed, no light was visible from outside. She turned the knob and eased the door to Conrad's room open, her heart thundering as she slid beneath the yellow crime scene tape. Since the room was at the back of the house, looking out over the bay, she chanced turning the light on, then gasped.

The room lay in shambles. Certainly the police wouldn't have done that. Clothes were strewn across the floor and suitcases were upended, their linings torn out and thrown aside. The mattress from the queen-size bed was propped against the wall, and the box spring lay crooked on its frame. Could Donald have trashed the room after she'd left him there? She struggled to remember how long it had been from the time she left him until she next saw him in the dining room. No use.

How could she possibly search this mess?

She peeked in the bathroom and flicked on the light. Makeup had been spilled into the sink, and the bag lay empty on the counter. The cabinet was open and empty. With the shower curtain pulled closed, the tub at the back of the bathroom was the only space she couldn't see. For the sake of being thorough, she pulled it aside. Spots of water still clung to the walls. Several puddles littered the floor, a faint tinge of rust coloring the one around the drain. Two shampoo bottles sat on a shelf beside a bar of soap.

Ugh . . . Cass gagged. Several pieces of short dark hair clung to the soap. That was one thing she didn't miss from her marriage. Every morning when she got in the shower, she had to wash Donald's hair off the soap. Even if she got her own bar, he still somehow managed to get hair on it. She started to pull the curtain closed, then froze, her gaze shooting back to the soap. If Tank was right, and Conrad was that much of a neat freak, he never would have left hair on the soap. Besides, this hair was dark. Conrad's hair was dirty blond. And Joan's hair was a mousy brown . . . and long. Who had dark hair?

Oh . . . oh no. No way.

She'd walked in on Donald wiping down the room. Emmett had heard Joan arguing with a man before he went to bed. It could have been Donald. Donald had made a comment about Cass contacting Conrad when he'd met her in the dining room. Joan had come to her seeking out answers from Conrad. Was it possible?

Cass turned and fled the room, thoughts of Donald and Joan chasing her out into the hallway. She reached back in and turned off the room light, but there was no way she was going back into the bathroom. That light would just have to stay on. Her mind whirled. Could Donald really be the killer? Was he having an affair with Joan Wellington? It would have taken two people to get Conrad up onto the rafter. Were Donald and Joan in cahoots? Someone had trashed the room. Why would Joan wreck her own room? What could they have been searching for?

Cass pressed her hands to her temples as questions ricocheted through her mind. A swirling mass of confusion enveloped her. Her head pounded. Okay. She had to calm down, had to think more clearly. She thrust her hands into her hair and squeezed. Suspicion pummeled her. She shoved it ruthlessly aside and slammed a block in place to keep thoughts from intruding.

With one quick glance down the empty stairway, she climbed up the stairs to the cupola. When she reached the top, she crouched low, careful to keep below the window ledges so Jim wouldn't see her if he returned. Jim. Oh crap. How long had she been in Conrad's room? It couldn't have been that long, could it? She'd totally lost track of time. She dropped onto her hands and knees and scrambled across the floor to the opening in the floor by the window. Nothing. The space still stood empty. The piece of wood flooring that had covered the hole was nowhere to be seen. Had the police taken it?

A band of light passed overhead. Headlights coming up

the hill? Panic seized her. She had to get out of there. Intent on making it back downstairs before Jim returned, Cass spun toward the stairway. Her gaze fell on Joan's body crumpled in the far corner, her eyes open, sheer terror frozen in the expression on her face.

A scream tore from Cass's throat, and she slapped a hand over her mouth. She ran to Joan and pressed trembling fingers to her neck. Nothing. A coiled rope was thrown on top of her. Cass stumbled across the room and almost nosedived down the steep stairs. She caught herself at the last minute by grabbing hold of the springs on either side of the opening.

Thud.

A car door? The front door? She ran down the stairs, launching herself down the last two.

"Cass?"

Jim. Oh no. What if he hadn't been on his way to the mansion? What if he'd been up here and killed Joan? Maybe he'd seen her slide off the road from the cupola. Fear threatened to choke her as she ran down the hallway, passing the room she'd stayed in while she was there.

"Cass? You up here?" He was already on the stairs.

Cass tried to run faster, tripped over her own feet, and face-planted on the rug a few feet from the stairs.

"Hey. Are you all right?" Jim grabbed her arm and helped her to her feet. He glanced at the open stairway to the cupola. "What are you doing up here?"

Cass sobbed. She couldn't help it. "I . . . uh . . ." She reached a hand into her coat pocket and felt around. A crumpled tissue, a dog treat, her cell phone . . . *oh crap* . . . when had she shoved it into her pocket? She prayed fervently that it wouldn't ring.

"Is something wrong?"

"No . . . I . . . uh . . ." There had to be something. Her fingers fell on a small cylinder. *Yes*. She pulled out the tube of lipstick. "I forgot this in the nightstand when I left." She sucked in a deep shuddering breath. "It's my favorite color."

"You shouldn't have come up here."

"I know. I got dizzy when I was almost to the stairs and fell. Did you find my phone?"

He studied her a moment longer, the intensity of his gaze penetrating the haze of fear. "No. I did find your purse, though. It's on the table in the ballroom."

"Thanks." She forced a smile—which probably looked more like a grimace—and pressed a hand to her head. "You know what? I think maybe I do need to go to the hospital after all. I'm really not feeling very well. I think I'm going to be sick."

With a firm grip on her arm, and a last suspicious glance around the empty hallway, Jim frowned as he led her toward the stairs and guided her down.

"Are you sure you don't want me to come in with you?" Jim's SUV sat idling in front of the emergency room entrance.

"No. Thank you." Cass studied his expression. Was that suspicion darkening his eyes? She swallowed hard. "I'm fine. They'll probably just check me out and send me home. My friend Bee is up all night working anyway. He won't mind coming to get me. I've already put you out enough. Thank you, again, for everything." *Shut up and get out of the car, Cass.* "Well, see you."

"Sure." He squeezed her hand and, for one fleeting moment, she was afraid he wouldn't let go. "I hear there's going to be a group reading tomorrow night. Maybe I'll see you there."

Oh crap. She'd forgotten about the readings. She hadn't even called Henry. It was probably too late now. She'd have to call him in the morning. She glanced at the dashboard clock. Twelve thirty? She couldn't possibly have been at the mansion that long. How long had she been unconscious in the car before Jim found her?

Jim's eyes narrowed. "Are you sure you're all right?" He opened his door and got out. Shoot, she should have moved faster. He kept his gaze on her as he rounded the front of the SUV and opened her door. "Watch the ice on the sidewalk."

Most of the sidewalk was covered with salt, but a few icy patches still remained.

"Thank you. I'm okay now." The emergency room doors slid open, and Cass had one moment of panic before Jim said good night and returned to his truck. She crossed the waiting room and stood beside the reception desk, positioning herself so she could keep an eye on Jim's truck in her peripheral vision.

"Can I help you, miss?" The receptionist glanced at Cass and winced.

Cass smoothed her hair. She hadn't given any thought to her appearance. What on earth did she look like? She checked her reflection in the glass cabinet door on the wall behind the desk. *Yikes!* Jim's truck was still there. *Dang.*

"Are you okay, miss?" The woman's brows drew together as she pushed her chair back from the desk. She gathered some paperwork and clipped it to a board then handed it to Cass and gestured to a cup of pens at the side of the counter.

Cass took the clipboard and moved to the edge of the counter. She grabbed a pen and waved to Jim, who was still idling at the curb.

"May I see your insurance card and ID, please?" The woman held out her hand. "It'll be faster if I make the copies while you fill out the paperwork. We're pretty slow right now, so you shouldn't have to wait long."

Apparently satisfied she was in good hands, Jim finally pulled away.

Cass blew out a pent-up breath, tossed the paperwork on the counter, and pulled out her phone. "Excuse me." She left the startled receptionist staring after her and fled the waiting room. No way was she going out into the parking lot. She couldn't take a chance Jim was waiting around out there somewhere. Instead, she locked herself in a bathroom stall. If he did come back, she could always say she was sick.

Her hands were shaking so violently, it took three tries to dial Bee's number.

Bee picked up on the fifth ring. "Hey, sweetie. You're lucky you caught me. I just turned the phone back on. In the zone, you know?" Only Bee would answer the phone in the middle of the night as if it were a perfectly normal time to chat. She guessed, for Bee, it was. "I was just getting ready to head home from the shop. Can I call you back in a little bit?" Bee often worked on his dress designs late into the night. Any distractions broke his ability to concentrate, so he'd set up a room in the back of Dreamweaver where he could turn off his phone, crank up his music, and escape from the world long enough to create what he needed. The results were breathtaking. "Cass? Hon? You there?"

Cass sighed, relief finally seeping some of the tension from her tight, aching muscles. "I need you to come get me."

Bee must have sensed the urgency in her voice, because he immediately sobered. "Where?"

"The hospital." No need to specify which hospital, since Bay Island only had one.

"Oh, dear. What happened? Are you all right?"

"Nothing. I'm fine. Well . . . not exactly fine . . . I crashed my car."

Bee gasped.

"Oh, and I found a body." Dead silence followed for a moment. Had he hung up? "Are you still there?"

"Jeez, sweetie. I can't leave you alone for one minute, can I?"

With a small chuckle, Cass swiped at the tears streaming down her face.

"I'm on my way. Where are you, the emergency room?"

"Uh . . ." What if Jim was still out there waiting to see if she came back? That was stupid. Why would he wait? And why would he care? Did he know Joan's body was in the cupola? Did he suspect Cass knew?

"Cass?"

"No. Pick me up out front."

"The main entrance is closed this late at night, Cass."

"Oh. Right." She'd been gone from Bay Island for too long. Even though Manhattan was less than a hundred miles from Bay Island, they were very different worlds. "Okay.

Pick me up right outside the ER." She hesitated. She couldn't wait out there. "But pull right up to the doors and call when you get here."

"I'm on my way."

When Bee ended the call, Cass just stood in the stall—careful not to touch the walls—unsure what to do next. She tucked the phone back into her pocket, opened the stall door, and peered out. No one. Even with the icy roads tonight, Bay Island's only emergency room was quiet. People must have stayed home. Smart people. At least, smarter than her.

Catching sight of her reflection in the mirror above the small row of sinks, Cass cringed. "Ah jeez . . . Bee's gonna freak." Blood streaked her face. Apparently, the head wound had bled more than she realized. While the car was lying on its side, it must have flowed into her hair, because her hair was matted with blood and sticking out where she'd run her hands through it. She had a small cut on her bottom lip. Her left eye and cheekbone were bruised, although not too badly. And her coat and shirt were stained with coffee. *Ugh* . . .

She stuck her hands beneath the faucet, then soaped them vigorously. The water ran pink as she rinsed. How had she not noticed the blood on her hands?

The door opened, and Cass jumped and spun toward the intrusion, splattering water across the floor, her heart thundering.

"There you are." The receptionist pushed through the door, a nurturing smile on her face. "Do you need help? Are you sick to your stomach? I can bring a wheelchair if you need one."

Cass grabbed a few paper towels and blotted her hands

dry. "Oh, no. Thank you. I actually feel much better now. I just called a friend to come get me."

The woman frowned. When she spoke next, her voice had turned gentle. "Did someone do this to you? You're safe here, you know, we can call—"

"No." Cass held up her hands. "Oh. No. No one hurt me. I flipped my car on the icy roads. It was hours ago, but I wasn't feeling well, so I came in, but now I feel better. I think I was just nervous." She almost choked on the giggle she offered. It came out sounding like more of a high-pitched squeak. Did she look as hysterical as she felt? If so, the woman would probably call for a straitjacket instead of a wheelchair.

With a suspicious stare, the woman started to back away. "So, you no longer want to see a doctor?"

"No. Thank you. I'm fine now."

"I'm afraid I'm going to have to insist." The woman's brow lifted. "You shouldn't play games with a head injury."

Okay, so maybe fine was too strong a word. "It's not even bleeding anymore." Cass was saved from having to argue further when her cell phone rang. She answered as she fled the bathroom with the woman's protests following after her.

13

Pulling her hood up against the frigid wind, Cass crossed the sidewalk, careful not to slip and fall, and climbed into Bee's bad-weather car. She was surprised the beat-up, four-wheel-drive pickup truck even still ran, but it was a better alternative than taking his Trans-Am out on icy, salt-and-sand covered roads.

"Oh my." Bee's hand fluttered to his chest. "They didn't clean you up very well."

She pressed her hands to the vents, grateful for the warmth. "I didn't see the doctor."

"What? Why not?" Turning in the seat so he could face her, Bee examined her face. "Well, the bleeding's stopped, but it doesn't mean you don't have a concussion or something. You should really be seen."

"No. I'm okay, Bee. Please, can we just get out of here?"

She glanced around the dark parking lot. No sign of Jim's SUV, but still . . .

"Look, hon. I know you're spooked—especially after the . . . incident . . . with finding Marge Hawkins in the theater and all—but there are bodies in the hospital all the time." He placed a hand gently on top of one of hers. "Unfortunately, people die. It's no reason to go home without getting checked out. They obviously felt you needed to see a doctor, or they wouldn't have brought you to the hospital." He squeezed her hand, released it, turned back around, and gripped his door handle. "Now, come on. I'll walk you in and stay with you. You can squeeze my hand if you want. Not too hard, mind you. I still have work to do on the evening gown . . ."

When he started to open the door, Cass grabbed his arm, confusion making her head pound harder. "What are you talking about?" Her head started to spin trying to make sense of the one-sided conversation. "Who's 'they'?"

"They?"

"You said they brought me to the hospital. Who's 'they'? And who died?"

Bee made a face and turned back to her. "'*They*' is whoever was in the ambulance, and I don't know who died. You're the one who said you found a body."

Oh, right. She had said that.

He leaned closer, staring into her eyes. His warm breath, and the lingering scent of peppermint, washed over her.

"What are you doing?"

"Checking your pupils."

Cass sighed and turned to scan the parking lot again. She rubbed her temples. "I'm fine, Bee. The ambulance didn't bring me to the hospital, Jim Wellington did. And the body I found wasn't in the hospital, it was in the cupola at the old Madison Estate. And the only other person there with me was Jim." A barrage of mental questions assailed her, bringing an immediate headache. Ignoring the sense of urgency, she shoved the questions aside to focus on Bee.

He held up a hand. "Okay. Just start at the beginning." He shook his head. "No. Wait. Actually, never mind that. Skip the beginning, I'll catch up. Just start with what you were doing alone at the Madison Estate with Jim Wellington—and don't skip a single detail." He fanned himself with both hands. "Then you can tell me the rest."

Cass couldn't help but laugh. She dropped her head against the seat back and closed her eyes. "I'll give up all the juicy dirt, but only if you drive while I do." She opened her eyes.

"You've got yourself a deal." He shifted into drive, checked the side-view mirror—giving Cass a moment of terror while he waited for another car to pass—then pulled out. "Spill it, sister."

With a sigh, Cass started at the vet's office.

Bee clucked sympathetically, and she assured him Beast would be fine and that she was going to start a strict training program. He laughed at that, and Cass bristled.

"What? I can train him."

"Of course you can, dear. Now, let's get to the part where you're alone in an empty mansion with Jim Wellington."

"Grrr . . ."

Bee laughed again.

Wiseass. Just for that, she should clam up and not tell him anything.

"Want me to stop at 7-Eleven and get you a cup of coffee?"

Okay. He's forgiven. "Oh, yes. Thank you."

He hit the turn signal and made a quick right into the small parking lot. Pulling into a spot right in front of the door, he glanced at her. "Do you want something to eat?"

Did she? Her stomach was no longer queasy, and she couldn't remember the last time she'd eaten. Probably the McDonald's she had for lunch, which seemed like days ago.

"They have donuts. They're not Tony's, but in an emergency, they'll do." He grinned and hopped out of the truck without waiting for an answer.

Cass marveled again at what a good friend he had become. Bee was already living on Bay Island when Cass returned home. He had his own troubled past, his own demons to battle, and yet he never failed to offer a sympathetic ear or a helping hand. Warmth finally began to return to her. Bee always made her feel safe, loved, protected, and happy.

How had she ever considered Sylvia a friend? Her best friend, in fact. The woman had always put Cass down in subtle ways that made her feel inferior and encouraged her to be clingy and needy. Then she'd crept in and stolen Cass's husband when she was at her most vulnerable. Cass obviously had a lot to learn about choosing her friends.

Bee shouldered open the door and headed for the car, a cup holder and bag in his hands. At least she was off to a good start.

Cass reached across and pushed the door open for him.

"Thanks." He handed her the drinks and climbed in. After dropping the bag on the seat between them, he rubbed his hands together. "It's absolutely freezing out there, but at least it stopped snowing."

A tear slid down Cass's cheek.

"Oh, honey. Are you okay?" Bee opened the glove compartment and riffled through it, then pulled out a couple of napkins. "Here."

"Thank you, Bee." She held his gaze, trying to convey the depth of her gratitude for his friendship.

"It's just a napkin."

She laughed and let her gaze drop as she took the napkin and wiped her cheeks. "No, Bee. Not for the napkin, but that too. I meant thank you for everything. You're one of the best friends I've ever had. You're always there for me whenever I need you. You came out in the middle of the night in terrible weather to get me, then didn't harass me for answers . . . much anyway." She smiled. "Even though the curiosity has to be killing you."

Tears shimmered in his eyes, and he lowered his gaze and patted her hand. "Well, now that I'm appreciated, start talking before that curiosity does kill me."

Cass laughed and wiped her face again. She took the chocolate donut Bee held out to her.

"Just to hold you over till we can get something else. Do you want me to go through Taco Bell?"

"Nah. Thanks, though. This is perfect." She took a big bite of the donut and savored it for a moment, then swallowed and started to talk.

Bee didn't bother to drive, just sat with her, eating donuts, drinking coffee, and listening to her story. He scolded her for heading up to Emmett's by herself. She should have called him and asked him to take a ride, but she'd been upset about Beast and hadn't thought of it. Better she hadn't anyway. The thought of him having been hurt in the accident brought the chill rushing back.

When she finished, he ran back in for more coffee, giving her a few minutes to think about where to go from there. By the time he returned, she was more in control than she'd been all night.

She opened the door for him again, and he handed her a cup holder. "Four cups?"

"Stephanie and Tank are gonna be pissed if we show up there before dawn without coffee. Don't you think?"

"Stephanie and Tank?" Cass's hands started to shake.

Offering her a sympathetic look, Bee slid the truck into reverse and backed out of the parking spot. "You do realize you have to go to the police, right?"

Cass shrugged, a moody pout her only answer.

"If you'd rather go to the police station . . ."

"No."

"Well then, quit sulking and help me figure out who killed Joan and Conrad."

Cass perked up a little. "At first, when I found the hair on the soap, I was sure it was Donald. And I can see why he'd kill Conrad if he was having an affair with Joan. Especially since she probably inherited Conrad's share of the family fortune. But what would they have been looking for?"

Bee sat quietly. "Maybe the will? If Joan was the beneficiary, they might have needed a copy of the will. Maybe Conrad hid it somewhere."

"I guess." That did make sense, at least until Joan was killed. "But why would Donald kill Joan? It's not like he'd inherit anything if he wasn't with her."

"Hmm . . . true. But who would?"

Cass frowned. "You think there were two different killers? Donald and Joan killed Conrad, and then someone else killed Joan?"

Bee shrugged. "I guess it could have happened that way, but that would be kind of weird, no?"

"This whole thing is kind of weird."

"True enough." Bee hit the turn signal and turned onto Stephanie's street. "Three killers seems like a bit much to me."

"Well, there had to be at least two to kill Conrad. No one could have gotten him up there by themselves. Do you think?"

"Probably not. Even if you were strong enough, it seems you'd need at least three hands." Bee pulled into Stephanie's driveway. The house was dark. "Do you think we should call first?"

Leaning forward, she searched for any sign of life. Nothing. "Probably."

He pulled out his cell phone and dialed. "And what about Jim Wellington? If he was alone at the house with Joan's bod—" He held up a finger. "Hey, Tank. Yes, everything's all right. Well . . . sort of. Listen. I'm sorry to bother you in the middle of the night, but Cass had an accident and . . . no . . . yes, she's all right. No, Beast wasn't with her, he's at the vet. Yes, he's okay too . . . no . . . picked her up at the hospital. She also found a body. Yes. In your driveway." Bee clicked off and tucked the phone back into his pocket. "That went well." He grinned as the front porch light flicked on.

"What were you saying about Jim?"

"Just that if he was alone in the house with Joan's body, who else could have killed her? It almost has to be him, no?"

Cass shook her head. "I have no idea. He acted suspicious of me, but in a *she's-acting-like-a-lunatic* sort of way, more than a *does-she-know-I-killed-my-sister-in-law* kind of way. If you know what I mean."

Bee nodded. "Makes perfect sense."

Tank held the front door open, and Bee handed him a coffee cup on his way past by way of greeting. They trudged to the kitchen and sat at the table.

Tank looked good for just having been woken from a dead sleep. Of course, he was probably used to waking suddenly in the middle of the night and having to be alert. He spun a chair around and straddled it, resting his forearms on the chair back.

Stephanie arrived a moment later, the beat-up red bathrobe she refused to get rid of tied over a pair of plaid pajama pants. Her hair was a tangled mess. "This had better be good." Apparently Tank hadn't had time to fill her in.

"Oh, it's good. Well worth getting up for." Bee leaned back, crossed his legs, and draped an elbow over the chair back.

"Would you be saying that if it was seven in the morning?"

He studied her for a moment then handed her a cup of coffee. "This time, I'd have to say yes. I would have gotten up at that ungodly hour to go pick Cass up from the hospital."

"Hospital!" Stephanie's gaze shot to Cass. As if seeing her for the first time, Stephanie winced. "Oh, man. What happened?" She set her coffee cup down and went to the sink, pulled out a dish towel, and filled it with ice. "Here, press this to your eye. It's already bruising. What did the doctor say?"

"She didn't see the doctor." Bee sat looking smug while Stephanie reprimanded her.

Tank took a sip of his coffee, seeming to take it all in before he finally interrupted. "Enough."

Silence descended on the room.

"Cass, are you all right?" His eyes narrowed as he examined her.

"Yeah. I'm fine."

"Okay, then. Start somewhere, anywhere, and tell me what's going on." He smoothed a hand over his near crew cut.

"When I left Doc Martin's office—Beast is going to be fine but had to stay overnight—I decided to head past Emmett's to see if he was sure it was Conrad Joan had been arguing with."

Tank frowned. "What made you think it wasn't?"

"Nothing specific. We were talking about it over lunch and Bee suggested someone else could have been in there with Joan. And I don't think Emmett specifically said she was arguing with Conrad. I might have just assumed it." It could just as easily have been Donald. The soap popped into Cass's mind. "Then when I was searching Conrad's room, there was dark hair on the soap. Conrad had dirty blond hair, so I thought . . . uhh . . ." *Oops.* Apparently the knock on her head loosened her lips. She'd have to remember that.

Tank lowered his head for a minute. With his elbows propped on the back of the chair, he clasped his hands behind his neck. "I don't even want to know yet, just back up."

Cass had a sudden revelation. Tank was a patient man. "Right." Lifting the coffee cup to her mouth to stall for a minute, Cass tried to remember what else she should probably leave out. At this point, it seemed pretty safe to tell him everything. There was no other way she could explain finding Joan's body without confessing to searching the cupola anyway.

"When I was heading toward Emmett's, I passed the Madison Estate, and I noticed the cupola was lit, but the rest of the house was dark. Then, as I was heading down the hill toward Emmett's, my car slid off the road and rolled. I don't know how long I was unconscious, but . . ."

Tank held up a hand to stop her. "You were knocked out?"

Oh crap. Maybe she should have skipped that. The last thing she needed was to get hauled back to the hospital. "A little. I think."

"You think? How do you get a little knocked out? Are you sure you're okay? I could take you to the hospital, and we could talk about all of this there."

The concern in his voice and the warmth in his eyes made Cass choke up. She swallowed hard and shook her head. She couldn't possibly drink any more coffee, so she settled for twirling the cup in circles on the table. "I'm good. If I don't feel well later, I'll go back to the hospital."

Tank didn't push the issue.

"The next thing I knew, Jim Wellington pulled me out of the car." Thankfully, she was still clear-headed enough not to mention her reaction to him. She remembered the feel of his warm fingers sizzling against her skin. Surely someone who looked like him, with such a sensitive, caring touch, couldn't be a killer.

"Cass?"

Her cheeks heated. "Oh, sorry. Jim brought me to the estate; he said he was on his way there to clean up and pick up a few things he forgot. Then I sent him back to the car to look for my phone, ran up and looked in Conrad's room—which is where I found the soap—and the cupola—which is where I found Joan Wellington." Cass swallowed hard, wishing she hadn't drank so much coffee or eaten anything. Her stomach lurched. "Her body."

Tank jerked upright. "You found Joan Wellington's body?"

Cass nodded.

He jumped up and pulled a phone from the pocket of his pajama pants.

"No. Wait."

He paused and stared at her.

"Please, you can't tell anyone I found her."

"What?"

How could she explain that she didn't want Jim to think she'd lied to him? Okay, that would probably look bad. "Uh . . ."

"Tell me, quickly, where is she? Are you sure she was dead?"

Cass was already nodding. "She's definitely dead. I checked her pulse, and her skin was ice cold. There's no doubt. She was curled up, kind of, by the window in the cupola."

"What were you looking for up there?" Tank wiped a hand across his mouth.

"When Joan came in for the reading, she—"

"When? What reading?"

"She came into the shop this afternoon. Uh . . . well, I guess yesterday afternoon, and she was looking for something. She wanted me to contact Conrad and ask him where it was."

"What was she looking for?"

Cass shrugged. "She wouldn't tell me."

"All right. I'm going to have to check it out. You realize that, right?"

Cass shrugged. "I guess."

Bee put a hand on her arm. He looked at Tank pleadingly. "Maybe you could wait till morning and then just go back and look around the cupola again. Then you wouldn't have to say Cass found the body."

Cass shuddered, the thought of dealing with the questions and the police investigation more than she could deal with right now.

Tank just stared at Bee as if he had ten heads.

"What?" Bee feigned innocence. "It's not like she's going anywhere."

Massaging his temples between his thumb and forefinger, Tank closed his eyes. The phone rang in his hand, and he checked the screen before answering. "Yeah, Emmett?" He glanced at Cass. "It's all right. She's here . . . a little banged up, but okay." He listened for a few more minutes. "Calm down, Emmett. What ghost?"

Cass sat up straighter, the exhaustion weighing on her only moments ago suddenly lifted.

"Wait there. I'm on my way." Tucking the phone back into his pocket, he met Cass's gaze. "That was Emmett, in a panic because he found your car on his way back from the Madison Estate, where he'd gone to plow out the driveway and lot." He heaved in a deep breath, and his expression softened. "Which he didn't do, because he saw a ghost."

"A ghost?"

"The cupola lights were on, and he could see a body hanging. He thinks it's Conrad's ghost, so he won't plow up there."

Fear clenched Cass's gut. An urgent whisper was all she could manage. "There was a coil of rope on top of Joan's body."

"Looks like someone either went back to finish the job, or was there the whole time you and Jim Wellington were." Tank strode from the room, leaving Cass, Bee, and Stephanie staring after him.

Exhaustion finally got the better of her, and Cass folded her arms on the table and laid her head down.

"Come on, Cass. You can lie down in the guest bedroom for a while." Stephanie emptied the remainder of Cass's coffee down the drain and tossed the cup in the garbage.

Cass reluctantly lifted her head. "Thanks, Steph, but I have to go home and take a shower."

"There's a shower in the guest room."

Cass looked at the coffee staining her shirt and jeans. She slid her jacket—also stained with coffee—from the back of the chair. Bee took it from her and helped her into it. "I need a change of clothes and stuff, too. Besides, I only have a few hours before I have to be at the shop for the individual readings. I'd like to at least close my eyes for a little while."

"You're going to do the readings?"

Cass shrugged. "If I don't do the readings and set up the group reading for tonight, I'll have to refund all of the money."

"You didn't set that up yet?"

"I never got a chance." She rubbed her eyes.

"I'll tell you what. Go get some sleep. I'll call Henry in a little while and work something out." Stephanie frowned. "I don't really think you should be alone."

"I'll be okay."

"I'll take care of her." Bee put an arm around her shoulder. "Come on. I'll take you home and hang out on the couch while you sleep for a little while. I'll make sure you get up in time and take you to the shop."

"You're a sweetheart, Bee. Thank you. You too, Stephanie."

Squeezing her shoulder, Bee led her toward the door. "No problem. Now let's go. But you're getting up in time to eat a real breakfast." He turned to Stephanie. "Why don't you meet us at the diner at eight? Then we can figure out what to do next."

14

A shower, three ibuprofen, a few hours of sleep, and a good makeup job worked wonders. Other than some residual achiness and stiffness, Cass didn't feel too bad, all things considered. Rubbing her lower back, she stood waiting by the front door of the diner with Bee and Stephanie, while the hostess ran around trying to find seats for the steady stream of customers. A few people cast discreet stares in her direction, and she gingerly touched her bandaged forehead. No doubt the whole town already knew she'd wrecked her car. "I can't believe they're this crowded at eight o'clock on a Tuesday morning."

Bee leaned close, pitching his voice low. "Two murders—though I've only heard Conrad's mentioned so far—and two ghost sightings, in four days. The deli and Tony's are probably mobbed too." The diner, deli, and bakery were the town's central gathering points. When there was good dirt

to be had, you could always expect a long line and a group
of people who didn't mind waiting in each establishment.

"Two ghosts?"

"Yeah, yours and the one Emmett saw." Bee had a knack
for deciphering gossip, weeding through what was important
and what was too far-fetched to be relevant, and coming up
with a fairly accurate summary within seconds of walking
into a room. Bee's bushy eyebrows drew together, creasing
his brow. "But there's another undercurrent buzzing I can't
quite pick up on yet."

"Hey, guys. I have your usual table in the back with
Elaina."

The back of the diner had a small room that could be
reserved for parties, but they often used it for extra seating
at busier times. Cass couldn't ever remember it being open
on a Tuesday morning. "Thanks, Gabby."

They squeezed through the crowd, dodging harried wait-
resses as they crossed the main section on their way to the
back. Chrome and mirrors filled the space, reflecting the
animated conversations and adding to the excitement. A
frosted glass wall etched with the image of a lighthouse
separated the back from the main section of the diner. Bee
slid into one side of the booth facing the open doorway—
wouldn't want to miss anything—and Cass and Stephanie
slid into the other.

Elaina Stevens ran over with a coffeepot in each hand.
She poured Stephanie and Cass regular coffee and Bee decaf.
Everyone knew Bee only drank decaf in the morning before
he went to bed. "Do you guys know what you want yet?"

They ate at the diner often enough none of them needed
to look at a menu, but Bee obviously wanted to linger. He

opened his menu on the table. "Could you give us a few minutes, dear?"

"Sure. Just yell when you're ready." She leaned over the table and pointed to a random spot on the menu. "Have you guys heard the news?"

"Which news?"

"Guess who's back in town?"

Bingo. There was the undercurrent Bee had picked up on. He nodded discreetly to Cass, his expression smug.

"Elaina?"

The young girl turned as Frankie Mandola, the diner's owner, entered the room. "Yes?"

"Could you do me a favor and quick set up table three back here?" The older man rolled his eyes. "The Talbots just parked."

"Be right back." Elaina rushed to set up the table before Joe and Marie Talbot made it to the front door with their pack of brats. Everyone knew not to let those four boys run free in the main room. One set of eight-year-old twins, a six year old, and a four year old, who was following right in his brothers' footsteps. Cass would bet her last dollar their parents had never once said the word *no* to them.

The paper placemats on the table were covered with ads for local businesses. Cass traced a finger around her small ad in the top right corner. "Do you think maybe I should try a bigger ad next time?"

Bee slid his menu over to check out the ad he'd no doubt seen a million times already. "I don't think it needs to be bigger, but maybe you should add some color, or a logo or something. You know, a little something to make it pop off the page and stand out among the others."

Exactly. "Good idea. Any suggestions?"

Stephanie studied her placemat too. "What about a light-house? Your shop is really close to the lighthouse, and you sell lighthouse souvenirs."

"I don't know." She scanned the placemat. "There are three other ads featuring lighthouses."

"Four." Bee pointed out a small silhouette of a light-house in the background of one ad. "This one's kind of hard to see."

"How about a crystal ball?"

"Maybe." Cass shrugged.

"Hi, guys. Ready to order yet?" Elaina held a pen poised over her pad.

"Sure. Can I have a vegetable omelet with whole wheat toast?" Since Cass couldn't get her daily exercise walking down the beach from her house to the shop in this weather, she really had to watch what she ate. "And a diet coke, please."

"Got it. Stephanie?"

"Umm . . . I'll have hash and eggs, over easy, and an orange juice."

"Sure. Bee?"

"I'll have a bacon cheeseburger—medium-well—with fries and a root beer." He closed his menu and handed it to Elaina, but he didn't release it when she grabbed hold. "Who's in town?"

Elaina laughed and glanced over her shoulder then leaned closer. "Horatio Madison's widow and son."

"Get out of here." Bee released the menu. "What for?"

Elaina shrugged and collected the menus from Stephanie

and Cass. "No one knows. Supposedly, they arrived some-time really early this morning."

"The ferry's running again?"

"Nah. They showed up in a small, private boat."

Cass wracked her brain for any reason the Madisons could have returned. "That's all you know?"

"That's it. But if I hear anything else, I'll be sure to let you know." She pulled the top page from her pad and tucked the pad into the front of her apron. On her way to the back, she stopped to grab ketchup for another table.

The hostess led the Talbots back and seated them at the other side of the room.

"It's not going to be far enough."

"Huh? What's not?" Cass scanned the room. Had she missed something?

"The Talbots." Bee gestured toward the boys, two of whom were already fighting over some kind of handheld video game. "They are definitely not far enough away."

The youngest boy started running around the room, weaving between the tables, arms extended like an airplane. One of his brothers made banging noises as he tried to shoot the little guy down.

"Okay, that's enough." Bee leaned over out of the booth, and crooked a finger at the two oldest boys.

They approached the table warily.

"How'd you like to each earn a dollar?" Bee smiled.

The twins looked at each other before shrugging. "Sure," they answered together.

"You stay calm and keep your brothers calm, and I'll give each of you a dollar on my way out."

The two hooted and high-fived each other.

Bee held up a finger. "Uh-uh . . . I said calm. I want to eat my dinner in peace and quiet."

"Dinner?"

"Yes, dinner. I haven't gone to bed yet, so this is my dinner."

The boys shrugged again and ran off to whisper with their brothers. All of them stared at Bee.

He pulled four dollar bills from his pocket and waved them back and forth then laid them on the table.

The boys conferred again then sat in their seats.

"See. They're good boys. They just need a little incentive."

Cass laughed. More likely, they just didn't know what to make of Bee.

Stephanie leaned forward and spoke quietly. "So what do you think the Madisons are doing back?"

Sipping her coffee, Cass shook her head. "I have no idea." She looked at Bee.

"Nope. Me neither."

"Hmmm . . . Anyway, I was able to get in touch with Henry, and the group reading is all set up for tonight. He's giving you the ballroom. Some of the guys are going to take the big table from the mansion and bring it to the hotel for you."

"That's great, Stephanie. Thank you."

Stephanie waved her off. "No problem. I also called Isabella. She's going to cater it for you. She said she may as well since she already had all the food. No sense letting it all go to waste."

"Perfect."

"Hey!" One of the Talbot twins ripped the game from his brother's hands then glanced over at Bee.

Bee lifted a dollar from the table, folded it, and started to stick it back into his pocket.

Kurt or Kyle—they were identical twins—quieted instantly.

Bee tossed the bill back on top of the others.

Cass turned to Stephanie. "Have you heard from Tank?"

Stephanie shook her head. "No. Not since he left."

"That's a long time."

"Yeah."

That didn't bode well for Joan. If Tank had found anything, he'd have already called Stephanie. The fact that he hadn't probably meant Joan was dead. Which Cass already knew; though, she desperately wanted to be wrong.

Elaina returned and placed a small bowl of coleslaw and a pickle in front of Bee.

"Thanks, hon."

"You're welcome." She hurried off.

Stephanie turned back to Cass. "I talked to Emmett, though. He towed your car to the shop, and he has a loaner for you. I'll take you by to pick it up when we leave here."

"Awesome. Thanks."

Bee bit into his pickle.

"No problem."

Gesturing toward Cass with the remainder of the pickle, Bee frowned. "Who do you think inherits Conrad's share of the fortune now that Joan and Conrad are both dead?"

"I don't know. Why?"

"Just thinking." He leaned close, keeping his voice low. "Joan would have inherited it if she lived. Now that she's gone, too, someone's going to be pretty rich."

Cass hadn't thought of that.

Stephanie leaned in too. "You can't assume the motivation for killing them is money."

"Why not?" Bee lifted a brow.

"Could just as easily be jealousy, especially if Joan was having an affair." Stephanie slid back to her spot with a shrug. "Who knows? Maybe she was having more than one."

Try as she might, Cass just couldn't imagine Joan in the role of Jezebel—even the new, nasty Joan she'd met in the shop.

"Let's say, for argument's sake, she had one lover," Bee said. "Jealousy makes sense when Conrad got knocked off— her lover killed him—but how does Joan's death figure in?" He stopped talking as Elaina crossed the room with their food.

Why would Joan's lover kill her? It didn't really make sense. Unless they were the ones arguing in her room. Maybe he killed her over whatever they were arguing about someone taking. Cass was definitely going to have to chat with Emmett again.

Elaina slid their orders in front of them.

Cass eyed Bee's plate—a thick hamburger piled high with cheese, bacon, lettuce, tomato, and two big, fat onion rings. He doused the entire thing in ketchup. How on earth did he manage to stay in shape? She returned her gaze to her plate and sighed.

Elaina returned with extra napkins and bent close.

"Rumor has it the Madisons and Wellingtons had a meeting at the Bay Side Hotel early this morning."

Bee's eyes widened. "Do you know what it was about?"

"No idea. No one seems to know, but they were in there a long time." Elaina turned when someone called her and hurried off.

"Wonder what they could possibly be meeting about?" Cass broke off a piece of toast.

"No idea." Bee waggled his eyebrows. "But I'll definitely try to find out."

Cass laughed. She turned to Stephanie and caught a glimpse of the Talbot boys quietly shoveling pancakes into their mouths. "I can't believe those boys are sitting so quietly."

Bee winked at her. "Works every time."

S tephanie pulled up in front of Emmett's Garage. "I'll meet you at the shop in a little while."

"Thanks, Stephanie. If I'm not there yet, can you open? I want to talk to Emmett for a few minutes, and I have to pick up Beast."

"No problem."

"Thank you." Cass climbed out of the car, wincing at the ache in her back.

Stephanie leaned over the passenger seat and glanced up at her through the still open door. "Are you all right?"

"Yeah. Just a little sore this morning." She pushed the door shut and waved as Stephanie pulled away then turned and entered the waiting room.

Emmett looked up from whatever paperwork he was

doing behind the counter. When he spotted her, he dropped his pen on the desk and rounded the counter. Lifting his red baseball cap from his head, he smoothed a hand over his long mane of greying hair. "Man, am I glad you're okay. Gave me a good scare this morning." He fitted his cap back into place and chuckled.

"Sorry." Cass grinned.

"I have your car in the garage if you want to get anything out of it."

"Thank you. I left Beast's leash in there, and I have to pick him up."

He turned and pushed through the door to the garage, then held it open.

Cass followed. Her car sat in the center of the first bay. The little silver Jetta had definitely seen better days. Cass reached to open the passenger door.

"You have to go around. That one doesn't open."

She walked around the front of the car. "Are you going to be able to fix this?"

Emmett surveyed the damage. "I just got it in here a little while ago and haven't had a chance to take a look yet." He smiled. "You weren't the only one to go off the road last night. I had to tow in three other cars. Luckily, no one was hurt."

She nodded. From the damage she could see, she was very lucky. The passenger side was pretty smashed up and the front window was shattered, but still in place. The driver's side fender was crumpled. The roof was sort of crushed in the middle. Must have happened when she hit the tree. A chill raced up her spine.

Blocking out the vision of the accident, Cass opened the

door then closed it again. "You know what? I don't really need the leash." The vet's office had a small selection of supplies for sale. She'd just buy a new leash when she stopped to pick up Beast. She turned her back to the car. "Stephanie said you had something I could drive for now."

"Yeah, out back." He started walking toward the back door of the shop. "I keep a few loaners, just in case of something like this." He opened the door and held it for her, then gestured toward the back corner of a small parking lot. "You can use either one while we figure out what's going on with yours."

"Thanks, Emmett. You're a lifesaver."

His cheeks flushed red.

Tucking her hands in her coat pockets, she crossed the lot with Emmett at her side. She inhaled deeply, the salty scent of the sea filling her lungs, soothing her even as the wind whipped sand across the open lot. She lifted a hand to block what felt like shards of glass from hitting her face. "There's something I want to ask you."

He pulled his cap down against the wind. "Oh?"

It was too cold to find a tactful way to lead into the conversation. "When Joan was arguing the other night, was she arguing with Conrad?"

Emmett hesitated, which surprised Cass. She expected him to just say yes.

"I'm not sure. No reason to think it wasn't, but I couldn't say for sure."

Hmm . . . They reached the two SUVs. An old, black Suburban—way too big—or a pretty light green Forester. "Can I have this one?"

"You bet." He pulled two keys from his pocket, selected

one, and put the other back. "Here." He handed her the key on a small ring.

"Thank you, Emmett." He was obviously not going to expand on his answer, and she couldn't think of a way to ask about the ghost he'd seen without saying Tank told her.

"I'll see you tonight." He tipped the brim of his hat and walked off.

That's right. She'd forgotten about the group reading tonight. She had less than an hour before she had to open the shop. She climbed into the Forester and started the engine, then took a minute to familiarize herself with where everything was. She turned on the radio and pulled out of the lot heading toward the Madison Estate. She'd swing around quickly and see if anything was going on, then stop and pick up Beast and head to the shop. Perfect.

Thankfully, between the sun shining and the salt and sand that had been spread on the roads, they were now covered in slush rather than ice. She snapped off the radio and slowed as she rounded the curve by the mansion. Police cars, a crime scene van, Tank's SUV, and a news van from a local TV station. She braked gently, mindful of the road conditions, and slowed to a crawl.

Tank was standing by the front gate talking to two uniformed police officers. She stopped and rolled down her window, waving to get his attention.

When the two officers nodded, he looked around and approached her. "What are you doing here?"

"I just left Emmett's and had to swing by Doc Martin's to pick up Beast. I figured I'd take a ride past and see if anything's going on." She swallowed hard and looked past him. "I guess there is."

Tank rubbed a hand over his head. "Yeah. It was Joan." He folded his arms against the roof and leaned in the open window, keeping his voice low. "I want you to stay out of this, okay, Cass? I mean it. We don't know what's going on, and I don't want you involved."

"Did you talk to Jim Wellington?"

"Yeah. Seems you're part of his alibi for the evening."

Tank didn't look happy about that, but Cass let it drop.

Guilt prickled her conscience. "Do you know what time she died?" Catching her lower lip between her teeth, she prayed it was before Jim had pulled her out of the car.

Apparently sensing her unease, Tank's expression softened. "It was late in the afternoon, long before you got here."

Cass nodded, relief coursing through her. She'd never have forgiven herself if she'd left Joan there still alive. She glanced up at the cupola. She couldn't see anything but could imagine the crime scene techs collecting evidence and removing . . . better not to go there.

"Stephanie said she'll be at the shop with you all day. Can you tell her I'll give her a call in a little while?"

"Sure."

"Thanks. I'll see you later." Tank patted the roof then started up the walkway

"Tank?"

He turned and walked back to her. "What's up?"

"When I was up in the cupola, I noticed a small compartment in the floor. Do you know if they found anything in it?" She held her breath, waiting to see if he'd answer.

With a quick glance over his shoulder, he leaned closer. "Nah. Nothing. It was empty."

"One more thing?"

"One more. That's it."

She grinned. "Did the police trash Conrad's room?"

His eyebrows drew together when he frowned. "No. Why?"

"Well, you said something about Conrad being a neat freak. The condition his room was in . . . well . . ." She trailed off, remembering she hadn't told Tank she was in his room the first time when things on the dresser had been overturned, but without the level of destruction that was present the second time. "It seemed weird his room would be such a mess."

Tank held her gaze a moment longer than necessary, suspicion creeping into his eyes. "We don't know what happened yet." He pointed a finger at her. "I meant what I said, Cass. Stay out of it. I don't want you getting hurt."

She shot him her best innocent look. "Sure."

He held her gaze a moment longer then started away again.

"Wait."

He stopped and turned.

She grinned. "One more thing."

Propping his hands on his hips, he pursed his lips and waited.

She lowered her voice to a whisper. "Did you bag the soap?"

Laughter popped out. "Yes, Detective Donovan." He threw her a two-finger salute. "We bagged the soap. Now get out of here."

15

Cass pushed through the door of Mystical Musings with Beast in tow, content with being only five minutes late. Stephanie was already busy with a customer.

Cass took Beast to the back of the room and slid his basket of toys closer. "You don't chew on anything but these. Understand?"

He tipped his head and yelped.

"Good." She knelt beside him and petted his head, grateful to have him back. "I missed you, boy." With one last hug, she got up, grabbed her laptop from behind the counter, and took it to the back table. She pulled out the list Doc Martin gave her this morning, since the first one he'd given her had disappeared in the accident, and started researching how to train Beast.

The tinkle of the wind chimes above the door made her pause and glance up as Stephanie's customer left.

"How'd it go with Emmett?" Stephanie asked.

Cass shrugged, her attention still on the dog-training site. "Okay with the car, but he doesn't know if it was Conrad Joan was fighting with."

"We kind of figured that."

"Yeah. I guess."

"What are you doing?"

Cass moved onto the next site on the list. "I'm looking for ways to train Beast. Doc gave me a list." She scrolled down. "This one looks promising." She pointed to a small diagram in a box on the side bar. "That's how Doc did it, and Beast sat right down. How hard could it be?" She closed the computer and got up to get a treat. Beast jumped up as soon as she opened the canister, back end wagging furiously. "Okay." She held the treat up and started to move it toward him and over his head. "Sit."

Beast jumped up and snatched the treat from her hand.

"Ugh . . ." She dropped back into her chair, defeated.

Stephanie burst out laughing.

Cass shot her a glare. "By the way, Tank said to tell you he'd call you later."

"When did you talk to Tank?"

"I swung by the mansion on my way to the vet's."

Stephanie offered a sympathetic look. "He was still there?"

"Yup. With the crime scene crew."

"I'm sorry. I was hoping you were wrong."

"Yeah, me too."

"Did he have anything else to say?"

"Not really."

The wind chimes sounded, ending their conversation. Cass stood. "Good morning, can I help you?"

The young man pushed the door closed behind him. "I hope so. A friend of mine suggested I come in here." He looked around as Cass crossed to the counter. He ran his hand over the driftwood countertop. "This is really nice."

Cass smiled. "Thank you."

"Anyway. I graduated from college in June, and I've been filling out applications and dropping my resume off everywhere." His eyes lit up an instant before the smile started. He'd obviously gotten some kind of good news; though she couldn't guess what.

"Congratulations."

His eyes widened. "How'd you know?"

She tapped her head. "I'm gifted that way."

"Wow." Admiration filled his voice. "Yeah, so, I got a call yesterday from the advertising firm I really, really want to work for, and they asked me to come in for an interview. I've researched them meticulously, know exactly what they look for in a new employee and I'm sure I can do well, but I'm a nervous wreck." He laughed self-consciously, his cheeks flaming red. "I have my portfolio ready, and I've practiced what I want to say in front of a mirror, but . . . the truth is . . ." He huffed out a breath. "I'm terrible at interviews. It's scheduled for early in the morning, and I'm not really a morning person, so I tend to have a hard time focusing." A sheepish grin surfaced. "I also tend to babble a little when I'm nervous, in case you haven't noticed."

Cass laughed. This kid was adorable. She rested her forearms on the counter, clasped her hands, and continued to study the young boy as he spoke. Though she could tell he was nervous—little giggles, fidgety hands, rocking back and forth, a slight stammer now and then—he still carried himself confidently. He held his back straight and his head high and kept his gaze on her. He obviously knew his stuff. He just needed the confidence to sell it.

"So, I was wondering if there was anything you could give me that would keep me from making a total fool of myself?"

"I'm sure you'll do great, but I can definitely put a few things together that might help." She pulled out a tray of stones and laid it on the counter, then took out a small bag. Help with job interviews was a common request, so she kept a tray beneath the counter filled with the appropriate crystals; though she customized the bags for each individual client.

She held a transparent yellow stone up to the light. "This is citrine. It will help boost your self-confidence." She dropped the stone into the bag, then searched the tray for green aventurine, a good luck stone that promoted well-being. She selected one and held it up for him to see. "This one will help you to feel calm. It's also a great crystal for prosperity."

"Do these things really work?" He lifted a skeptical brow.

"My clients seem to think so." That was true enough. "Some people swear by them."

"Right now, I'm willing to try anything." He shot her a crooked grin. "And if they work, and I get the job, I'll swear by them too."

She couldn't help but smile at his enthusiasm. Next, she chose a ruby and rolled it around in her hand for a minute, but then put it back. A ruby could over-stimulate, and that was the last thing this kid needed. She lifted a sunstone instead. Yes, a much better choice. "Sunstone is a good luck stone. It helps alleviate stress and dispel fear." She returned the tray and tied the bag closed. "Make sure you keep this with you during the interview. I'm sure you'll do well."

He tucked the bag into his pocket and Cass rang up the purchase. She really hoped he got the job. It was always nice when someone came back in to let her know if the crystals had helped. Some people, like this kid, stuck in her mind and she had no way to follow up with them. "Good luck. Let me know how you make out."

"You bet. Trust me, if this works . . ." He patted the pocket where he'd put the stones. "I will definitely be back."

On his way out, he held the door open for an older woman Cass didn't recognize. Interest in Mystical Musings was definitely on the rise if the past two days were any indication.

"Hi. How are you?"

"Cold." The woman unwound her scarf. "This . . ." she gestured out the front window at the mess of slush, "is the reason I moved to Florida."

"How about a nice hot cup of tea?" Cass crossed to the pot at the counter. "What brings you up north in this weather?"

"Tea sounds lovely." She took her coat off and hung it on the rack. She wore a navy blue suit that screamed power. "Actually, I came to see you."

"Me?" Cass set out two cups, her interest piqued.

"Well, not exactly. I came up for a meeting, but after the meeting, I decided I had to come see you." The woman

LENA GREGORY

folded her hands in front of her and stood perfectly still, her face blank. No small movements, no change of expression, not one little tell to give Cass any indication of her mood.

"Now I'm intrigued. What for?" She started pouring water over the tea bags.

"I spoke to Priscilla Wellington this morning, and she said you were able to conjure Buford's ghost during a séance."

Cass looked up, one hand on the teacup, and the cup overflowed with hot water. "Ouch!" She jerked her hand away, knocking the cup over.

"Oh dear. Are you all right?"

Stephanie jumped up from the table and turned on the faucet. "Run your hand under the cold water."

Cass did as she was told. Her hand was fine, but she needed a few minutes to collect her thoughts. This was getting way out of hand now. Although, she had to admit, the boost in business sure was nice. But she was going to have to put a stop to these rumors. "I'm sorry. What did you say your name is?"

"I didn't." The woman leaned over to examine Cass's hand. "It looks okay."

Cass turned off the water and pressed a paper towel to her hand. "It's fine. I think I got more startled than anything. Only a little bit of water splashed onto my hand."

"In that case . . ." The woman extended a hand to Cass. "I'm Abigail Madison. I believe you've probably heard of my husband, Horatio."

Sucking in a sharp breath, Cass struggled to school her features. No sense letting her shock show. "Yes. Of course, Mrs. Madison." Cass took her hand. "What can I do for you?"

She sighed. "I saw Buford's ghost the night Horatio passed

· 206 ·

on. We both did. Everyone thought I was crazy—Horatio was crazy. The incident has tarnished his good name as well as his reputation. I'm hoping you can put a stop to that."

"Me? How can I help?"

"By contacting Buford again, of course."

Stunned, Cass made no move to make more tea. "What do you mean?"

"I want you to hold another séance and contact Buford. I want you to find out what he wants. Then I want you to help him get it so we can lay him to rest. Then, maybe, my Horatio can finally be at peace."

Cass opened her mouth, but when nothing came out, she snapped it shut again. The tinkling of the chimes announced another customer, saving her from having to give an immediate answer.

"What are you going to do?" Stephanie patted Beast's head and sat at the table with a bottle of water.

Cass shrugged and joined her. It was the first lull they'd had all day. Even with Stephanie taking care of sales while Cass did readings, there had been people milling around the store since they opened. She toyed with the business card Abigail had left with her, turning it over and over.

The front door opened, and Bee strode through, leaving a trail of snow in his wake. Concern filled his eyes when his gaze met Cass's.

"Is something wrong?" Cass stood as he stalked toward her.

He raked his fingers through his hair. "I'm not sure, but possibly."

"What happened?" Stephanie rounded the table to stand beside Cass, facing Bee.

"I was in the deli—"

Stephanie narrowed her gaze. "And you didn't bring coffee?"

Bee waved her off. "I left without buying anything. I ran out of there after I heard the latest gossip." He looked back and forth between Stephanie and Cass, before finally letting his gaze land on Cass. "Rumor has it, you might know who killed Conrad."

"What!" Cass and Stephanie shouted in unison. "How . . . what—"

Bee held up a hand. "Isabella was there. She's been helping out at the hotel with feeding all of the unexpected guests. She worked something out with Henry to provide some meals. It helped him out, and all of the stuff she had prepared didn't go to waste." He pressed a hand to his forehead. "I can't even think straight."

"Here." Cass pulled out a chair. "Sit for a minute."

"No. I'm fine. I can't sit yet. Cass. You have to listen. People are saying Joan planned to come ask you who killed Conrad. Then she came in for a private reading. No one knows what you told her, but next thing you know, she turned up dead."

"So everyone knows she's dead?"

"Yes, but that doesn't matter." Bee grabbed her by both arms, intensity darkening his deep brown eyes. "Don't you get it?"

Startled, Cass simply shook her head.

"If Joan was killed it was because the killer thought she knew who he was. And the killer thinks you told her. Who do you think he'll come after next?"

Laughter erupted before she could stop it.

Bee released her arms. "Well, I'm glad you think it's funny. I was a wreck all the way over here."

"I'm sorry, Bee. I wasn't laughing at you. I just can't believe all these people think I can just . . ." What was the phrase Donald had used? "Ring up the dead and ask them things. This is getting ridiculous." She returned to the table and flopped into the chair. "Sit. You may as well get comfortable while we tell you the rest."

"There's more?" Bee perched on the edge of a chair, forearms resting on the table.

Stephanie pulled her chair out and sat. "No wonder the store's been packed all morning."

They brought Bee up to date on Abigail's visit.

He frowned. "Are you going to do it?"

"I don't know yet. All of a sudden everyone is asking me to contact the dead. It's a little unnerving."

Stephanie lifted a brow. "Uh . . . Cass . . . that's what you do for a living. Remember?"

Cass tossed Abigail's card, which was still in her hand, onto the table and laughed. "I guess, but before now I wasn't all that popular." She shook her head. "I guess I'm going to have to repeat the séance, but what if nothing happens?"

Stephanie shrugged. "You could always give the Ouija Board a try."

Bee lurched to his feet.

When Cass shot her a dirty look, Stephanie laughed. She knew full well Cass wouldn't touch a Ouija Board again. "Sit down, Bee. I'm not using the Ouija Board."

Stephanie lifted her hands in a gesture of surrender. "I'm

just kidding. If nothing happens, nothing happens. Maybe people will think Bee scared him off the last time."

Bee glared at her and returned to his seat.

"You think?" A small flicker of hope flared.

"Probably not. But what else can you do? If you have the group reading and the séance, no one could possibly ask for their money back, even if nothing happens."

"Except for the Dobbs'." Cass lowered her head into her hands.

Bee bristled. "You just tell those crackpots no."

That sounded good in theory, but the last thing she needed was those two saying she ripped them off. "And what if something does happen?"

"What do you mean?"

The true source of Cass's apprehension bubbled to the surface. She'd never really talked about how she did what she did with anyone. At least not seriously. The words didn't come easy. "I don't know." She shrugged uncomfortably. "I've never really thought about how I do readings or séances. I just notice things and say them. Somehow, it always seems to work out. I'm not sure how I feel about really trying to bring the dead back."

"Are you scared?" Stephanie asked.

"Maybe a little."

"Hmm . . ." Stephanie propped her elbows on the table and rested her chin on her clasped hands. "Of what exactly?"

Cass took a deep breath then blew it out slowly. "When I left my practice, I wanted to do something that would make people feel good. But I didn't want any responsibility for anyone else." She massaged her temples. "This feels an awful lot like responsibility, like people are counting on me to figure out what's going on." She shook her head, unable to find words to express her fear of failing and having someone get hurt. "People are dying. And I don't want to feel responsible for that."

Stephanie tilted her head and studied Cass. "I think things got a little out of hand this time. In the past, people have sought you out for entertainment, or to feel comforted by the presence of loved ones who've passed on. This is different."

Cass nodded, relieved Stephanie could understand her fears.

Bee had remained unusually quiet through the conversation, and Cass spared him a quick glance. A deep frown marred his features.

When he looked up, he sat back. "And now there's a killer out there who thinks you can possibly point a finger at him."

When the chimes sounded, they all jumped.

16

When Cass returned to the table after taking care of her customer, Bee was thoroughly engrossed in something on the laptop screen, with Stephanie staring over his shoulder.

"What are you looking at?"

"Well," Bee glanced at Stephanie, who nodded, "we have an idea." Bee rubbed his hands together, obviously eager to share. "You're going to do the séance."

"I am?"

"Yup. We'll announce it tonight at the group reading. We'll try to have it at the mansion again, but if the police won't let us in, we'll do it here or at the hotel. It doesn't really matter, although it will seem more authentic if you do it at the mansion."

"Seem?"

"Yup." Bee gripped her hand in his. "Look, Cass. You're

not charging anyone for the séance. Everyone who paid was present at the first séance. Plus, you did all of the individual readings, and you'll do the group reading tonight. So, technically, this next one is a freebie."

She opened her mouth to respond, but he held up a hand to stop her.

"Hear me out before you say anything. Part of what you do is entertainment, but there's another part that's different. The part where people believe in this driv . . . uh . . . well, you know what I mean. Anyway, we don't want you to deceive anyone but, let's be honest, this whole situation is out of control." He paused to glance at Stephanie. "So we want you to have the séance, but we want to script it." He winced.

"What do you mean, 'script it'?" She leaned over to see what he was looking at on the computer. Some kind of chart was up, but she couldn't make out what it was.

Apparently relieved she hadn't blown up at the idea, Bee settled more comfortably. "The way I see it, there are a few things we need to let everyone know." He held up a hand, ticking each point off on his fingers. "One, we need to make it very clear you have no idea who the killer is. That keeps you safe, and it also keeps anyone else you've talked to safe. We don't want the killer targeting everyone you were alone with who has some involvement in this case. Let's face it, anyone at that séance could have been involved, and you were alone with a lot of them today, doing individual readings."

Cass nodded. "True." *Crap.* She hadn't thought of that. Had she placed everyone in danger by continuing with the readings? Maybe she should heed Tank's advice and just stay out of the whole thing.

"Okay, that brings me to point number two. At the last séance, you said Buford wanted to reveal a secret someone had. The killer obviously has a secret." He shrugged and leaned back. "So all we have to do is come up with a believable secret that's unrelated to the murders."

"Is that all?" It didn't really sound all that hard, and it just might work.

"Not exactly."

She frowned. She knew it sounded too easy.

"Three . . ." He lowered another finger. "We have to figure out who actually killed Conrad and Joan, and why."

She frowned. They couldn't possibly think that was a good idea. "Why do we have to do that?"

"Just in case our plan backfires. I mean, this is going to look totally believable. Some people are going to believe you talked to Buford Wellington. It's not that far a jump to think, eventually, the killer might try to silence you. Just in case you could contact someone else, like maybe Conrad, who presumably knows who killed him. Think of it as insurance."

Cass struggled to digest it all. Overall, it wasn't a bad plan. *If* they could pull it off. "There's just one thing."

Bee's laughter echoed through the shop. "Just one?"

Actually two. The first being Tank told her to keep out of this. But that one didn't really count. He didn't specifically say to not have a séance. Right?

"Probably more, but just one I can think of right now."

"Fair enough. What is it?"

"What happens if Buford actually shows up?"

Bee pressed a splayed hand to his chest. "Bite your tongue if you want my help, sweetheart."

Cass laughed and shook her head. "All right." *I must be out of my mind.* "Where do we start?"

"I guess we start with, how do you do what you do? I have to give you props, what you do sure does look real. But we need to figure out how you do it if we're going to re-create it and have it look authentic to people who regularly attend your events."

She'd never put a lot of thought into the how of it before. "I don't really know. Stuff just kind of comes to me and I say it. How can I make something up when I don't know what will come to me in the moment?"

"Can you think about it ahead of time?" Stephanie asked. "What if we could get you into the mansion by yourself beforehand and you could see what comes?" She leaned forward on the table.

Hmmm . . . that just might work. "I would feel better doing it that way." Cass pulled her chair closer to the table, warming to the idea. "You know what would help a lot? If the two of you could help me out at the group reading."

"Help you do what?" Stephanie asked.

"I need you to notice everything you can about everyone. Who they talk to, who looks nervous, who seems skeptical . . . The more information I have on each person, the easier things come to me."

Bee clapped his hands together. "Sure. We can do that."

Excitement sparked. This might just be crazy enough to work. "Okay, so we'll meet up at my house around lunchtime tomorrow and compare notes."

"Sounds good. Now, for the hard part." Rubbing his hands together, Bee leaned over the computer.

"What's that?"

"Figuring out who had reason to kill Conrad."

Stephanie reached for the stack of paper.

"Uh . . . uh . . ." Bee swatted her hand away.

"Hey, what was that for?"

He glared pointedly at Cass. "This time, *I'm* in charge of the suspect list." He pulled the computer closer. "Now. There's no way the three of us can watch everyone, so we're going to have to narrow it down some. Something's been bothering me all along. If the motivation for Conrad's murder was money, why stage a suicide? That would stop the life insurance from paying out. Why not stage an accident? Seems it would have been even easier to knock the old boy on the head and give him a shove down the stairs than it would be to haul him up into the rafters. No?"

Hmm . . . Cass hadn't thought of that.

"Maybe they don't need the life insurance. Maybe he's worth enough without it," Stephanie offered.

Bee started typing. "While I try to figure out Conrad's net worth, what other reasons could there be for murder?"

Stephanie tapped a pencil against the table, the rhythmic *click, click, click* making it hard for Cass to concentrate.

She propped her elbows on the table, pressed the heels of her hands to her eyes, and worked to block everything out. Why would someone kill? Greed for sure, but Bee was already checking that angle. What else did they know? "Jealousy. Maybe Joan was having an affair and her lover killed Conrad." She remembered the dark hair on the soap in Conrad's shower. "Conrad had light hair, yet the soap was covered in dark hair."

Bee shrugged. "Could be his hair was colored and his body hair was still dark. His brother has dark hair."

"I didn't think of that."

"Or maybe Conrad was having an affair with a woman with short dark hair, and Joan found out and killed Conrad out of jealousy?"

Tension gathered at the base of Cass's neck. She reached to rub it. "But then who killed Joan?"

"Maybe Conrad's lover?" Stephanie was shaking her head before she even finished the statement. "I find it hard to believe there were two killers."

"Me too," Cass agreed. "But there almost had to be two people working together, didn't there? One person couldn't have gotten him up onto the rafter."

Bee pursed his lips. "That doesn't necessarily mean there are two killers, though. It's possible one person killed him and another helped stage the suicide." Bee tapped his pen against his lip. "But I still go back to, why hang him in the cupola?"

"Hey. Wait." Stephanie sat up straighter. "What was that you said at the séance, Cass? About Buford hanging himself in the cupola? Where did you get that from?"

"I don't remember. I thought maybe Bee found it in one of the books he brought."

Bee frowned. "I don't remember seeing it before the séance. The first I remember hearing Buford hung himself was from Carly Dobbs."

Had that been the first time Cass had heard the story? No use. She couldn't remember.

Bee's low whistle pulled Cass's attention from thoughts she really didn't want to contemplate anyway.

"Well, well, well. Lookie what we have here." He leaned back to allow Cass and Stephanie a better view as he turned the computer toward them and pointed to the screen.

Stephanie gasped. "Is that billions?"

Cass's mouth fell open.

"Yup. Someone certainly stands to gain a fortune."

"Yeah, but who?"

"Presumably, Joan. But we have to figure out who her heir is."

"Okay." Cass pressed a thumb and forefinger to the bridge of her nose. "I'm getting a headache, and I have to be able to concentrate tonight." She stood and stretched her back. A quick glance at the clock above the counter told her it was time to get going. "I'm starved and I have to drop Beast off at home before the reading."

"You're going to leave him at the house?" Stephanie's gaze shot to Beast.

"Alone?" Bee's eyebrows shot up into his hairline.

"What else can I do?"

Beast scrambled to his feet as if he knew they were talking about him.

"I don't understand why he behaves so well here." She thought of the three beds he'd already chewed through this week. "Mostly."

Bee ruffled the big dog's mane. "Probably because he sits right here with you most of the day. You give him treats, pet him, and pay attention to him. So do your regular customers. It's leaving him alone that seems to be the biggest problem."

"Yeah." Cass sighed. She might have to think about getting that crate Doc Martin suggested when she picked him up. "Come on, boy. Let's get you home and fed so I'm not late for the reading."

"This looks fabulous." Bee squeezed her arm.

The scent of his aftershave drifted over Cass, bringing a sense of comfort and calm. She could do this, with the help of her friends, despite the nerves churning in her gut. "It does, doesn't it? They did a great job."

Stephanie smiled. "It helps that Elaina has been to enough readings to understand the ambiance you like to create."

Elaina Stevens—Henry's niece, who worked part-time as a maid at the hotel, in addition to her waitressing job at the diner—had seen to the decorations. She and some friends had done a wonderful job setting things up. Round tables covered with dark blue tablecloths filled the room. Soft lighting enhanced the casual atmosphere, as did white candles in mason jars filled with seashells, set in the center of each table. The soft jazz playing from overhead speakers created a relaxed, soothing mood.

"Maybe I'll ask her to come in and do the same thing in the shop when we do the regular monthly readings there." Cass relaxed. She tilted her head from side to side, loosening the knotted muscles in her neck.

"Come on." Bee took her arm and led her to a table toward the front of the ballroom. "Let's get your microphone on and tested before the guests start to arrive."

"I'll catch up in a little bit. I want to start filling the cases." Stephanie would remain in the lobby, where Cass had set up a few small display cases, until the reading began, in case anyone wanted to buy crystals or souvenirs. She'd also watch who was coming and going and take notes on their behaviors.

"Thank you."

Stephanie smiled. "Good luck."

When they reached the large round table with the number one on a card in the center, Cass chose the seat that afforded her the best view of the room and hung her bag over the back of the chair. "Who else is sitting with us?"

"I'm not sure. I only looked for our names on the way in." Bee extracted the microphone from the case and tested it. He didn't seem to be in a chatty mood. "Here. Slip this on." He handed her the small box attached to a belt.

Cass pulled off her sweater. Clad in only her leggings and camisole, she wound the belt around her waist, fixing the pack at the small of her back, and secured the Velcro to hold it in place.

Bee plugged a wire into the top of the battery pack, then wove it up beneath the back of her shirt and handed her the small microphone. "Make sure it's comfortable."

Though she'd used the microphone before to speak at Bee's fashion shows, this was the first time she'd used one for a reading. "You'll make sure it's not too loud, right?" When she did readings at Mystical Musings, she didn't need the microphone.

"Don't worry about a thing, dear. It'll be perfect."

While Bee fiddled with another box on the table, Cass pulled the microphone wire up over her ear and pressed it to her cheek a couple of inches from her mouth.

"Hold it right there, hon." Preoccupied with his preparations, Bee didn't look up.

Anxious to get started, Cass began to fidget, rolling her right ankle over, then her left, rocking back and forth. If she wasn't staring through the open doorway when Priscilla Wellington entered, she might have missed the furtive glance over her shoulder as she folded a piece of yellow paper in half and shoved it into her pants pocket.

"I'm almost done." Bee tore off a small piece of clear tape and secured the microphone. He stepped back then ran his fingers through her hair, fluffing it to cover much of the wire and tape. "There. Perfect."

Priscilla glanced up and met Cass's gaze. Plastering a smile on her face, she started across the room.

"Thanks, Bee." She left him to gather his things from the table and stuff them into his briefcase, while she started forward to intercept Priscilla. If she could get her alone for a minute, she could ask about having the séance Friday.

"Priscilla. There you are." Jim Wellington strode through the far door and headed straight to his sister. "I've been looking all over for you." The statement sounded an awful lot like a reprimand as he gripped her arms and kissed her cheek.

Priscilla's gaze locked onto Jim's. "I . . . um . . . had a f-f-few things to d-d-do."

Cass stopped short. And, with any luck at all, maybe she'd find out why the powerhouse of a woman was acting so weird. Priscilla Wellington stuttering? Something was definitely up.

Jim stared at her another moment, some sort of silent communication passing between them, then squeezed her arms and released her.

Cass offered what she hoped was a warm smile and

extended her hand. "It's good to see both of you. I'm so sorry to hear about Joan."

Priscilla gripped her hand but glanced at Jim before she spoke. "Thank you."

Jim took Cass's hand in both of his. "It's good to see you again. I wasn't sure we'd be able to make tonight's reading, but with Conrad and Joan unable to leave the island yet, we felt it only right to stay with them." He released her and stepped back. "I'm only sorry Priscilla won't be able to enjoy it more. She does so love anything to do with ghosts."

A visible shiver ran through Priscilla, and she dropped her gaze to her entwined hands.

Cass jumped at the opening. "Speaking of ghosts, I was wondering if you'd allow me to complete the séance for the guests who've already bought tickets."

The siblings silently conferred before Jim shrugged and Priscilla turned to Cass. "Sure. I don't see why not."

"Would Friday work?"

Priscilla's eyes widened and her hand fluttered to her chest.

Uh-oh. Too forward?

Jim's eyes narrowed, his gaze firmly locked on his sister. "At the bed-and-breakfast?"

"As long as the police will allow us in, I'd like to pick up where I left off."

"Fair enough."

Cass quickly scanned the room in search of Bee, but he was nowhere to be found. She needed a distraction to take Jim's attention so she could get Priscilla alone and see if everything was all right.

Priscilla lifted a shaky hand and tucked her hair behind her ear.

"If you'd like, I can give you a private reading as well, Priscilla. Either tonight or Friday." Cass held her breath, hoping she'd accept the offer.

"That'd be very nice. Thank you. Perhaps Friday." She offered an apologetic look. "I have a bit of a headache tonight."

Dang. "Friday it is then."

"If you'll excuse me, I must attend to a few things before we start." Priscilla turned and left without acknowledging her brother, who stared after her.

Once she had hurried through the ballroom doors, Jim turned a charming smile on Cass. "I apologize for my sister. This has all been quite hard on her. She and Joan were rather close."

That's not what I heard. Cass bit the inside of her cheek to keep from blurting out the rumors she'd heard about all of them fighting like cats and dogs. "Of course, I understand."

"I'll also apologize in advance in case we can't make it Friday. It will depend on if the medical examiner releases Conrad and Joan. Once they're released, we'll have arrangements to attend to."

Okay. How tacky would it be to ask how they died? She searched for a discreet way to inquire. "Have they figured out what happened yet?" *Duh. They were killed, obviously. Ugh* . . . Discreet was not one of her strong suits.

Jim didn't seem to notice. His gaze ran over her, searching her eyes, capturing her gaze.

A tingle fluttered in her stomach.

"I know the timing is a bit off, with everything going on, but I don't want to lose the opportunity. If I'm still here Friday, maybe you'd like to go to dinner with me afterward?" He took her hand, running his thumb over her palm.

Oh boy. Should she accept? An image of Luke popped unbidden into her mind. His dark, shaggy hair and those deep blue eyes. Though she hadn't seen him in a while, she kind of wanted to see where it was going.

Where what's going?

She ignored the voice of reason. Of course, she might be able to get some information from Jim if she could get him alone.

She was saved from answering when Bee pushed open the doors and entered with Stephanie and Priscilla.

Cass jumped back, pulling her hand from the warmth of Jim's.

Propping the door open, Bee gestured to someone in the lobby.

Donald nodded to Bee on his way through the doors, Sylvia clinging to his arm. *Figures they'd be the first to show up.*

Ignoring them, Cass returned to her table. She lifted her bag from the chair and slung it over her shoulder, more for something to do than any great need. She'd find the ladies' room and fix her hair and makeup. With any luck, the ballroom would be full by the time she returned and she could avoid her exes altogether.

17

Cass pulled a couple of tissues from the dispenser on the counter. While the Bay Side Hotel didn't boast the most luxurious bathrooms in town, they certainly had one of the cleanest. She ran the water and wet the tissue a little then used it to wipe the eyeliner that was smudged beneath her eyes.

She separated her blond curls, leaving some in front of her shoulder to cover part of the microphone wire. Then she smoothed lipstick over her lips. She surveyed the finished product in the mirror. Still clad in her leggings and camisole, Cass shivered. She'd left her sweater back at the table. Oh well. She rubbed her hands up and down her arms, trying to chase away the goose bumps. No easy task when most of the chill came from within.

Cass turned away from the mirror and headed for the door. *Time to get this show on the road.* She pushed through the doorway and almost ran right over Donald, who was waiting in the hallway on the other side.

He lifted both hands as if to catch her, but she jumped back before he could make contact.

"Look, Cass." Donald scratched his head, a sure sign he was nervous.

Good.

He cleared his throat. "I'd like to talk to you, if you have a minute."

She lifted a brow, shooting for her best *you have got to be kidding me* look. "Where's your sidekick?" Yikes, had she really said that out loud? She clenched her fists to keep from slapping a hand over her big, fat mouth and stalked past him toward the open ballroom door.

"Please, Cass." He kept pace at her side. "You have to listen to me."

"Fine." No way was she going to be alone with Donald. "If you want to talk to me, you can talk to me in the ballroom. I have to get ready."

He grabbed her arm.

Startled, she froze.

He whispered urgently, "I have to talk to you alone, Cass."

She shot a glare at his hand on her arm then lifted her gaze back to his.

Apparently, he got the hint, because he dropped her arm and stepped back, holding his hands up in an *I surrender* gesture. "Please."

She'd always had a hard time saying no to Donald, and if he'd have used his charming routine, she'd have left him standing there for sure. As it was, the usually smooth Donald was looking a bit disheveled. His hair stuck up in spots, as if he'd run his hand through it a hundred times—which he only did when he was nervous—a gesture he repeated as he stood there, hammering her suspicions home. "Look, Donald, I have things to do. I will give you two minutes while we walk."

"Come on, Cass," he whined.

"Take it." She started down the hallway toward the ballroom. "It's that or nothing."

He growled but hurried after her. When he reached her side, he pitched his voice low. "You have to do something."

"Do something about what?"

He glanced around the empty hallway. "I think the police suspect I had something to do with Conrad's death."

She slowed, stunned by his admission and unsure of what to say. She'd suspected as much herself, but hearing it said out loud sent chills racing up her spine. "So what do you want me to do?"

"Listen. Please."

"Talk fast, Donald." She stopped walking and looked around, his paranoia contagious. "What is it you want from me?"

He blew out a breath. "An alibi."

"What?!"

He slapped a hand over her mouth, his other hand gripping the back of her head, and leaned close, whispering urgently in her ear. "After the séance, Sylvia and I had a fight. She stormed off, and I went to my room alone. I was still alone when the screaming started. I ran out and Sylvia was already in the hallway." He lowered his hand but didn't step back. Sweat poured down the sides of his face. The urgency dropped off, his next words filled with defeat. "Then, when Joan was murdered, I was alone again."

Cass's head spun. Donald had no alibi for the time in question? She'd assumed he and Sylvia were together. Of course, she'd also assumed there were two killers. Or one killer and one person who helped clean up afterward. She couldn't make sense of any of it.

Donald's hot breath washed over her. Claustrophobia threatened. He was too close, crowding her. She needed room to think. Splaying a hand on his chest, she shoved him back.

"So what did you tell the police when they questioned you?"

He raked a hand through his messy hair again. "I said I was alone." His eyes lit up. "But I could change it. If you tell them I was with you, I can just say I was trying to respect your privacy."

"Respect?" Anger surged like a slap in the face, wiping out some of the shock. "Since when do you have any respect for me? Leave me alone, Donald. I have things to do." Holding her breath, afraid he might grab her, she pushed past him and hurried into the ballroom.

Cass stopped in the doorway, trying to collect her thoughts, and surveyed the room. Although a few more guests had arrived, the room was still fairly empty. Most of the guests must still be hanging around the lobby. With any luck, they were buying something.

The Dobbs' had arrived and were seated at a table in the center of the room, heads bent together in some kind of deep discussion.

Two women she didn't recognize stood beside a table.

One of them held up a small pouch and emptied stones into her palm. *Yes.* At least someone had bought something.

Her gaze fell on Jim, who stood with his back to her, facing Sylvia.

Sylvia smiled, fluttering her lashes and lowering her gaze. When she next spoke, she peered up from beneath her lashes—the same flirtatious gaze she used to aim at Donald.

Was she on the hunt, or was there something going on between her and Jim Wellington? That could explain some of the jewelry and furs Donald probably couldn't afford. There was no way Sylvia could have paid for the full-length fur coat she now wore on her receptionist's salary.

Sylvia laughed and laid her fingers on Jim's arm in that touchy-feely way she'd always had with men.

Cass thought back to the night they'd found Conrad. Sylvia had been glued to Donald's arm, wearing a barely there negligee. Had she been with someone else? Jim? Conrad? Maybe Donald had killed Conrad because he found out Sylvia was having an affair with the billionaire. But why kill Joan? Did she figure out he was the killer?

Cass pressed the heels of her hands to her temples. *Time to shake things up a bit.*

Cass put her sweater back on before she took her seat. She lifted her glass with a shaky hand, splashing water onto the blue tablecloth, then put it down without drinking. She had to collect herself if she was going to pull off this reading.

Guests began to filter in, some stopping to chat, others going straight to their tables. Dinner would be served after the reading, but may of the guests carried drinks from the bar in the lobby.

Bee pulled out his chair and sat. "Are you all right? You

seem a little pale." He took her bag from the back of the chair and riffled through it.

"I have a problem."

"Oh?" Opening her makeup bag, he removed the blush. "Come here." He lifted her chin and examined her face. "What's the problem?" After brushing a little blush on each cheek, he sat back to study his work. "There. So, what's the problem?" He stuffed everything back in her bag and hung it on the back of the chair.

Unable to wrap her mind around Donald's request, Cass turned her mind to the reading. Readings were lighter than séances, and more fun. The mood was dramatically different from the more somber atmosphere she created for a séance. But her nerves were strung taut. How was she going to pull this off?

"Are you going to share what the problem is, or do I have to sit here worrying all night?"

"I'm sorry. My mind was elsewhere."

"I'll say." He peered at her expectantly over the rim of his glass as he took a big gulp of water.

Sighing, she relented. "Donald asked me to give him an alibi for the time when Conrad was murdered."

Bee choked and dropped his glass.

Jumping up to avoid the spill, Cass moved behind Bee. She patted his back a few times until he held his hand up to stop her.

Heaving in a deep, shaky breath, Bee tried to talk. It came out as more of a wheeze.

"Are you all right?"

He glared at her.

"Oh fine, maybe my timing could have been a little better."

"You." *Wheeze.* "Think?"

Laughter bubbled out. Cass couldn't help it. This entire situation was ridiculous. "I'm sorry, Bee. Are you really all right?"

"Yeah." He nodded. "Tell me."

Looking around to be sure no one was paying attention to them, she launched into a quiet tirade. "Can you believe that guy? Sylvia wasn't with him when Conrad was killed, and he wants me to say I was." She shook her head. "Unbelievable."

Bee frowned an instant before one eyebrow shot up beneath his bleached blond bangs. "Then who was enjoying the lingerie she was sporting in the hallway, while freezing her bahungas off, I might add?"

Bahungas? "How do you know she was freezing?"

"Oh, puh-leeeease, honey, that garment left nothing to the imagination."

Leave it to Bee to go right for the gossip angle. Never mind where Donald was or what he was doing. Who Sylvia was doing topped his list of interests. Actually, Cass couldn't help but wonder the same thing, and her mind jumped right to Conrad Wellington.

Had she been in the cupola with Conrad? It would make sense, since Conrad was found without a shirt. Maybe Donald went up and found them together and killed Conrad. Logically, that situation worked. Then Sylvia could have helped him try to cover up the murder with a lame attempt to disguise it as a suicide. The perfect scenario. Motive. Opportunity. So why didn't it sit right in her gut?

Cass grabbed a couple of white linen napkins from the table and helped Bee mop up the water he'd spilled.

"You did tell him no, right?" Bee glared across the room at Donald, who now sat beside Sylvia at a small table in the farthest corner of the room.

She'd have to remember to thank Stephanie for the seating arrangement.

Cass caught her lower lip between her teeth, knowing she was about to earn Bee's wrath. "Not exactly."

"Well, now you can just march yourself right over there and *exactly* tell him no." He shooed her toward Donald's table.

"It's not like I said yes. I didn't answer him."

Bee rolled his eyes.

"First, I'd like to thank all of you for coming." Stephanie's voice filled the room, saving Cass from any further discussion about Donald.

Bee righted his glass and pulled his chair back in as he sat, then rested his clasped hands on the table.

Cass laid a hand on his. "Don't worry, Bee. I'm not stupid."

"I know, dear." He patted her hand. "But you don't always have the most common sense."

"Hey!" Cass bristled.

"Cass Donovan." Stephanie gestured toward her.

Applause erupted as Cass stood and took Stephanie's place at the center of the room. Heat flared in her cheeks. She didn't love being the center of attention, and this was the largest crowd she'd ever performed for. Come to think of it, there seemed to be a lot more people here than there had been at the mansion. Had they sold more tickets? She'd have to remember to ask Stephanie.

Cass scanned the faces of the guests. Was one of them a killer? Most likely, yes. But how could she figure out who? "Thank you all for coming." The applause died out as everyone settled more comfortably for the show.

Readings were a lot less formal than séances, so Cass kept the lighting at a comfortable level for her to interact. She liked to roam the crowded room, searching for someone to read. The perfect target would have their emotions well displayed for Cass to interpret. "I'd like to start with a moment of silence for Conrad and Joan Wellington." She dipped her chin but continued to scan the room. Chairs scraped as everyone stood, and most everyone bowed their heads.

Sylvia cocked a hip, looking impatient.

Donald continued to stare at Cass, the plea for help clear in his expression.

Wiping a tear from her cheek, Priscilla lowered her gaze.

Jim held his clasped hands in front of him but chanced a quick glance at his sister.

Mitch and Carly Dobbs stood with their heads bent together, whispering. At least Carly kept her voice down this time.

Emmett and Sara stood side by side, fingers entwined. A jolt of joy flared in Cass. They were good for each other.

Cass's gaze caught on a stranger. A tall man with dark hair and a muscular build. He wore a black suit, and his tie was loosened. Not only did he hold his head upright, he glared toward Priscilla with undisguised contempt.

"Thank you." She lifted her head as everyone took their seats.

Grace Collins waved from across the room, and Rudy winked. Cass's heart warmed at the sight of the elderly couple. They'd never attended a group reading before, and she couldn't help but wonder if they'd come to lend support.

She relaxed. She was in her element now, the place she was most comfortable. These people had gathered to see her, to support her. Most of them, anyway. Her gaze skipped back to the intense stranger. Should she start with him? He pulsed with negative energy. Could he be a killer? Possibly. Better to leave him alone and not draw his attention.

"Many of you have attended readings before, and I thank you for coming back." Making eye contact with as many return clients as possible, Cass hoped to convey her gratitude and make them feel welcome. "I also see a lot of new faces. Welcome."

She started to move through the room, ignoring anyone who made her feel uncomfortable. It was imperative her full concentration be focused on what she was doing. Bee and Stephanie would worry about everything else.

She approached Sara Ryan. Sara was a regular customer. She blushed as she glanced at Emmett. Emmett's cheeks flamed bright red. Sensing they would be uncomfortable having attention drawn to them, Cass smiled and moved past them.

An older woman sat with three younger women. She clasped and unclasped her fingers. One of the women reached over and squeezed her hands, offering a reassuring smile. *Hmmm* . . . something. Not exactly nervous, but stressed. "You have something on your mind."

The older woman fidgeted but nodded.

Most people who attended readings were seeking to communicate with a loved one who had passed on. "There's someone here, someone you want to reach."

The woman nodded again and lowered her gaze to her left hand. She twisted the plain gold band around her finger.

"Your husband."

She sucked in a breath as her gaze shot to Cass. "Yes."

Tears shimmered in the woman's eyes. The look on her face was one of fondness, the look of someone who'd long since come to terms with her loved one's passing. It wasn't the raw grief of a woman recently widowed.

"He's been gone a long time now." Indecision prickled Cass's nerves when the woman didn't answer immediately. *Ah jeez, I hope that's right.* Should she backpedal? She waited. Confident.

The woman smiled and finally spoke. "Fifteen years, now. Eddie's been gone since the girls were teenagers." Her gaze softened as she looked at the women seated around her, women who all had to be in their thirties by now. Their love for their mother was very obvious in the way they looked at her, the silent encouragement they offered.

"He's very proud of them." Cass moved closer, making the contact more intimate, less of a group event.

"Yes. I knew he would be. They've taken good care of me over the years."

Fifteen years. What would she want to ask her husband who'd been gone for so long? Certainly not where something was. That was a common request. People died, leaving behind loved ones who needed something only the deceased knew where to find.

The women all looked healthy. All of them kept their gazes firmly on their mother. Obviously, it was the older woman who needed some sort of guidance. Cass focused her attention on her. An attractive woman, probably in her late fifties or early sixties. A tear trickled down her cheek. The loyalty she felt toward her departed husband was evident in the pained expression on her face. Loyalty? Odd word choice, but it definitely fit the woman's expression.

What would trouble her so? What could make her feel disloyal? Cass softened her voice. "Eddie is concerned."

The woman's breath hitched, and she stared at Cass, a plea in her eyes.

"He's afraid you're having trouble moving on."

A soft sob escaped, and the woman nodded. One of her daughters gripped her hand, and another offered her a drink of water. The woman sipped slowly then placed the glass on the table, a newfound confidence straightening her back. "I am. I love my husband. I always will."

Though she didn't say it, Cass sensed the *but*. "It can be lonely being the one who's left behind."

"Yes." Relief relaxed the woman's shoulders, loosening the tension.

Cass approached and knelt on one knee in front of her. She took the woman's hands in hers. "He understands that. He loves you, and he'll be waiting for you when it's time for you to move on." Cass searched for the right words, the words that would offer the comfort this woman needed to move forward with her life. "You have a lot of love inside you. There's nothing wrong with loving someone else while you're here. It doesn't take away from the love you feel for your husband. He knows that. He wants you to be happy, to have someone here to love who will love you back."

The woman cried softly. "Thank you."

Cass patted her hands then stood and moved on, leaving her to the privacy she needed. One of the daughters' hushed words followed Cass through the room. "See. I told you he'd be okay with you getting married again."

18

Cass worked her way through the room, sometimes stopping to chat, other times just saying hello before moving on. Smiles met her at every turn. The reading was progressing wonderfully.

A scatterbrained old man needed help finding the watch he'd misplaced. He swore his deceased wife had put it somewhere. As it turned out, he'd always made the same accusation when she was alive, too. Cass gently reminded him of that fact while she led him to remember where he'd put it.

She helped a young woman contact her mother to apologize for the argument they had the night she died. Unable to forgive herself, and certain her mother would never forgive her, the woman had been tormented by the argument for three years. She'd lost weight, couldn't sleep, and suffered from severe depression. Hopefully, Cass had helped her start on the road to recovery, but she'd also discreetly passed on a colleague's business card and suggested the woman seek counseling to help her work through her depression.

Tears had flowed down more than one face during that exchange. Even Bee had pulled out a tissue and blotted his eyes. She loved bringing people peace, or even some small measure of comfort, without having to shoulder too much responsibility. She'd helped more than one person seek forgiveness over the years. It was a need she understood well. Too well. The patient she'd failed weighed heavily on her still. She shook off the image, needing to concentrate on the here and now.

All in all, she had to consider the evening a great success, but it was about time to wrap things up. It was getting late, and Isabella would be ready to serve dinner soon. Cass had wanted to do the reading before dinner so she'd be available for a while afterward. It was common for people to seek her out to discuss a private reading or ask questions they were too shy to ask publically.

Of course, one extra minute to stir things up a bit wouldn't hurt. You never could tell what information you'd accidently unearth with a well-placed shove.

Weaving casually between the tables, Cass angled herself toward her target.

Sylvia sat slumped in her chair and tapped a quiet staccato against the table with her long, hot pink, rhinestone-studded nails. Her eyes opened wide and she straightened when Cass stopped at the table beside her.

"I sense you've lost something."

Donald rolled his eyes, but Cass ignored him.

Sylvia snorted, but she glanced at the rock on her left

finger an instant before shooting Donald a suspicious glare. Apparently, she'd already made him replace the missing ring. Or perhaps Donald had been in a hurry to claim the woman Cass suspected was straying. Was that why she'd removed her engagement ring? Maybe she hadn't forgotten the ring when they changed rooms. Maybe she'd deliberately removed it for her midnight rendezvous. Had she been in the room with Conrad?

Wait.

The realization struck hard, and Cass froze. Sylvia hadn't left the ring in Conrad's room. Cass knew that with absolute certainty. Not only because the awareness sucker punched her in the gut, but because Beast had never been in Conrad's room. Where could he have picked it up? She stood still, waiting to see if more would come. Someone—Stephanie? Bee?—had said maybe Beast picked it up in the hallway. Could be. Somehow, it didn't feel right. But where else had he been?

Sylvia squirmed then glanced at Donald but cast her gaze quickly away. Was she afraid Cass would tell him where she'd dropped the ring?

No matter how hard she tried, Cass couldn't come up with where the ring had been. Beast could have picked it up anywhere. Maybe it *had* been in the hallway. "Hmm . . . Sorry, it seems I've lost the connection."

Sylvia visibly relaxed.

An image popped into Cass's mind. "All I can tell you for sure is, the ring is exactly where it belongs." She smiled and moved back toward the front of the room.

Stephanie was shaking her head but smiling, and Bee had his head lowered, laughter rocking his shoulders.

When she reached the front of the room, she suppressed a grin and turned. "Thank you all for coming. I hope you enjoyed yourselves." Applause thundered through the room, bringing a rush of joy. "If you have any questions, feel free to ask now, or come to me during dinner."

Carly Dobbs nudged her husband with an elbow.

Mitch lurched to his feet, and his hand shot into the air. "I have a question."

Was there a tactful way to ignore him? Not that she could think of. *Crap.* "What would you like to know?"

"Can you do anything to break the curse?" He finally dropped his hand to his side.

"Curse? What curse?"

"You know. The curse on the old Madison Estate." He pointed a finger at her, his stance combative. "My wife told you all about it the other night. That curse brings misfortune and death to everyone who owns that house."

Death? She couldn't remember if the Dobbs' had specifically mentioned the curse brought death. Was he embellishing?

Bee stood and started around the perimeter of the room toward Mitch. *Uh-oh.*

"I'm sorry, I'd have to look into it more, but I doubt it." She smiled and leaned her hip against the table, hoping to ease some of the tension.

He clenched his fist but kept it in the air. "Well, then, can you tell us who's going to be next?"

"Next?"

"Yeah. Can you look into your crystal ball, or whatever it is you do, and figure out who the curse is going to take next?"

"Uh . . ." Bee still hadn't reached him, but she wanted to avoid the scene that would incur if Bee tried to throw him out and Mitch fought back.

"Because someone else *is* going to die."

The certainty with which he spoke sparked a small niggle of fear. How could he be so sure? Could he have concocted the whole curse thing as a way to get the Wellingtons to turn over the mansion? He had to be out of his mind.

She noted his dark hair. Was he Joan's secret lover? He seemed like enough of a lowlife to threaten a woman. She aimed a quick glance at Emmett, perched on the edge of his seat as if ready to pounce. Did he recognize Mitch's voice from the argument with Joan the night Conrad died?

Mitch tilted his head, and some of the anger left his voice. "Funny, don't you think, that everyone associated with that place meets a tragic end?"

Priscilla gasped, and Mitch turned on her. "Of course, you don't have to die. You could re-think your decision and hand the estate over to me . . . uh . . . us, now. Before anyone else loses their life."

Jim shot to his feet, tumbling the chair behind him. "Is that a threat?"

Ah jeez . . .

Mitch took a step back from the table and turned to Jim. "Why don't we call it more of an observation?"

Jim started toward him.

Mitch held up his hands in surrender. "What? I'm just saying I'm willing to take the problem off your hands."

Thankfully, Bee reached Mitch before Jim did. He put a hand on his shoulder and whispered something in his ear.

Mitch paled, then clamped his teeth closed and dropped into the chair.

Carly wore a self-satisfied grin, her eyes shining with greed.

Bee rested a hand on his cocked hip and turned to meet Jim's attack. He lifted the other hand in a stop gesture, and Jim skidded to a halt. The two conversed in a hushed whisper, Bee gesturing wildly.

In the end, whatever Bee said worked, because Jim shot a glare at Mitch but returned to his seat. He righted his chair but didn't sit. Instead, he stood behind Priscilla with his hands resting on her shoulders. He leaned close to her ear. A moment later she nodded and patted one of his hands.

A flood of relief poured through Cass. The last thing she needed was a brawl in the middle of the ballroom. She shot Bee a grateful glance.

He waved his fingers and continued to stand beside the Dobbs' table. Hopefully, he'd be able to fend off any more problems through dinner.

With another thank-you, Cass took her seat at the table beside Stephanie.

"That was weird, huh?" Stephanie's gaze continued to jump back and forth between Mitch and Jim. "You think the Dobbs' had something to do with the murders?"

Cass shrugged. "I don't know what to think."

Jim pulled Priscilla's chair back and helped her stand. Then he guided her from the room with a hand on her elbow.

"Hmm . . . What do you make of that?" Cass asked Stephanie.

"I honestly don't know what to make of any of it."

Stephanie waved her off. "Don't think about it anymore tonight. Enjoy your dinner, and we'll get together tomorrow and see what we can figure out." She patted a small spiral notebook at the side of her plate. "Bee and I have been trying to keep an eye on everyone all night. We're going to meet for lunch tomorrow and go over everything. I hope it's okay, I've asked Tank to join us."

Cass glanced at Bee before turning her gaze back to Stephanie and lifting a brow. Tank and Bee didn't always hit it off; though, Tank had been trying a little harder lately to be tolerant.

"Don't worry. I asked Bee before I invited Tank, and he was okay with it."

"Oh, good. I'd like to see the two of them get along."

"Yeah. I know what you mean. It's not easy. Tank doesn't really know what to make of Bee, and Bee's distrust of the police doesn't help matters. He's on edge whenever Tank's around."

"I'm sure they'll work it out."

"I hope so. Anyway, Bee said he'll pick you up around one tomorrow then meet us at the diner."

"Sounds good." But her mind was already a million miles away.

"Let's go, Beast. In the crate." Cass stood beside the brand-new, shiny cage she'd bought from the vet's office that morning. Sue had assured her she was doing the right thing, but she didn't have to like it. "Now."

Beast tipped his head to the side, his eyes filled with confusion.

"Don't look at me like that. You wouldn't have to go in the crate if you hadn't eaten the leg off the table while I was at the reading last night." Well, maybe not all the way off the table, but the table definitely tilted to the side he'd chewed on all night. "Now, let's go. I don't have time for this."

She glanced at the clock on the stove. Bee would be there in five minutes.

"Come on, boy. Please?" Okay. She hadn't had time to check out many of the websites Doc Martin had given her yet, but she was pretty sure whining wasn't the way to go. Maybe he just didn't know what he was supposed to do. She'd put a brand-new bed and a blanket and toys in there, but maybe he still didn't realize he was supposed to go in. Or maybe he was afraid of it. *Hmm* . . .

She dropped to her knees in front of the crate and leaned in. "See, boy. You go inside. It's your bed."

Beast woofed once and ran out of the room.

Frustrated, Cass blew her hair up off her forehead and followed.

"Ugh . . . No, boy, not that bed."

Beast sat in the center of her bed, wagging happily.

"Come here." She took his collar and led him back to the kitchen. He followed willingly, until they reached the cage. Then he stopped short, planted his bottom on the floor, and held his ground. He wasn't going anywhere near that cage.

"Okay." She scratched her head. Maybe she had time to look it up on the computer quickly. She bolted toward the bedroom for her laptop.

The sound of tires crunching on the gravel driveway stopped her short. *Crap.* She ran back to the kitchen.

"Look, Beast. This is not that hard. You just go in." She

tried to shoo him, but the big dog wasn't budging. His stubbornness showed her why it was all the more important she get him trained. She raked her hands into her hair and squeezed. "All right . . ." She turned around and dropped onto all fours in front of the cage. "Like this, boy. Look. It's fun. There are toys and a blanket."

He continued to stare at her.

"Please, boy. I have to go."

He tilted his head, and his tongue dropped out the side of his mouth.

Sighing, she backed into the cage. "See." She backed onto the dog bed. "It's comfy."

The back door opened, and Beast swung around to greet Bee—who stopped short the instant he laid eyes on her. He frowned as he caught Beast's paws when he jumped up. "Down." He dropped Beast back to the floor and petted his head when he sat.

That's it. I give up. I have to buy a new table anyway. Let him eat the rest of it while I'm gone, and I'll look up how to get him in the stupid cage—I mean crate—as soon as I get home.

Bee pressed a hand to his chest and fluttered his false lashes. "Far be it from me to tell you how to train your dog, dear . . ."

Yeah right!

"But I have to say, I don't think you're doing it right." He burst out laughing, clutching his side.

Cass crawled out of the cage, stood and brushed off her jeans. "Ha-ha. Very funny."

"I could be wrong, but I'm pretty sure *he's* supposed to be on the inside of the crate."

"Ya think?"

He wiped a tear from the corner of his eye. "Are you ready?"

"Yeah." She grabbed her bag from the counter and slung it over her shoulder. "Let's go."

When she started for the door, he held out a hand to stop her. "Aren't you going to crate him?"

"Not right now. I think I'll let him get used to it for a while first."

"From the outside?"

She glared at him.

Laughter erupted again. He held up his hands. "I'm sorry . . ." *gasp*, "I . . ."

"Give it up, and let's go." She strode past him and out the door. Squinting against the sun glaring off all of the white snow, she fished her sunglasses out of her bag and put them on. With a quick glance over her shoulder to be sure Bee was coming, she climbed into the pickup truck.

Bee pulled the house door shut and followed her.

They sat in silence for a few minutes, Bee shaking his head and laughing every so often as he backed out of the driveway and headed for the diner.

Fields were covered with a foot of snow, and the branches of the trees dipped with the weight of the snow and ice, and smoke poured from chimneys of the small farmhouses they passed. "So, did you guys figure out who the killer is?"

"No clue." He shot her a grin. "But I can tell you whose car was parked in front of Amanda Cabot's all night while her husband was off visiting his mother." He waggled his eyebrows.

"Jeb Simon's?"

"Yup. I told you last month there was something fishy going on between those two."

"Hmm . . . You did say that."

Bee smirked, his expression smug.

"Anything else interesting?"

"I had a run-in with Mitch Dobbs and Jim Wellington in the men's room before I left the hotel last night."

"What?" She sat up straighter, her interest suddenly piqued. "Why didn't you tell me?"

"I didn't see you afterward. And this morning, well, you were kind of . . . busy." His smile softened the teasing.

Better to just accept she wasn't going to live this one down for a while and ignore him. "What happened?"

"Nothing."

"Nothing?"

"Nope. Jim walked in when Mitch was on his way out. Jim puffed up his chest a bit, and Mitch stared at the floor and scurried out like a rodent. That's it."

"Strange."

"Stranger, still, is Priscilla was nowhere to be found. I dillydallied until Jim left and followed him out. He got in his car and drove off. No Priscilla. That's the first time I've seen him stray that far from her since they got here."

Cass pressed a finger to her lips, thinking back over the times she'd seen Jim. He'd arrived at the Madison Estate alone, but Priscilla had come in very soon after. "Actually, the night I crashed, he was alone. At least, he was when I woke up. I guess it's possible he had Priscilla with him when he found me, then dropped her off somewhere and came back for me after."

"Seems a little far-fetched."

"You're probably right. Let's just hope another body doesn't turn up this time. Where did he go, anyway? Aren't the Wellingtons staying at the Bay Side Hotel with everyone else?"

"I don't know where he went. I tried to follow, but I'd parked out back so I could bring the sound equipment and stuff in. By the time I ran back through the lobby and out the back, he was gone. I drove past the Madison Estate—at night, by myself, you're welcome—and his car wasn't there." He paused for a minute as he hit the turn signal and turned into the diner's parking lot. "At least it wasn't out front. I guess it could have been around back, but no way was I going there to find out."

19

While they waited for the hostess to seat them, Cass scanned the room. It wasn't nearly as crowded as last time they were there; the bulk of the lunch crowd had already returned to work.

Stephanie waved from a large round table in the center of the room, and Cass pointed Bee in her direction. As they crossed the room, Cass couldn't help but wonder where Jim was going when he left the hotel last night. Her mind immediately jumped to Sylvia flirting with him in the ballroom. Had he run off to meet her somewhere? That didn't seem necessary with a hotel full of rooms at their disposal, but still, if they wanted to be discreet . . .

"Hey." Stephanie's greeting pulled her back to reality.

"Hi." She pulled out a chair and sat. Bee sat next to her, and she propped her bag on the empty chair on her other side.

Tank skipped saying hello, his eyes sparkling with humor.

Could Bee have told them about the cage incident already?

"So. I hear you guys are going to solve my case for me."

Cass laughed. "Someone's gotta figure out what's going on around here."

Tank scowled. "I seem to remember telling you to stay out of trouble."

"Hey." She furrowed her brow, pouting. "I haven't gotten in any more trouble."

"Not yet, anyway. Give it time."

Laughing—because he was probably right—she ignored him and opened her menu.

"Hi there. Sorry I'm late." The sexy southern drawl yanked her attention from her lunch options.

"Luke!" She jumped up and threw her arms around his neck. "What are you doing here?"

He hugged her tightly for a moment before answering, the woodsy scent of his aftershave invading her lungs, soothing her. When he released her and stepped back, disappointment surged.

"Tank called and said you guys were playing detective, and I didn't want to miss it." He grinned—that sexy, cocky, crooked grin that had attracted her in the first place. "It's good to see you, Cass." His fingers slid down her cheek then tucked her hair behind her ear.

Heat flared, creeping up her cheeks.

Bee mouthed *oh my,* and fanned himself behind Luke's back.

Tank couldn't drag his gaze from Bee.

"Here, sit." Luke pulled out her chair.

After she sat, she grabbed her bag from Luke's chair and hung it over the back of her chair then shot Bee what she hoped was a *behave yourself* stare. Since he grinned back at her, she had to assume he got the message. Now she just had to hope he'd listen.

"So, what is everyone having?" Bee opened his menu to the breakfast section, since this would be his first meal of the day. "I definitely want something with bacon."

"That sounds good." Luke opened his menu to breakfast as well.

While everyone chose and ordered their meals, Cass concentrated on the song playing in the background. "Chantilly Lace." For some reason, the lyrics brought images of Sylvia in her nightie. "Did anyone else notice Sylvia flirting with Jim Wellington last night?"

"Can you believe her?" Stephanie looked appalled.

"Oh, please." Bee blew it off. "I don't know why you're so surprised. If she'd steal her best friend's husband, a little flirting is nothing."

"I guess you're right." Cass traced an ad on the placemat with her finger. "But Donald said she wasn't with him the night of Conrad's murder, that's why he asked me to be his alibi—"

"What!" Tank and Luke both yelled together. Several customers turned to stare.

"Shh!" Cass chided.

"Sorry." Luke looked around and lowered his voice. "What are you talking about?" Anger darkened the already deep blue of his eyes.

"My ex asked me to tell the police I was with him when Conrad Wellington was killed."

Tank's jaw clenched before he spoke. Never a good sign. "And you didn't feel the need to tell me that?"

"What?" She feigned innocence. "I just told you."

"Cass . . ." Tank's tone held a note of warning.

"Oh, all right. I probably should have told you last night, but I forgot."

He massaged his temples.

Luke took over the interrogation. "What did you tell him?"

"Nothing. I walked away."

"All right. Hold on a minute here." Bee lifted a finger to halt the building anger. "We can possibly make this work to our advantage."

"Oh?" Tank sat back and folded his arms across his chest. "How's that?"

Luke just looked amused.

"Well. Since Cass didn't give him an answer, she could get him to talk about it again, and she could record him with her cell phone." He sat back, crossed one leg over the other, and smoothed the crease in his slacks. "It's brilliant."

Luke leaned forward, pushed his place setting away, and rested his forearms on the table. "What if he catches her?"

Bee paled. "Can't you guys be there?"

"I doubt he'd say anything incriminating with all of us standing around."

"What if she did it at the séance? Maybe the two of you could be there, you know, just in case."

"What séance?" Luke turned to Cass.

"I rescheduled the séance for this Friday. Priscilla called

late last night to say everyone will be there. Some of the guests are going to stay until Friday. Others are going to come back." Cass shrugged. "It seems, if everyone who was there the first time comes back, the killer has to be there. No?"

"So, naturally, you thought it would be a good idea to lock yourself back up in a mansion with a killer." Luke stared at her.

Tank rubbed a hand over his close-cut hair. "Welcome to my world."

"All right." Luke sighed and pulled a notebook from his pocket then patted himself, apparently looking for a pen.

Bee handed him one. "Sorry, dear, but it writes purple."

Luke shook his head and mumbled something that included "unbelievable," then opened the notebook. "I presume you have some suspects."

Stephanie leaned across the table and lowered her voice. "I think it was Joan's lover."

"What lover?"

"We don't know yet, but we figure she has one. Personally, I think he killed Conrad out of jealousy and then killed Joan." She looked thoughtful for a couple of seconds. "I'm just not sure why he killed Joan. Maybe she found out?"

"I think you're wrong," Bee interjected. "I think it was that wacko, Mitch Dobbs, and his loony wife. If greed is a motive for murder, those two have it in abundance." He shrugged. "Plus, they get the added bonus of revenge against a Wellington. They have a giant grudge against Buford, but maybe vengeance on any Wellington is good enough." He held up a finger. "And, the two of them definitely have the physical strength to have pulled it off."

All eyes fell on Cass. Should she voice her opinion? It

didn't feel right to tell the police she thought her exes killed Conrad and Joan. Then again, it wasn't really the police. It was just Tank and Luke.

She was saved from having to answer when the waitress arrived with their food. Luke closed the notebook and set the pen beside it.

The waitress placed Cass's chef's salad in front of her.

"Thank you."

Once everyone had been served, Cass pushed the food around her plate.

"Come on, Cass," Bee said. "We all know who you think did it, but what's his motive?"

That was the part that had her stuck. Unless Donald was Joan's lover. Or Sylvia was Conrad's lover. Then it made perfect sense either way. Why would Donald have been wiping down Conrad's room if he hadn't killed him? Maybe trying to get rid of any sign he'd been there with Joan? Was he the man Emmett had heard arguing with her the night of the murder?

Obviously sensing her discomfort, Bee changed the subject. Sort of. "Can you believe that tacky negligee Sylvia had on?"

Stephanie eyed Cass another few seconds before turning to Bee. "Yeah, but it's not a crime to wear tacky lingerie."

He huffed out a breath. "Maybe not, but it certainly should be." He forked a bit of hash and eggs into his mouth and chewed thoughtfully. "You know. It really wouldn't have been all that bad. A little less marabou, a few strategically placed scraps of material . . . could have made it enticing . . . alluring even." He lowered his fork. "Instead she just ended up looking trashy. Who knows? Maybe it's just her, not the garment." He thought for a minute then shook his head. "Nah."

"Have you ever considered doing a lingerie line?" Stephanie asked, looking genuinely intrigued.

"Nah." Bee waved her off. "Hmm . . . well . . . on the other hand . . . Maybe an offshoot, like a honeymoon line, to compliment my bridal line." Excitement lit his eyes.

Stephanie grabbed the notebook they'd been using to keep track of suspects and the pen and handed them to Bee. "Get together a list of what you'll need, and I'll work up the numbers for you later this afternoon." Stephanie was a genius with numbers and handled all of Bee's bookkeeping, and Cass's, too. She actually handled the books for a lot of Bay Island's businesses. Though she had a small office in her house, she often visited the shops she worked for, getting to know her clients and their needs. "If it would be profitable, I think you'd be great at it."

Tank stared at Bee then shifted his gaze to his wife. "Are we done here?" He started to laugh at their blank expressions. "I realize it's not quite as important as lingerie, but maybe we could discuss . . . oh, I don't know . . . murder?"

"Are you two going to attend the séance, then?" Bee tilted his head, waiting, while Tank and Luke stared at each other, some sort of silent communication passing between them. "It would be perfectly normal for Tank to attend with Stephanie. He is her husband, after all, not only a police officer."

Luke shrugged. "And I guess I could go as Cass's date, right?"

Bee pressed a hand to his chest and fluttered his lashes. "Unless you'd rather go with me, sweetie."

"You know . . ." Tank tossed his napkin on the table and leaned back. "That might not be a bad idea."

"No," Luke said.

"Less suspicious."

"Not happening."

"Aww, come on, Luke. Haven't you ever worked under-cover before?" Humor lit Tank's eyes.

L uke took the key from Cass's shaky hand, unlocked her front door and pushed it open, but made no move to enter. "Are you sure you're okay?"

Cass nodded. "Just a little tired."

Running his fingers gently over the bruise on her eye, he examined the small bandage she'd used to cover the cut on her head. "When Tank called and said you'd had an accident . . ." He pulled her into his arms.

Shivering, she curled into his protective embrace. His warmth enveloped her, bringing a sense of safety she hadn't had since the botched séance. Silence intruded on her mo-ment of peace. *Wait a minute.* She lifted her head and looked into the open front door. Where was Beast? He should have rocketed for the front door the minute it opened.

Luke released her and stood back. "What's wrong?"

"Beast should have come to the door." She started through the house, but Luke gripped her arm. He pressed a finger to his lips and motioned for her to let him search first.

This was ridiculous. She was going to have to put a stop to this. No way could she spend the rest of her life tiptoeing around, wondering if someone was going to try to kill her. She followed Luke through the living room, but paused when he stopped at the swinging door that led to the kitchen. She'd had Emmett install it for her so Beast could roam freely through the house. That might have been a mistake.

Luke eased the door open about an inch, then it hit something hard and stopped.

What the . . . ?

He peeked into the crack between the door and the jamb. Laughter rocked him.

Beast yelped once.

Ah jeez. What'd he do now?

Wedging his shoulder against the door, Luke pushed it open.

Apparently forgetting he was probably going to be in trouble for something, Beast jumped, landing his paws on Luke's chest.

"Hey, big guy." He looked past Beast's head and into the kitchen. "I think you're going to be in trouble." He ruffled the fur of Beast's mane then dropped him onto the floor and moved into the room.

Cass hesitated. How bad could it be, really? She braced herself and strode through the doorway Luke held open, then took a moment to survey the damage. All in all, not so bad. Tearing his new bed apart had apparently kept him busy most of the time. She perked up. At least he'd gone into the cage to get the bed. That was progress. Right? Sighing, she patted the big dog on the head and grabbed a garbage bag from beneath the sink.

Luke started picking up the larger pieces of the bed.

"Go run for a little while." She opened the back door to the fenced yard. "And stay out of trouble," she yelled after him. But he had already launched himself off the deck and was rolling in the deepest snow bank he could find. How she ever inherited this problem she'd never . . . *Wait. Inherited.* "Shoot."

"What's wrong?"

Cass shook her head. "I forgot to ask Tank something." She shut the door against the chill and held the bag open for Luke to drop the pieces of bed into. "Actually, it probably doesn't matter anymore, anyway."

He frowned but bent to clean up more of the mess. "Is everything all right?"

"Yeah." She waved it off. "I was talking to Bee and Stephanie, and we were trying to figure out why Conrad's death would have been staged as a suicide since that would stop the life insurance from paying out. But then Joan was killed, too, so I guess she wouldn't be able to inherit anyway." She shrugged. "So it doesn't matter."

Luke paused and stood. He studied her for a moment, then ran a hand over his face. "Look." Leaning back against the counter, he folded his arms across his chest and crossed his ankles. "You can't repeat this, okay?"

Ignoring the mess on the floor, Cass held her breath and nodded.

"Joan wasn't Conrad's beneficiary."

Cass gasped. "What?"

He shook his head. "When I talked to Tank earlier, he said Conrad's will was changed about the same time they bought the estate."

"So who inherited everything?"

He studied her for a moment, and she was afraid he wasn't going to answer. "You can't share this with anyone."

"I won't." *Except maybe Bee and Stephanie.*

He tilted his head and lifted a brow. "Cass."

Shoot. "Oh fine. I won't tell anyone." She held up a hand in oath. "I promise. Not even Bee and Stephanie."

"Conrad left everything to Priscilla."

"No way."

He nodded. "Tank said she didn't seem surprised at the news but didn't have too much to say about why the will was changed. James Wellington, however was a different story. He told them Conrad approached him a few months ago and said he was going to have his will changed. Said he finally figured out what a gold-digging witch Joan was." Luke frowned. "He also said something seemed weird about the whole thing. Especially when he asked James to keep it a secret, because he wasn't telling Joan. Apparently Jim had always thought it strange Conrad had up and married Joan in the first place. One minute she was his receptionist, the next his wife."

"And?"

"And nothing." He pushed away from the counter and started cleaning again. "That's all Tank said."

"Well, what does he think? Do you think Joan had something to do with Conrad's death?"

Luke held up his hands and started to laugh. "I didn't gossip with him, Cass. He shared that bit of evidence, among other things, when we were discussing the case."

Funny, she didn't see much difference between sharing details and gossiping. She checked to make sure all of the legs were still attached then dropped onto one of the kitchen chairs to sulk. "Do you think Joan would have been able to contest the will?"

"Who knows? Maybe, but it doesn't matter now."

"True."

"Do you think that's why James is so protective of his sister?" An image of Jim hovering close to Priscilla flashed through her mind, followed almost immediately by a vision of the stranger who'd been staring at her during the reading. "Do you think they're afraid she's next on the killer's hit list?" Mitch Dobbs' warning resonated through her head.

"No idea. If it was someone I cared about, I'd definitely have concerns for her safety." Luke pulled out a chair and sat close enough to reach across the table and grip both of her hands in his. "As it is, I have enough on my mind worrying about you." He ran a thumb over her wrist, sending a tingle all the way up her arm and into her chest. "Is there any way I can convince you to cancel the séance and stay out of this?"

She kept her gaze on their intertwined hands and shook her head. "I have to do this, Luke. I've worked too hard to establish Mystical Musings to allow this whole mess to ruin my reputation."

"Look at me, Cass."

She lifted her gaze to his, but his dark blue eyes were unreadable.

"I care about you. I may not get here to see you as often as I'd like, but you're important to me. If nothing else, I'd like the chance to see where this will lead." He lifted her hand to his lips and brushed feather-light kisses across her fingertips.

Her belly flip-flopped. His grin sent a wave of heat crashing through her.

"Thanks for letting me sleep on your couch."

She was relieved he'd let the séance issue drop, but probably more relieved he'd changed the subject about his feelings for her. She liked Luke. A lot. But she wasn't ready for any level of intimacy. Maybe it was a good thing he couldn't get away too often. At least they were forced to take things slow. She smiled. "Can't have you sleeping out in the cold. And the Bay Side Hotel is full with the guests from the bed-and-breakfast." She shrugged. "It's either the couch . . ." She gestured toward Beast's cage. "Or the crate. It's not like Beast's using it."

Luke captured her gaze with his, the intensity fluttering her stomach. "The couch is fine. Unless, of course, you'd like to share your room."

Her mouth fell open. "Uh . . . uh . . ."

Luke laughed. "I'm just playing with you, sweetie." He stood and kissed her head, then bent to finish cleaning up.

After a moment of admiring the view, Cass had to wonder if she was making a mistake.

20

Cass strolled through the empty mansion with Bee and Stephanie trailing a little behind. Their soft murmurs drifted to her but didn't interfere with her concentration. At least not too much. Beast padded softly at her side.

With no clue what to expect, Cass wandered aimlessly. The séance wouldn't start until later that night, but they still hadn't scripted the entire thing yet. Luke and Tank had balked about the idea at first but, with a little convincing, they'd grudgingly relented. They had even offered a few suggestions and agreed to wait outside and ensure she was left alone while she did the walk through. But Cass would have to figure most of what she would say on her own. After examining all of the downstairs rooms, except the ballroom, she climbed the stairs to the second floor. She'd go back to the ballroom later.

Bee cleared his throat. She tried to ignore the sound and the knowledge that they were both anxiously following her, pads and pens at the ready, waiting for her to have some sort of revelation so they could get started.

Goose bumps prickled her skin, and she shivered, but there was no obvious source of the cold invading her bones. She stopped at the bottom of the cupola stairs and glanced up. The police had agreed to allow the séance, and would have several plainclothes officers in attendance, but the cupola was strictly off limits. She chewed on a thumbnail, indecision grating on her already raw nerves.

She tilted her head back and forth, then rolled her shoulders, desperate to relieve some of the tension plaguing her. Turning away from the cupola, she stopped and stared at the closed door in front of her. Conrad's door. There was something in there. Of that she was certain. She'd been drawn to that room since the night of the murder. So had Conrad. And Donald. And whomever Joan had been arguing with. This was the source of Cass's current unease, not the cupola. Sucking in a breath, she turned the knob and eased the door open.

She hesitated. Her gut twisted into knots. Wiping beads of sweat from her forehead, despite the intensity of the chill, she glanced back at her friends. Neither of them said anything. Bee stood still. Waiting. Stephanie caught her lower lip between her teeth and shifted nervously. But neither of them discouraged her. She turned, lifted the crime scene tape, and ducked underneath.

Bee and Stephanie followed, closing the door quietly behind them. Bee gripped Beast's collar, and the big dog stopped and sat beside him. Even Beast seemed to feel the tension.

"There's something here. There has to be. It's the only thing that makes sense. Why else would Conrad have been so insistent on having this room?" The room had been cleaned up since she was last there. None of the Wellingtons' personal items remained. The box spring and mattress had been returned to their spot on the frame.

Bee crossed the room and looked out the window. "The view really is nice from here. You can see all the way across the bay to the lighthouse." He turned his back to the view, resting his hands against the sill, leaning back and crossing one leg over the other.

Cass shook her head. "It doesn't feel right." The same image she'd first seen when Joan came in for her reading assailed Cass, relentlessly playing over and over in her mind. "Help me." She started to lift the mattress.

"Wait. What are you doing?" Stephanie put a hand on her arm to stop her. "You can't move anything. You're not even supposed to be in here."

"We'll put it back when we're done. I have to roll up the rug and see if there's a compartment in the wood floor like the one up in the cupola."

Stephanie held her gaze a moment longer then sighed and gripped the other side of the mattress. They stood the mattress and box spring against the wall. The headboard was attached to the wall, so they couldn't budge it. "Okay. I'm going to roll up the rug on this side all the way to the bed. Stephanie, you do the other side. Bee, you see if you can lift the frame enough so we can pull the rug out from under it."

"You know there's no way this is going to work, right?"

Cass shrugged. "I have to try."

Without another word, Bee took his place and waited.

Beast tilted his head and studied them.

Cass searched the floor beneath the section of rug she'd rolled up. Nothing. "Anything on your side, Stephanie?"

"Not that I see."

Cass stood and propped her hands on her hips. She studied the sections of the floor that hadn't been covered by the rug. Again. She'd already searched every inch of the uncovered wood. There simply wasn't anything there. She looked back at the bed.

Bee lifted a brow and stared at her. "You do know, if we get that rug out from beneath that bed, it's not going back. Right?"

She realized that. She just couldn't figure out if it was worth it. Scanning the room, she tried to decide what to do. Her gaze skipped across the wall. It caught on the painting hanging above the bed. She moved closer.

A stormy sea, done in deep blues and blacks, with just a hint of the moon peeking from between the clouds. Gorgeous. She hadn't taken much notice before, but thinking back, she realized very little artwork adorned the walls throughout the mansion. The Wellingtons probably hadn't had time for little details like that yet. So, why this painting, in the room Conrad had to have badly enough to throw Donald and Sylvia out? Had he brought it with him?

Reaching out, she ran her fingers along the rough surface. A small, barely visible lighthouse sat in the deepest shadows on the rocky shore in the distance. She gripped both sides of the frame and tried to lift it. Nothing happened.

A small tingle of excitement sizzled through her. She tried again to lift the painting off the wall. It didn't budge. "Hey, Bee. Give me a hand."

"What's the matter?"

Beast looked up from where he lay chewing on the corner of the bed frame. He probably couldn't do too much damage to metal. Right?

She returned her attention to the painting. "I want to see what's behind this painting, but I can't move it."

"Here. Let me see." He took her place in front of the painting, grabbed the frame from either side, and lifted. Nothing. He looked beneath the frame on either side of the painting then stared at the front and frowned. "It seems like it's glued to the wall or something."

Cass climbed onto the bed frame and peeked down behind the top of the picture, running her fingers along the wall behind the frame. The painting was firmly lodged on the wall. She felt down the side, keeping her fingers pressed firmly against the seam between the wall and the back of the painting. Nothing.

Bracing one foot against the wall, Bee took a firm grip on both sides and yanked with all of his strength.

Just then, Cass's finger encountered something sticking out at the bottom of the frame. She wiggled it.

"Ahhh . . ." The painting swung down from the top, and Bee landed flat on his back, Cass tumbling with him as he went.

Beast jumped to his feet and barked once.

"Shhh . . ." Stephanie grabbed Cass's arm and pulled her up off Bee. "Are you two all right?"

"I'm fine." Brushing herself off, Cass turned to Bee.

He rolled onto his side and used the bed frame to help him climb to his feet. "That's because you had something soft to land on." He glanced at the box spring and mattress against the wall as he rubbed his back. "Probably should have put those back on first, huh?"

Cass laughed, but her interest had already turned to whatever Stephanie was pulling out of the hole in the wall behind the painting. "I guess now we know why he had to have this room."

"No kidding." Stephanie handed Cass a small, black, plastic box.

She looked around, unsure where to put it down.

"Here. Look out." Bee shooed Beast from where he'd returned to chewing on the bed frame, then dropped the box spring and mattress back onto the bed.

Cass pushed the box to the center and sat. A chill raced up her spine, and she shivered as she pulled the top off the box. Bee and Stephanie leaned over the small open box with her. Three heads crowded together, staring into a box the size of a shoebox.

"Don't touch anything," Stephanie reminded her.

As if I don't know that. Cass reached into the box and pulled out a small journal stuffed with papers. *Tank is so gonna kill me.* She held her breath and opened the cover. When no one protested, she set the small stack of papers aside and stared at the lists of numbers handwritten in neat print. She flipped through the pages. Column after column of numbers covered three quarters of the book. "I can make out dates . . ." She squinted and held the book closer to read the small print. "They go back more than ten years. But I have no clue what the rest of the numbers mean."

"Let me see." Stephanie held out her hand.

She handed Stephanie the journal and started sifting through the other pages. She unfolded a piece of computer paper. "Check this out. It's a family tree. Look." She shifted to allow Bee to see what she was reading and pointed to the name, *Celeste Garnier,* at the top of the page beside the name *Buford Wellington.* Skimming the page, she followed the branches down the line until she came to *Carly Garnier Dobbs.*

"Well, well, well . . ." Bee leaned closer over her shoulder. "Lookie what we have here." He pointed to a line on the opposite side of the family tree. A descendent of one of Celeste's granddaughters.

Cass sucked in a breath. "Joan Marris Wellington." Her gaze shot over her shoulder to Bee. "You think Joan was a descendent of Celeste and Buford?"

He shrugged. "According to that paper, she is."

Interest thoroughly piqued now, Cass turned over the page. Blank. "Give me those other papers."

Bee was already unfolding a sheet of yellow lined paper. He turned it over, then back to the front. There were only a few lines on the page, written in bold script. He read, "'Conrad. I know what you're doing, and I want in. Joan.'"

Cass frowned. "What was he doing?"

Bee shook his head. "No idea. It doesn't say."

"I might have an idea." Stephanie held her finger against a spot in the journal. "This is a ledger. From the looks of it, Conrad—assuming this was his—was stealing from their investment company, Wellington, Wellington, and Wellington." She looked into Cass's gaze. "A lot."

Cass sucked in a breath.

"See these numbers?" She ran her finger along a line of numbers in one of the columns. "They're account numbers. And these are dollar amounts. If the numbers are accurate, he syphoned off millions and invested it immediately, making even more money. The guy was worth a whole lot more than we figured."

Bee let out a low whistle. "So, with Joan out of the picture, whoever inherits is mega rich."

Priscilla Wellington. Biting her tongue to keep from saying the words out loud and betraying Luke's trust, Cass opened the last piece of paper. Unlike the others, this was yellowed with age, and she was careful not to damage it as she unfolded it. It was held together with tape in several places, where it appeared to have been torn at some point. She gasped. It was a copy of Buford Wellington's letter leaving the estate to Celeste. Quite possibly the original.

"Okay." Bee sat back as Cass started folding the pages back up and returning them to the box. "So obviously Joan was trying to get the fortune. And probably blackmailed him into marrying her. Do you think the Dobbs' killed them because Joan had the mansion and they wanted it? Maybe they were upset she wasn't the rightful heir, but she found a way to get their mansion anyway?"

Cass thought about that. Did it feel right in her gut? Not really, but not completely far-fetched either.

Beast jumped up and barked.

"Hurry. Get that stuff back in here."

Stephanie grabbed the box and slapped the top on the instant Cass returned everything to its original place. She stuffed it back into the hole, and Cass pushed the picture back into place just as the door to the room slammed open.

"Why did I have a feeling we'd find you three in here?"

After being reprimanded by Luke and Tank, and reluctantly handing over the box of evidence, Cass headed toward the ballroom. Bee had agreed to stay, since he knew the séance wouldn't be real this time. He took Beast to the kitchen, where Isabella would keep an eye on him until Cass was done. Stephanie went to see to the last-minute preparations—and probably beg Tank's forgiveness for tampering with his crime scene.

Cass hesitated before reaching for the knob, her hands slick with sweat. She wiped her hands on her pants. Was Bee right? Had Carly and Mitch killed Conrad and Joan? They certainly had the strength to have pulled it off. And probably the opportunity. Greed was definitely a powerful motive. And yet . . . She was still hesitant to point the finger at them. Or anyone, really.

She shook off the apprehension threatening to suffocate her. It really didn't matter who the killer was. Her goal tonight was to make it clear she had no clue who'd murdered Conrad and Joan. She'd let the police figure out the rest. With her mind set and her purpose clear, Cass pushed open the ballroom doors. And froze. Her heart thundered in her chest.

Sylvia stepped back, Jim's hands still on her hips, and wiped the smeared lipstick from around her mouth.

Cass's mouth fell open, but for once she couldn't think of a single thing to say, so she snapped it shut without saying anything.

Sylvia rolled her eyes. With one last sensual look at Jim, she sauntered past Cass then stopped and turned back. She aimed a glare at Cass and kept her voice low. "You can tell him, you know. But I'll just deny it."

Cass resisted the urge to wipe the self-satisfied smile off her face. Barely.

"And who do you think he's going to believe?" The echo of her laughter lingered as the door fell shut behind her.

Bitch. But really, what did it matter? Could Donald really expect loyalty from a woman who stole her best friend's husband? Aside from the initial shock of finding her in Jim's arms, in the grand scheme of things, Sylvia didn't matter.

She turned to Jim. "Uh, sorry. I just wanted to work out some last-minute preparations."

He turned on the charm as he approached her. "No problem. You weren't interrupting anything important."

She laughed, not because she found humor in the situation, but because he seemed to expect it.

"So . . ." Standing toe to toe with her, he held her gaze. "What did you decide about dinner later?"

He couldn't possibly be serious. "Thanks, anyway, but I'm seeing someone."

"So is Sylvia," he offered with a grin.

"True. But I'm not like Sylvia. When I make a commitment, I'm loyal." Not that she'd made any commitment to Luke, but Jim didn't have to know that. And if she had made a commitment, she certainly wouldn't be cheating on him. "Now, if you'll excuse me, I have a lot to do." *You rat.*

"Sure thing."

She noticed his swagger for the first time as he left her alone. How had she ever found him attractive? Wait until she told Bee she'd found Sylvia in Jim Wellington's arms. His voice filled her head. *Now that's a waste of a good-looking man.* This time her laughter was genuine.

Dismissing the incident, she closed the door and crossed the room to stand in front of the fireplace. She rubbed her hands up and down her arms, trying to ward off the chill. "So, Buford. Did I find the secret you were trying to share?" Did she really expect an answer? Who knew? She had no clue what to expect anymore. She jumped, startled by the squeak of the door opening.

A small gasp escaped as Priscilla Wellington entered the room. Dark circles ringed her eyes, deep lines etched into the sides of her mouth and furrows creased her forehead. Even her usually lustrous hair had lost some of its perk. "Are you almost ready to start?"

"Almost."

Priscilla closed the door behind her, the soft click like a shotgun blast in the empty ballroom.

"Is everything all right? You seem stressed." Heat rushed into Cass's face the moment the question left her lips. Of course Priscilla was stressed. She'd just lost her brother and sister-in-law.

The small flicker of a sad smile played at the corners of Priscilla's mouth. One tear tipped over her lashes and tracked down her cheek. "I know it seemed like we bickered a lot, but I loved my brother dearly, and his wife and I were true sisters." She sniffed and pulled a crumpled tissue from her pocket. A folded piece of yellow paper fell to the floor.

The same one she'd been studying when she entered the ballroom for the reading at the Bay Side Hotel?

Cass bent and retrieved it, then handed it to Priscilla. A shiver tore through her at Priscilla's ice-cold touch. "You're freezing."

Ignoring Cass, Priscilla unfolded the letter and held it out to Cass. Not really a letter. Only a few words written in large, neat cursive writing. *The curse will take you next.*

Cass's breath rushed out. She gripped Priscilla's hand to stop it from trembling. "Oh, no. I'm sorry." What else could she say?

"It's okay." She offered Cass a shaky smile, and Cass released her hand. "Unnerving, but I'm being careful. I don't believe in a hundred-year-old curse . . . though Conrad certainly did." She inhaled deeply. "I do, however, believe some wacko could possibly try to kill me, so I've taken precautions." She shook her head and stared at the paper. "I just can't help thinking the writing is somewhat familiar . . ." A frown creased her brow as she folded the note and stuffed it back into her pocket. "I'm sure I've seen it before, but I just can't place it." Her expression hardened. "But I will remember, and when I do . . ." She waved a hand dismissively. "Anyway, Jim's been hovering like crazy. He begged me not to attend, to return home and cower until the police figure out what's going on." She aimed a steady stare at Cass. "Like that's happening."

Cass grinned. "I bet Jim was none too happy."

Priscilla's laughter seemed genuine. "You could say that, but Jim has to learn he can't always get his way."

An image of him and Sylvia popped into Cass's head. *Hard to tell.* Cass kept the words to herself.

"Come on. The guests are getting restless." Priscilla opened the door and stepped to the side, gesturing for the guests to enter. As they began to file into the room, Cass stood beside Priscilla and greeted everyone, a sense of déjà vu assailing her. Only this time, Cass paid closer attention as everyone entered. She wouldn't be caught off guard again.

Cass leaned close to Priscilla's ear and pitched her voice low. "Why don't you go sit and relax a few minutes? I can finish up here."

"Thanks, hon." She patted Cass's arm and took her seat at the head of the table. With one quick glance to the side, where Conrad had been seated during the first séance, Priscilla sighed.

Donald entered the ballroom, with Sylvia draped on his arm. She offered Cass a smug smile then whispered something in Donald's ear and giggled. Donald pulled her closer.

Whatever.

Cass ripped her attention away from the pair, unwilling to give Sylvia the satisfaction of thinking she cared, and her gaze fell on the stranger from the reading. He walked along the back wall, his focus skipping from guest to guest as he continuously scanned the room, every so often returning his gaze to Priscilla. Priscilla who was now worth billions, if the information they'd found was correct. Priscilla, who'd already received at least one death threat. Who could have written that note? The neatly curved lines, a little swirly and overdone, seemed distinctly feminine to Cass.

"Come on, dear." Bee took her elbow and led her toward the table. "It's time to start." He smiled at everyone as they passed.

Cass looked around the room. Had she missed the Dobbs' coming in? "Have you seen Mitch and Carly?"

"They were here earlier. I saw them when I brought Beast down to the kitchen." Bee looked around, as if noticing they were missing for the first time. His eyebrows drew together. "Hmmm . . . Odd. They have to be around here somewhere. I'll keep an eye out for them." When they reached the table, he pulled out her chair and whispered in her ear, "You know what to do, right?"

She nodded as she took her place at the head of the table. Emmett sat on one side of her, Sara Ryan on the other.

"Good luck." Bee patted her shoulder then moved to stand against the wall beside Stephanie.

They'd all agreed Bee and Stephanie would stand in the back and survey the guests. Tank and Luke had wanted to stand there, but they looked too much like . . . well . . . cops. Bee and Stephanie would appear innocent, since they often stood during Cass's readings. Tank and Luke had agreed, albeit reluctantly, to wait outside of the ballroom during the séance.

Cass breathed in deeply, working to calm her nerves. She had one goal tonight: prove she had no knowledge of who the killer was. That was it. Surely she could pull that off. She just had to come up with a believable secret to share since she'd said one of the ghosts had a secret the last time. One more deep breath and she was ready to start. She'd offered a moment of silence out of respect for Conrad and Joan at the reading, so she'd skip it tonight. Better to keep the focus off the killings anyway.

"Thank you all for coming again." She smiled, hoping to ease some of the tension in the room. "Please, be seated."

Shuffling, they followed her instructions.

Bee turned off the lights, leaving only the wall sconces and the candles on the table lit. Flames flickered in the fireplace, sending shadows dancing across the walls.

The Dobbs' absence threw Cass off balance. Where could they have disappeared to? Had something happened to them? The candles sputtered, pulling her attention back to the matter at hand. During a reading, she relied on her "psychic" abilities to give her answers. At a séance, she relied on the spirits speaking to her. "There are definitely spirits here who'd like to communicate."

Someone gasped. "Is it Buford?"

Cass couldn't tell who'd spoken, but it was a woman's voice. "I'm not sure. I have a sense of a masculine presence."

"Conrad?" Someone else whispered.

How far to push this? "Possibly."

Stephanie leaned over her and pinched the back of her arm.

Oh, fine. "I don't think so, though. I get the feeling this spirit is comfortable in his surroundings, that he passed over some time ago."

Stephanie let out a pent-up breath and backed up.

What had they discussed? She had to make everyone know she hadn't contacted Conrad. But Mitch and Carly weren't there. What if they were the killers? Then this was a waste. She studied the guests gathered around the table.

"Definitely a man. He's warning of a secret."

A few hushed whispers filled the air.

A secret. That was true enough. The feeling someone was hiding something was stronger than ever, a physical weight on her chest. "An old secret."

No. That didn't feel right. She'd go with it anyway. She scanned the guests, deciphering their features as best she could in the dim lighting. Did anyone seem disturbed by what she was saying? The story Carly Dobbs had told popped into her mind. How many of the guests knew the tale?

"A former resident of Wellington Manor, as the house was originally called." *Way off base.* Her gaze met Donald's. He swallowed hard. Guilt? Maybe. But at what? The way he'd treated Cass, or something more sinister?

"He killed himself, hung . . ." Her gaze jumped from guest to guest. The stranger no longer stood against the wall. She didn't see him seated at the table either. Where had he gone?

What had she been saying? Oh. Right. "No. That's not right. Everyone thinks he killed himself." Did it really matter if she implicated a woman who'd lived a hundred years ago in a murder? Probably not, but it still didn't feel right accusing Buford's wife of his murder when she had no real evidence to support her claims. "He didn't, though." She paused. Partly to increase the drama, but more because she was uncertain which way she wanted to go. "He was murdered."

The urgency of the whispers increased. Would this secret satisfy the killer that she wasn't going to point the finger at him? Was the killer—or killers—present? One more glance at each of the guests. The tension was suitably high. People held their breaths, hanging on her next words.

"He . . ."

Her gaze landed on Jim Wellington. "Had a . . ." He

stared at her, his dark eyes made even darker by the dim lighting. "Mistress." His longish shaggy hair cast shadows over his features. An image flashed into her mind. His face staring in as he pulled her from the car. His hair soaking wet, as if he'd just come from . . . the . . . A surge of adrenaline rushed through her, squeezing the breath from her lungs. Shower. He'd just come from the shower. Joan's shower. After he'd left her in the cupola. It was his dark hair on the soap.

Ah jeez.

His eyes narrowed, knowledge darkening his expression. He knew she'd figured it out.

"I'm sorry." How was she going to let someone know? "I'm getting flashes. Images. I have to interpret them." She glanced at Bee but couldn't get his attention. Stephanie had wandered to the other side of the room. She couldn't get a message to either of them with Jim staring at her.

Jim leaned over and whispered in Priscilla's ear. Her eyes went wide. Taking her hand, he led her quickly toward the exit.

Oh crap. All rational thought fled. She had to follow them. If she was right, Priscilla just left with the man who'd threatened to kill her. "It was his wife. Buford's wife had someone kill him because he was having an affair." She jumped up from the table. "Excuse me." She ran from the room after the Wellingtons, leaving a confused babble behind her. She couldn't lose them.

The pounding of footsteps on the stairs told her which direction to run. She glanced around the hallway, but Luke and Tank were nowhere to be found. Where was everyone? No matter, Bee and Stephanie would be right behind her. She bolted up the stairs, reaching the top just in time to see the door to Conrad's room falling shut. She dove for the door, getting her hand between the door and the jamb in time to keep it from closing. She glanced over her shoulder. No one. Indecision beat at her. Go for help or follow them?

She was saved from having to make a decision when a strong hand gripped her wrist and yanked her into the room.

21

Cass sucked in a breath to scream, but Jim Wellington clamped a hand over her mouth before she could get it out and wrestled her into the room. Priscilla lay in a crumpled heap in the corner, perfectly still, a small but steady stream of blood seeping into the hair at the back of her head.

"If I uncover your mouth, are you going to scream?"

She shook her head and tried to say *no*, but the word was too muffled by his hand to understand.

He released her, and she worked her jaw from side to side. "What are you doing?"

"Look, Cass. I don't know what's going on here, or what you have in your head, but I'm no killer."

He's lying. The certainty slammed into her with the force of a physical blow. "Okay."

"Okay?" He scrubbed his hands over his face. It was the first time she'd seen the super laid-back, smooth James

Wellington out of control. His hand trembled as he raked it through his hair in a nervous gesture that seemed out of character for him.

She shrugged. "I never accused you of killing anyone." Her heart jackhammered against her ribs. Could he hear the pounding?

He laughed, a mocking laugh that held no humor. "Please. It was written all over your face. I thought your eyes were going to pop out of your head."

Dang. She never was good at schooling her expressions. No wonder she was such a terrible liar.

He propped his hands on his hips, sparing Priscilla a quick glance before turning his attention back to Cass. "You know, we were going to open anyway—Conrad's obsession with this house was too good an opportunity to pass up—but Conrad wanted to open in the spring, when there would probably have been a full house. It was such a brilliant idea to open in the middle of winter, when there shouldn't have been many people in attendance to witness his murder." He paced back and forth, his agitation increasing with each step. "Two years we spent planning his murder, finding and setting up a scapegoat, and then you came along with this psychic nonsense and ruined everything."

We? She knew there were two killers. She spared a quick glance at Priscilla crumpled in the corner. His accomplice?

"I wasn't happy about this psychic weekend at first, but my sister is so into that nonsense, and I couldn't come up with any logical reason to say no. How could I explain wanting to open with only a few guests?" He clenched his fist and plowed it through the wall beside the door.

Cass jumped, true terror beginning to take hold.

Pieces of sheetrock and dust rained down when he pulled his hand back out. "I thought I could make it work to our advantage." He shot Priscilla a look of complete disgust. "And Mitch and Carly Dobbs, with their stupid stories about the past, only added to the confusion." He shook his head. "Who'd have thought you'd actually be able to talk to the dead?"

Talk to the dead? What was he talking about?

"Who was it that ratted me out? My dear brother, or that conniving wife of his?"

"Uh . . ."

"I asked you a question." He pulled a gun from his waistband and aimed it at her with a shaky hand.

She lifted her hands. "I don't know what you're talking about."

"Don't play innocent with me. Which one of them did you contact, or whatever it is you do?"

Shaking her head, she took a step backward. "I wasn't able to contact anyone." A soft knock on the door made her freeze.

Jim held the gun aimed at her as he sidestepped toward the door. "Who is it?"

"It's me, baby."

Cass recognized the voice. Sylvia. Her breath rushed out. Did she dare risk Jim's wrath to warn her? Her gut screamed no, but her conscience wouldn't allow her to let anyone—not even Sylvia—walk into danger.

Jim unlocked the door and started to pull it open.

"Sylvia, run! He has a gun!"

He pulled the door open wide and peered down the hallway, then closed it and turned the lock.

Sylvia grinned as she strode toward Priscilla. "Run? Why on earth would I run?"

Ice water rushed through Cass's veins.

Sylvia gripped a handful of Priscilla's hair and lifted her head, studying her intently, then dropped her and turned a glare on Jim. "Why is she still alive?"

"I already told you, she doesn't die until after she collects the inheritance."

Cass massaged her temples, contemplating whether or not to ask what was going on. Morbid curiosity demanded she ask, but common sense held her tongue.

If looks could kill, the one Sylvia shot Jim would have dropped him on the spot. "If she dies, you collect anyway. What's the difference?"

"We've been through this. If she dies now, the police are going to look too hard at me."

Sylvia rolled her eyes. "I already told you, Donald is going to take the fall no matter what."

Shock slammed through Cass.

"What's the difference if we pin one more murder on him?" She eyed Cass, her gaze lingering only a moment before she shrugged. "Or two?"

"We've already established a motive for him killing Conrad and Joan. Did you do what you were supposed to?"

She smiled slyly. "Of course, baby. I threw his stupid engagement ring in the garbage and sent him to Conrad's room to look for it, so his fingerprints will show up once they arrest him. The pictures you took of me seducing Conrad in the cupola are safely tucked in his suitcase, along with the length of rope." She approached him and ran a hand along his arm. "And the last page in his diary is filled with regret for having to kill Joan when she figured out it was him."

Cass's mind raced. What had Jim said? Two years they'd planned this? Two years ago, she'd still been married to Donald. The truth sucker punched her, knocking the breath from her lungs. Anger started to take root. "You did it on purpose."

Sylvia turned to face her. "Did what?"

"You seduced Donald for the sole purpose of setting him up. You destroyed my marriage just to use Donald as a scapegoat?"

"Of course I did, dear." She held Cass's gaze, her expression more smug than ever. "Why else would I want that spineless, sniveling loser? And why else would I befriend someone like you?" Her condescending laughter scraped Cass's last nerve raw. If Jim ever lowered that gun . . .

Jim used his free hand to steady his shaking wrist, holding the gun in a two-handed grip and pinning Cass with a hard stare. "I'll only ask one more time, how did you figure it out? Who ratted me out?"

Confusion warred with fear. Curiosity—nosiness—beat out both. She struggled to steady her voice. "Why did you kill them?"

He tilted his head. "Why don't you tell me?"

Hmm . . . He obviously knew he wasn't going to be able to walk away—she swallowed the lump of fear gagging her—or let her walk away. Could she talk her way out of this mess? "He was stealing."

Shock widened Jim's eyes.

"He'd been embezzling money from the company for years. Had stolen millions. Maybe more. It's understandable you'd have been angry . . ." *Greedy.* ". . . when you found out." Cass had no doubt it was greed that motivated him. His actions had nothing to do with revenge.

"I don't know how you do it, but you're pretty good. Shame all that talent is going to go to waste."

If she could stall long enough, surely someone would find them. Of course, there were a lot of rooms to search. And this room was off limits, so it might be the last one they checked. "The only thing I don't understand is what the old letter from Buford had to do with anything?"

Eagerness lit Jim's eyes. "Did my dearly departed brother tell you where it is?" He shook his head. "Can you believe that idiot was going to give the Dobbs' the mansion? Said he had proof of the familial line and the original letter from Buford Wellington. He believed the curse and was terrified we would all meet a tragic end." His laughter sent a chill up her spine. "Turns out he was partly right, anyway."

She licked her lips, but since her spit felt like paste, it didn't help ease the dryness. Keeping him talking shouldn't be too hard. He seemed more than willing to brag.

Jim screwed something onto the front of the gun she suspected might be a silencer. *Uh-oh* . . . Maybe she was wrong.

Her stomach cramped. Urgency beat at her. "But why did you kill Joan?"

"Couldn't have her contesting the will, could we? Now . . ." He lifted the gun toward Cass.

"Wait. Don't shoot. I know where the letter is."

He lowered the gun, just a little.

The door burst open, slamming into the wall behind it, and Bee exploded into the room, pointing a really big handgun at Jim. "Freeze, dirtbag." He offered Cass a quick grin. "I have always wanted to say that."

Jim's eyes narrowed, and Cass knew with every fiber of her being that he was about to pull the trigger. "Bee!"

The shot echoed through the room.

The breath Cass had been holding whooshed out. "Oh, crap."

"Lift that gun again, buddy, and I'll take out more than just your knee." Bee stood over Jim—who lay curled on the floor clutching his knee—his gun hand rock steady.

Sylvia dove for Jim's gun.

Cass grabbed a handful of her hair, pulled her head back, and punched her full force in the face. The crunch, followed by a spurt of blood from her nose, sent a rush of satisfaction shooting through her. She shoved Sylvia to the floor and heaved in a shaky breath.

Bee grinned. "Remind me not to get on your bad side, honey."

Cass lifted her gaze at the tinkle of the wind chimes. Luke's smile warmed her heart.

"Hey, beautiful."

"Hey, yourself."

Bee made kissy sounds behind her back, and she did her best to ignore him. He had saved her life, after all.

"Did you and Tank wrap things up?"

"More or less." He looked over Cass's shoulder at Stephanie. "He should be here in a few minutes."

"Took long enough. You guys have been there all night."

"There was a lot to sort out."

They moved to the table and sat with Bee and Stephanie, just as Tank strode through the door. After dropping a quick kiss on Stephanie's head, he joined them.

Cass opened her mouth to ask . . . well . . . everything, but Tank held up a hand to stop her. "Can I at least get a cup of coffee before you hammer me? I've been up all night."

She laughed. "Sure." She grabbed the two pots of coffee from the burners and put them on trivets in the center of the table then grabbed the cups, milk, and sugar. "There. Help yourselves." She grinned. "But talk while you're doing it."

Tank laughed and grabbed a cup. "Fine. What do you want to know?"

"Everything, of course. Starting with, is Priscilla going to be okay?"

"She's going to be fine, should be out of the hospital in a day or two." He grinned at Cass. "Supposedly, she can't get rid of that mansion fast enough. She and Jim had already met with the Madisons before the séance. Though Jim was . . . reluctant, Priscilla wanted to ditch the mansion immediately after Conrad was killed." Tank sat beside Stephanie, blew on his coffee, and took a sip. "Anyway, Horatio Madison's son is buying the place and keeping it a bed-and-breakfast. He's going to reopen Memorial Day weekend, and rumor has it, he's going to ask you to do an occasional psychic weekend."

Excitement surged. "Really?"

Tank shrugged. "That's what I heard. Anyway, you know we arrested James Wellington. And we're positive it was him. We have the evidence we need to prove it."

A relieved sigh escaped. She'd known that, but it was good to hear it confirmed.

"Once he gets out of the hospital, that is." He shot a pointed glare at Bee.

"Hey. Don't look at me like that. What was I supposed to do, let him shoot her?"

Tank grinned. "You were supposed to yell if you found her. Remember?"

"Oh. Right. Of course, he might have killed her while I was busy yelling for help."

Then Tank sobered. "I suppose it could have happened that way. Luckily, you were there and it didn't."

Bee lowered his gaze to his hands, and Cass noticed the slight tremor there. He'd faced a gunman with a steady hand, but the thought of what could have happened to her made them shake. She reached out and placed her hand on top of his. Meeting her gaze for just a moment, he smiled then turned away, an adorable blush creeping up his cheeks.

"Do you know what happened to Mitch and Carly Dobbs?"

"They were escorted out of the mansion before the séance, when they were found in the cupola searching for something. That's why we weren't right outside the ballroom when you left. We were dealing with that mess."

"Who found them?"

"Apparently, Priscilla hired a bodyguard after Conrad was killed. He suspected the Dobbs' might have something to do with the murders, so he went in search of them when they didn't show up in the ballroom. When he found them in the cupola, he called the police. He also had his suspicions about James Wellington, but figured Priscilla would be safe enough in a room full of people."

Cass thought back to the night of the reading. She'd

thought the strange man was staring at Priscilla. If that was her bodyguard, maybe he'd been glaring at Jim hovering over her.

"What kind of evidence did you find?" Stephanie asked, bringing Cass back to the present.

"When we searched Jim's room at the Bay Side Hotel, we found a backpack with rope and a knife in it. Among other things. And the handgun he had when he was arrested was the same caliber used to shoot Joan Wellington. We're pretty sure it'll match."

Cass looked around the table at her friends. Tears prickled the backs of her eyes, and she reached over to take Luke's hand. Maybe she was finally on her way to recovering from Donald's betrayal. "Oh. What about Sylvia?"

"Jim ratted her out before we even had him in the ambulance. According to him, she helped him kill Conrad and clean up the mess after he killed Joan."

She had a moment of sympathy for Donald, but then it passed. Yeah. She was definitely ready to move on. She'd find some way to make Mystical Musings work through the winter months, because there was no way she was leaving Bay Island. It was good to be home.

Lena Gregory is also the author of *Death at First Sight*, the previous Bay Island Psychic Mystery. She lives in a small town on the south shore of eastern Long Island. Visit her online at lenagregory.com, facebook.com/Lena .Gregory, and twitter.com/lenagregory03.

The Bay Island
Psychic Mysteries
by Lena Gregory

**At her psychic shop, Mystical Musings, Cass Donovan
gives readings to locals and tourists. But it's the killer
visions that really keep her on her toes.**

Find more books by Lena Gregory
by visiting prh.com/nextread

"As breezy and salty as a gust of wind off the
chilly bay waters."—Juliet Blackwell, *New York Times*
bestselling author on *Death at First Sight*

lenagregory.com
Lena.Gregory.Author
LenaGregory03